Praise

"Funny, warm, and terrifying at times, *Wonton Terror* adds yet another delicious dish to Vivien Chien's growing menu of enticing, cozy mysteries."

—*Suspense* magazine

DIM SUM OF ALL FEARS

"I am so delighted by this cozy mystery series!"

—*Book Riot*

"Provides plenty of twists and turns and a perky, albeit conflicted, sleuth." —*Kirkus Reviews*

"Thoroughly entertaining . . . fun and delicious."

—*RT Book Reviews*

DEATH BY DUMPLING

"Vivien Chien serves up a delicious mystery with a side order of soy sauce and sass. A tasty start to a new mystery series!"

—Kylie Logan, bestselling author of
Gone with the Twins

"*Death by Dumpling* is a fun and sassy debut with unique flavor, local flair, and heart."

—Amanda Flower, Agatha
Award–winning author of *Lethal Licorice*

"A charming debut, with plenty of red herrings. The heroine's future looks bright." —*Kirkus Reviews*

EGG DROP

DEAD

VIVIEN CHIEN

St. Martin's Paperbacks

This is a work of fiction. All of the characters, organizations, and events portrayed in this novel are either products of the author's imagination or are used fictitiously.

First published in the United States by St. Martin's Paperbacks, an imprint of St. Martin's Publishing Group.

EGG DROP DEAD

For information, address St. Martin's Publishing Group, 120 Broadway, New York, NY 10271.

www.stmartins.com

ISBN: 978-1-250-22832-1

Printed in the United States of America

St. Martin's Paperbacks edition / March 2020

10 9 8 7 6 5 4 3 2 1

For Margaret,
Thank you for encouraging me to chase
my dreams.

AUTHOR'S NOTE

- - - - - - - - - - - - - - - -

In the fall of 2008, I created the character of Lydia Shepard for a college course I was taking on fiction writing. The main objective of the class was to create a short story in the mystery genre by the end of the semester—a task that seemed rather daunting as I was not *that* familiar with the genre at the time.

However, with the guidance and knowledge of an amazing teacher, I learned more in one semester of her class than I ever had before . . . (and actually retained it!). Her clear love of mystery helped me cobble my way through a short story featuring a female private investigator with a sassy attitude and one heck of a story to tell. I was a little skeptical on how the story would turn out, but I had my fingers crossed it would at least get a passing grade.

Then three things happened that I hadn't expected: I got an A!, my teacher suggested I submit the short story to a mystery magazine (which I never did end up doing), and I fell so in love with the story and the characters that I wanted to turn it into a full-length novel. And though I began that process, the project took a backseat as life went about its business.

Fast forward a decade later, on a drive in to work, I began to contemplate my writing journey as a whole, thinking about the twists and turns that it's taken along the way. I started to contemplate the idea of our different selves through various parts of life, and wondered what past versions would think of future ones. And that thought turned into characters I have created over the years. While Lana and Lydia are vastly different people from myself, they both contain a piece of me and my life at very distinct times, shaping the development of their character. What might they think of each other and how would they interact if they met? I loved the thought so much that it inspired the sub-story for *Egg Drop Dead*.

With all that in mind, it seemed natural to dedicate this book to that wonderful teacher who changed my life and set me on a path I never would have imagined in my wildest dreams.

And even though Lydia's full story has yet to be told, I am so happy to awaken her voice on the page with Lana Lee. I hope you enjoy reading it as much as I enjoyed writing it.

ACKNOWLEDGMENTS

A zillion thank yous to my agent, Gail Fortune; my editors, Hannah Braaten and Nettie Finn; to Kayla Janas, Allison Ziegler and Mary Ann Asher. And to my publisher, St. Martin's Paperbacks, I appreciate all of you so much.

My gratitude and respect to the Sisters in Crime, locally and nationally. Your existence has helped me and so many others seek out our passions and not feel alone while doing it.

Much love to my family and friends for the continuation of support and encouragement. I am lucky beyond words to have you guys in my life.

And to all my readers . . . many hugs. Thank you for going on this journey with me.

CHAPTER
1

"I am not going to wear a qi-pao to Donna Feng's party, Mother!" I was standing in front of the mirror that hangs on my bedroom closet door while my mother, Betty Lee, held the Asian-style dress against my body, the plastic hanger pushing firmly into my neck.

"Why not?" my mother returned in somewhat of a whine. "You look *so* cute."

I think most of us can agree that women in their late twenties do not want to be labeled as "cute." And you could definitely put me on that list. Who am I? Lana Lee, nice to meet you. I'm your not-so-average Asian American gal, recently turned twenty-eight, with not a clue in the areas of martial arts, math that goes beyond long division, or how to speak any dialect of Chinese. But I can use chopsticks like a son of a gun. So that's something, right?

If you had to find me in a crowd, it wouldn't be a problem because 50 percent of my hair is currently pink. I love hamburgers and pizza almost as much as I love noodles, and if you asked me to cook you a proper Chinese meal, we'd both starve that night. That's why I manage my parents' Chinese restaurant instead of cooking there. Trust me when I say, no one wants me behind a wok.

In recent weeks, I'd come up with the idea of adding a catering service to the family business as a way to help bring in extra money. Summer months at the noodle shop could be slow, and we were dead smack in the middle of July. With Peter's artistic help, we put together a flyer advertising the new service and left a healthy stack at the plaza's community center and included them in all our take-out bags.

Our first catering job was for Donna Feng, the owner of Asia Village—the shopping plaza my family's restaurant was part of. It was Donna's birthday, and she wanted to have a fancy dinner party at her house. When she first proposed the idea, I of course jumped at the opportunity, thinking that it would include food for maybe ten to fifteen of her closest friends and family.

That was not the case. It turned out she was thinking more along the lines of a small, intimate gathering of fifty. You know, because all of us have a close-knit group of fifty friends. Regardless, I was up for the challenge, which was nothing Ho-Lee Noodle House couldn't handle. At least that's what I had to keep telling myself in order to keep the butterflies from causing a frenzy in my stomach.

I'd had a very specific dress in mind for the party, and it did not resemble this navy-blue qi-pao covered in dragons and clouds that my mother had picked out. The black dress I had chosen, with its high lace collar and cap sleeves, was feminine, sleek, and most of all mature. It didn't make me feel like a little kid playing dress-up.

My mother is a small Taiwanese woman with an extreme desire to keep me at the age of seven, and this dress was evidence of that. She released the hanger's hold on my neck and waved the dress in front of me. "But this is so beautiful. If Mommy was younger, I would keep this for myself."

"Well, Mother, as they say, age is just a number. It looks like it will fit you just fine." I smiled sweetly at her.

She scowled in return and laid the dress on my bed next to Kikkoman, my black pug, who had been watching our every move with intrigue. Kikko sniffed the satiny material before letting out a groan that might be mistaken for a very human sound of misery.

When my mother turned around to face me, she planted her dainty hands on her hips—as was her customary stance when speaking to me—and jutted her head forward with determination set in her dark-brown eyes. "Everyone else who is working will wear the same dress. This will show high class."

"So Peter's going to wear *that* dress?" I responded with a smirk.

My mother did not find it amusing. "You are not funny, Lana Lee."

I glanced back at the dress on my bed. "Neither is making me wear that dress."

"Why?" my mother asked. "Your sister is okay wearing this dress. She did not give Mommy such a hard time."

"That's because she's a kiss—"

"Hello!" a cheerful voice yelled from the living room.

"We're in here!" I shouted back.

It was my best friend and roommate, Megan Riley. And hopefully she could talk some sense into my mother. Kikko hopped down onto the floor and wiggled her curly tail as she went to greet Megan, who was on her way to join us in my bedroom.

Her blond hair was ironing-board straight, and she was dressed in a black T-shirt and skinny jeans, most likely coming home from a shift at the Zodiac, the bar where she works. Lately she had been working a mixture of random hours due to staffing problems they were having. I couldn't ever be sure when she'd get home, and when she'd need to run off to start pouring drinks. "Oh hey, Mama Lee," she said, giving my mother a hug. "It's nice to see you."

My mother looked up at her, squinting as she assessed her. "You look skinny."

"Ma, you always say that." She squeezed my mom's arm playfully and turned to me. "What are you guys up to? Want to get some dinner or something?"

"You came just in time," I told her, grabbing the dress from my bed. "My mother wants me to wear this." I shook it at her. "Isn't it ridiculous?"

Megan took the dress from me and looked it over. "What's wrong with it?"

"Don't you think it's a bit cliché?"

"I think it's cute."

I threw my hands in the air. "Exactly."

My mother groaned.

Megan laughed and handed the dress back to me. "Stop being so stubborn, Lana. It's just one night."

"I'm not being stubborn," I replied as I gave the dress in my hands the stink eye.

Okay, in truth, when it comes to the must-knows about Lana Lee . . . stubborn makes the list.

The next evening, after lots of internal debate on the merits of wearing the dress I had purchased for myself versus the dress my mother was insisting I wear, I decided not to create unnecessary waves and give in to her request. So I dutifully put on the qi-pao and a pair of black patent-leather stiletto heels to add some edge and went on my way to Donna Feng's house in Westlake, one of the wealthier suburbs of Cleveland, without another thought about it.

The upper-class widow lived with her two teenage daughters in a house that was large enough to host two full-sized families. Donna had confided in my mother on a few occasions about how difficult things had become after her husband, Thomas, died. She found herself struggling to handle a lot of the affairs that come along with taking care of a house that size. And what with raising two teens, the charity work she did within the Asian community, *and* her mild involvement with Asia Village, she'd quickly found her hands full. So instead of minimizing her responsibilities, she'd recently hired a maid, a live-in nanny, and a gardener to help with the various tasks around the house.

I pulled onto Donna's street and parked a few houses down behind my sister's car. We'd been instructed to park a little way away from the house itself to give the guests the best parking options.

It was approaching sunset, and the humidity of

the day had mostly dissipated. A light, refreshing breeze ruffled the leaves on the trees ever so gently.

The dress was a little tight—probably from all the doughnuts I'd been eating recently—and I shimmied myself out of the car, thankful for the respectable slit down the side. As I walked along the sidewalk listening to my heels click-clack, I began to regret my choice of footwear—like I always do.

My sister, Anna May, and Peter Huang, our head chef, were in Donna's driveway unloading the food trays and dining accessories that we needed for the evening. Peter had borrowed his cousin's beat-up work van, and it stuck out like a sore thumb in this ritzy neighborhood. I made a mental note that we might need a catering van if we were going to get serious about this side business.

Peter noticed me approaching and gave a casual nod in my direction. His normally ball-cap-covered head was bare, and his shaggy, black hair looked like it had been trimmed and slicked back. Also missing from his typical apparel were the beat-up combat boots he wore in the kitchen at Ho-Lee Noodle House every day without fail. In their place were polished, square-toed dress shoes. He noticed my assessment and spoke before I could say anything. "My mom said I had to, so don't give me a hard time, okay?"

"I wasn't planning to say anything," I lied, biting back a quip about being a mama's boy. Even though we often teased each other about these kinds of things, I knew that him dressing up was a no-joke zone. "You look sharp."

"Thanks. I feel weird, though. And they're so not cool to cook in. I told my mom they were going to get ruined, but she didn't care." He shrugged. "So whatever."

Anna May batted his arm. "Stop saying you look weird. You actually look like a grown-up for once."

I regarded my sister with a quick assessment. Of course, we looked very similar in our matching qi-paos, but she had gone for classy and I'd gone for sassy. Her hair was impeccably done, a French bun, not a hair out of place. Classic pearl necklace and matching bracelet, French-manicured nails and sensible kitten heels. Whereas my hair was French-braided and swept up to the side in a messy sort of way with strands of pink left down to frame my face, thanks to Megan's ability to copy hairstyles from magazines. I'd chosen bold silver jewelry, chunky rings, a cuff bracelet, sparkly chandelier earrings, and of course these blasted stilettos.

As I thought about them, my sister's eyes landed on my feet and she snorted. "Lana, you're going to die in those shoes within the first hour."

"I'll be fine. Let's hurry and get this stuff inside so Peter can move this van. I'm surprised Donna hasn't said anything about it yet."

As the three of us walked inside, I cringed as the toes of my shoes started to pinch. But you know how sometimes you focus on the smallest inconveniences of life, not realizing that things could be so much worse?

Yeah, it was going to be one of those times.

CHAPTER
2

Donna Feng is the kind of woman that makes a statement just by walking into a room. She is bold, she is coiffed, and she exudes the kind of confidence any woman would covet. Even when her husband was killed several months ago, she'd carried herself with a poise that seemed almost superhuman. I often found myself searching within for the same type of self-assurance. Only rarely had I seen her at all flustered.

When we entered through the front door, we found Donna in the sitting room standing next to a slightly shorter woman in a sleek black suit, barking orders at a team of people in crisp white shirts and black dress pants. I had no idea who any of them were, but my best guess told me they were here to help make Donna's party the best in the city.

Donna, though, in a stunning, dark-gray A-line dress, appeared less than confident for the first time since I'd known her. Her fists were clenched at her sides, and I could see the anxiety in her eyes as the other woman spoke to the lineup of staff members. We stood off to the side so as not to interrupt.

"Okay, people, guests will start to arrive shortly, and everything has to be absolutely on point! I expect nothing less!" The woman clapped her hands together in quick succession. "Flower arrangements on all the tables, settings placed to perfection . . . if anything is out of place, put it in place. Now move!"

The workers left the room in single file.

My sister and I shared a look as we followed behind Peter. Donna caught the movement from the corner of her eye and clasped her hands in excitement. "Oh, Lana, darling," she cooed, ignoring both Anna May and Peter. "You've arrived! Come in, come in. I'm so happy you're here!"

She greeted me and my sister with a hug and gave a respectful nod to Peter. "Lana, I'd love for you to meet my party planner. This is Yvette Howard, and she is absolutely brilliant at what she does. I don't know what I'd do without her."

The shorter woman stepped up and smiled brightly. She had the exact same air of confidence that Donna carried, and I could see why Donna would choose her. "It's nice to meet you."

"Yvette," Donna said, putting an arm around me. "This is my caterer, Lana Lee, her sister, Anna May, and their cook, Peter Huang. Lana was so gracious as to handle all of the food prep, and since she's a family friend, you can see why I didn't need any help in that department."

Donna and I had sort of bonded around the time of her husband's death a few months back, and ever since then she'd seemingly taken more of a liking to me, while continuing to regard Anna May with the same cool politeness she used with most people. She wasn't a huge fan of Peter, because he happened to be the illegitimate son of her deceased husband. However, because of this, she did show him a level of respect. I knew it must be painful for her to see him since he was a living reminder of her husband's infidelity, so considering the circumstances, I think she handled her encounters with him pretty well.

"That's wonderful," Yvette replied with what was clearly fake enthusiasm. "It's really nice to meet all of you, but I should go check on things on the back deck and make sure we're just about ready. After all, time is of the essence."

Donna patted Peter on the shoulder, gesturing to the kitchen entrance with her other hand. "Let's get you three situated. You can set everything down in here. You'll have to excuse the mess, it's been absolutely chaotic all day. I can't seem to find any competent help except for Yvette, and the girls have been driving me nuts since the moment they got out of bed this morning. I feel as though I'm living in a zoo."

Jill and Jessica Feng were Donna's twin teenage girls, who were a bit of a handful these days. Both of them had decided it was a good time to go through their rebellious phase. I had a suspicion it might have something to do with their father's death, and everything that came out about Peter being their half brother didn't help the situation.

No one talked about it, either . . . including Peter. The girls never spent any time with Peter and he had never offered to get to know them. According to my mother, neither Donna nor Peter's mother, Nancy, had ever encouraged the half siblings to become friendly with one another.

I set my armload of items down on the flawless marble countertop of the kitchen island and assessed the room. The stainless-steel appliances were sparkling and definitely cleaner than anything you'd find in my apartment. The ceramic floors were equally clean; you could've eaten off them if the situation called for it. "Donna, everything is immaculate as usual. You're worrying over nothing."

She released a heavy sigh, leaning against the island. "Everything just feels absolutely out of order. How's my hair?" she said, quickly changing subjects.

"It looks great!" my sister chimed in from behind me. "And your dress is amazing."

"Thanks, dear," she said, smoothing out the lines near her waist. "Calvin Klein never lets me down, I can tell you that. And you girls look lovely as well." She assessed our matching qi-paos. "It was a great idea of your mother's to have the ladies wear matching outfits. Uniformity is a clear sign of classic professionalism."

I bit my tongue because I didn't agree. I thought it was an awful idea, but now wasn't the time to express my true feelings about my attire to the birthday girl. "Donna, why don't you go and relax for a little while and let us handle everything down here. I can get the door as the guests start to arrive. And Yvette seems to have everything else under control."

"Oh sure, I suppose you're right about that. I probably should check on the girls one last time as well. They invited a few of their little friends over and I want to make sure they understand the ground rules. After all, this is an adult party." As she started to walk away, she turned around to say, "Just send everybody out onto the back deck and I'll be down in a little while."

After she left the room, Peter, who had remained silent during the whole conversation, let out a low whistle. "Dude, someone needs to chill."

Easy for Peter to say: I'd seen him emote maybe a whole two times since the day we met. Although it was odd for Donna to act out like this. The Donna I knew was calm, collected, and ate social functions for breakfast.

"Give her a break," my sister said, swatting his arm. "Women get weird on their birthdays as they get older. Life is passing, things haven't happened, things have gone by the wayside, whatever. There's always something. And she's already a widow."

"Age is just a number," I said, knowing full well what would happen next. But there are moments when I just can't help myself.

My sister rolled her eyes at me. "That's because you're not even thirty yet, Lana. Trust me. You're going to be singing a different tune in two years. Mark my words."

"Doubt it," I replied. "You've said this to me every year for how many years and I still don't agree."

"Lana, *I* am the big sister, so trust me. I know."

My sister is only three years older than me, but she acts like there's twenty years in between us. She is always warning me about this and that and how things are just all heading down from here.

On more than one occasion, I've been called an idealist, and truly, I think it's a blessing if anything. Yes, I'd like to believe in the good of life and humanity. Is that so wrong?

Instead of caving to the typical argument that

follows between us on the subject, I decided to busy myself with the actual task at hand.

The bulk of the party would be outside in the backyard around the pool. My friends from Asia Village, Kimmy Tran—who was also Peter's girlfriend—and Rina Su would assist in serving food. Since the size of the party had been larger than we expected, the two women had offered to help out. I was more than grateful to them considering I knew how much they had going on in their own lives.

Not only did Kimmy help run her parents' entertainment store, China Cinema and Song, but she also moonlighted at a local strip club as a cocktail waitress to help ends meet. Her second job was pretty hush-hush; the only people who knew about it were me, my boyfriend Adam, Megan, and Peter. If her parents ever caught wind of this, their heads would probably explode as they were a little on the reserved side.

Rina was a newer friend of mine who'd just moved to Cleveland a short while ago. The tragic death of her sister and brother-in-law had brought her here from New York, and she'd decided to stay and open her own business. She now owned the cosmetics shop at Asia Village, The Ivory Doll, which so far had been a smashing success. My own makeup collection could be testament to that.

The menu was predominantly appetizers, and we would be circulating throughout the party with trays. But as manager of Ho-Lee Noodle House, it was also my job to make sure that everything ran smoothly. My parents would be in attendance at the party, but they were coming as guests. It was just the Lee girls working tonight, since Peter's mother,

Nancy, usually our most reliable waitress at the restaurant, had been exempt from the evening because of the weirdness between her and Donna. I thought at first that it might hurt her feelings, but she was actually quite relieved. She and our other cook were at the noodle house keeping the place running so we didn't have to close to cater the party.

Peter went out to move the van, and my sister got busy finishing up the final tasks before the party started. We were being extra particular, not only because this was Donna's birthday party, but also because it was our first catering gig and there would be many prominent guests here that might want our catering services for themselves in the future. I'd had special menus and extra business cards printed to hand out to guests if anyone asked. Nothing could go wrong tonight. Absolutely nothing.

CHAPTER
3

An hour after the guests had begun to arrive, the party was in full swing. Donna had hired a DJ to give the party a more carefree vibe. She told me originally the plan was to hire a pianist to provide the music, but her new nanny, Alice Kam, had assured her that something more upbeat would make a better atmosphere for birthday party time. I was grateful to the new young woman in Donna's life for the suggestion, since I'd much rather be listening to lively dance music as I worked than a lone piano, which seemed more fitting for a casual, sit-down dinner.

I did loops around the pool with my tray of teriyaki beef sticks while Kimmy, Rina, and my sister carried trays of various appetizers. We had shrimp toast wedges, mini egg rolls, crab Rangoon wonton cups, and sweet-and-sour chicken balls circulating the party. The beverage service was handled by Penny Cho from the Bamboo Lounge, and while she staffed the bar, her helper worked the crowd with flutes of champagne.

I returned to the kitchen to grab more appetizers from Peter when Kimmy stopped me. "I am seriously super mad at your mom right now," she said, pointing at her dress. "I feel absolutely ridiculous. Like a stereotypical Asian girl. Now all I need are chopsticks in my hair and we can get this party started for real."

Rina sidled up next to us. Her tray was empty as well. "Is Kimmy complaining about her outfit again? I told her she looks great in it. It really compliments her curves."

"It's true," I agreed. "You look great, Kimmy. I don't know why you're so upset about it. At least you have actual hips." I pointed to my own hips, which barely existed.

"Whatever," she replied. Kimmy was known to dismiss compliments or anything positive you said to her. Most of the time she acted as if nothing affected her. But I knew her well, and I knew that she had a big heart. She actually cared quite a bit more than your average bear. She just didn't like to do it while people were looking. "I can't wait to get out of this dress."

Peter smirked.

"Peter Huang, what is *that* supposed to mean?"

"Nothing," he replied, avoiding eye contact. "Lana's here."

"Oh, ew." I made fake gagging noises. "Let us fill up our trays and get out of here before you guys continue this conversation."

Rina chuckled and nodded in agreement.

After Peter filled my tray with freshly made teriyaki sticks, I started to head back out the French doors into the backyard, but right as I opened the door, Jill, Jessica, and a girl about their age with black, braided hair came flying through in the direction of the backyard. They jumped into the pool while one of the girls yelled, "Cannonball!"

The three teenagers leapt into the pool at the same time, and large waves of water erupted out onto the surrounding area, splashing a majority of the guests. Shrieks and "what the hecks" filled the party.

Kimmy, Rina, and I gawked at one another before rushing out to see what was going on.

My eyes immediately landed on Donna, whose face had turned a bright red. She screamed at the girls to get out of the pool. The three teenagers, sensing the severity of what they'd done by the tone in Donna's voice, swam to the edge and hoisted themselves out of the water as if their bodies were made out of lead.

"What did I tell you girls not even two hours ago?" Donna yelled with a bit of a slur in her voice. "Where is Alice!"

Jill or Jessica, I could never tell them apart, said, "We don't know . . ."

Donna regarded the other twin and she shrugged, tucking her chin inward.

"The three of you, go back upstairs to your room this instant and I will deal with you later."

As the girls turned to leave, Alice the nanny came out onto the deck in an obvious state of panic. When she put together what had happened in her absence, her hands flew up to her gaping mouth. "Ms. Feng, I am so sorry! I was only in the restroom for a minute and when I came back, they were gone!"

"You are an absolute moron!" Donna shouted, stomping a foot. "Look at my beautiful dress! Look at my guests! I told you specifically to keep those girls upstairs and out of my hair, but you couldn't even do that right. What do I even pay you for, Alice?"

Alice's cheeks flushed with embarrassment. "I'm sorry, ma'am."

We all watched on as if it were an episode of *As the World Turns*. I could barely believe my eyes. In all the years I'd known her, I'd never seen Donna act like this before. As I watched her now, I felt slightly embarrassed at her outburst. She'd clearly had too much to drink, and I wondered if she was even aware of how she was coming off in front of her guests.

Out of the corner of my eye, I saw my mother sidle up slowly to Donna and squeeze her arm, whispering something in her ear.

Donna teetered back and forth, shaking off my mother's hand. "I will deal with you later," she spat at Alice. "You just wait! I will not stand for this! Now get out of my sight!"

"Yes, ma'am." Alice lowered her head and disappeared back inside the house.

The music had stopped and everyone stared blankly at Donna, unsure as to what we'd just witnessed. It was so quiet that all you heard was the lapping of water against the pool's walls. I don't think anyone here had ever seen her act this way.

"Well," she said, breathing heavily. "I apologize for the inconvenience. I have fresh towels in the pool room if you'd like to dry yourself off. Follow me." She signaled the DJ to turn the music back on. "Let's continue this party, shall we?"

I squeezed into a trio of well-dressed women who were whispering among themselves. "If you ask me," a petite woman in a blue dress said to the other two, "she's totally lost her mind since her husband passed away. Poor thing can't handle it all."

The second woman, wearing a gold, gauzy dress, nodded in agreement. "Can you blame her? Those kids are a nightmare. Then there's that other *thing* to deal with."

They didn't say what *thing* they were specifically talking about, but I was sure they meant the situation with Peter. The two women bobbed their heads in unison, understanding the unspoken words, while the third woman, whom I recognized as Ms. Evelyn Chang, turned away as if she would rather not participate in the conversation.

The woman in the blue dress spoke again. "If you ask me, it's only a matter of time before she goes totally insane and does something to completely ruin her reputation."

Ms. Chang jutted out her chin. "If the two of you ask me, you both need hobbies to keep yourselves busy instead of judging something you know nothing about."

The woman in the blue dress sneered. "As if *you* know what it's like to lose a spouse."

Ms. Chang turned her nose up. "It's called 'empathy,' darling, you may want to look it up."

The three women noticed me eavesdropping and I blushed, holding up the tray as my disguise for being there. "Would you like a teriyaki skewer? They're fresh off the grill."

With polite smiles they shook their heads in unison. I slunk away to the next group of partygoers.

It's true that Donna had seemed out of sorts recently, and it appeared to be getting worse as time went on instead of any better. Tonight was proof enough of that. My only hope was that they were wrong and she didn't end up doing something that she'd regret.

While Donna was helping her guests put themselves back together, I decided to slip inside and check on Alice. I didn't know the woman, but I felt sorry for her nonetheless. As I headed up the stairs, I could hear loud pop music coming from one of the closed doors and figured the girls were keeping themselves entertained and wouldn't be heard from again that night . . . at least if they knew what was good for them.

From a previous visit to the Feng household, I remembered which room had been the guest room, and I found that door to be closed as well. I lightly tapped on the hollow wood. "Alice? Are you in there?"

"Who is it?" a muffled voice returned.

"My name is Lana. I'm the one handling the catering."

There was silence for a moment, and then the doorknob turned. She opened the door a crack, and I immediately noted that she'd been crying. Her eyes were puffy and bloodshot, and her nose was reddened. "Did you need something?"

"Actually I came to check on you," I said quietly. "Make sure that you were okay."

She forced a smile. "Thanks, I appreciate that, but I'd like to be alone right now."

"Donna doesn't mean it, you know. I'm sure

everything will be fine once she's calmed down. She's just under a lot of stress right now."

Alice snorted. "Are you kidding me? She's been like this since the moment I walked in the door that very first day. I was beyond shocked with the instant change in her attitude."

"What do you mean?"

"She certainly didn't act like that when I interviewed with her. She was very pleasant and practically begged me to move in here as soon as possible. I could see she was struggling with everything she has going on. I mean, these society women . . . they just don't sit still. So I agreed. I moved in that week. And as soon as I stepped foot in the house, she was always barking orders, always yelling. It's like I can't do anything right according to her. It's tiresome and I don't know if I can work for her much longer. I will not be someone's punching bag."

My eyes widened. "Really? I can't—"

"There are things . . ." Alice paused. She opened the door a little more and stuck her head out, glancing down the hallway. "There are things that people don't know about her. Things she wouldn't *want* anyone to know."

I felt a knot form in my stomach. "Like what?"

Alice looked down at her feet. "Nothing I care to share at the moment. But she's lucky that I'm a loyal employee. At least I have been . . . so far." She lifted her head, sniffled, and gave another weak smile. "I'm sorry, if you'll excuse me, I really would like to be alone. I'm sure you understand."

"Sure." I nodded. "No problem."

Before shutting the door, she said, "Hope the rest of the party goes without incident."

"Yeah, me too," I mumbled to myself as I hurried back down the stairs.

It was nearing eleven p.m. and the party had thinned out considerably. My parents left shortly after Donna flipped out on Alice. They used the need to get back to my grandmother as an excuse to leave.

The DJ had closed up shop and the stragglers that stayed behind seemed to be Donna's closest friends. The party had now moved into the house, and most of the remaining guests lounged in the living room area.

Donna had disappeared several times throughout the night to check on what was happening upstairs. She appeared on edge, and my guess was that she would have a hard time relaxing the rest of the evening.

The DJ stopped me in the kitchen while I was cleaning off party platters. His shaggy hair was tousled and hung down to his eyelids. He tilted his head and swept it out of the way. "Do you know where the boss lady is? I need to get paid."

"She's around here somewhere," I said. "I can look upstairs, she might be with her kids."

"Nah, on second thought, that's okay. I gotta take off. I'm sure I'll get my money one way or another."

I gave him a once-over. The entire right side of his black, button-down dress shirt was drenched. "You got splashed by the kids messing around in the pool too, huh? I hope none of your equipment got ruined in the process."

He shrugged. "It's all good. Kids will be kids,

right?" He jerked his chin toward the door and
started to walk away. "I'll be seein' ya."

"Okay, I'll let her know you left."

He gave me a nod as he headed out of the house
carrying the rest of his equipment.

Peter had pulled the van back up into the driveway and was hauling things out. Since my feet
were throbbing, Peter cut me some slack and suggested that I clean up in the kitchen and pack up for
him to take things out instead of me making trips
in and out of the house. I'd sent Rina and Anna May
home half an hour before. They'd both busted their
tails all night, and seeing as I was manager, I felt it
was my responsibility to finish the cleanup. I tried
to send Kimmy home, too, but she stayed behind
because she planned to leave with Peter.

One of the guests stopped over. "Excuse me,
young lady, have you seen my handbag? It's a teal
sequined clamshell about this big." She held up her
hands to show me.

I thought for a few seconds but couldn't remember seeing anything like that. "No, I'm sorry, did
you maybe leave it outside?"

She smacked her forehead. "I probably did. After
all the commotion, I slipped inside and must have
left it at one of the patio tables." She headed for the
French doors, and I turned my attention back to the
packing box I was filling in front of me.

Not even five seconds later, that same woman
let out a bloodcurdling scream that startled me so
much, I dropped the silver party platter I'd been
holding on the floor. It clanked loudly as it hit the
ceramic tiles, and I cringed from the sound. Leaving

the platter where it had fallen, I ran out the door to see if the woman had slipped and fallen.

But she hadn't. She was standing about three feet away from the edge of the pool, where a lump of black clothing floated ominously in the water.

I froze, staring at the form, trying to register what I was seeing.

The woman turned around to look at me, her eyes filled with terror. "Call 911!"

Peter came running out from behind me, grabbed my shoulders, and moved me out of the way. Without hesitation, he jumped into the pool and swam toward the black mass.

The woman turned to me again. "Young lady!"

I snapped out of my trance and ran to my purse, digging frantically for my phone. It had taken me a few moments to realize the thing I was looking at was a dead body.

CHAPTER
4

The body in the pool turned out to be Alice Kam. Peter had attempted to administer CPR, but it was useless. She was already dead.

The Westlake police arrived minutes later to secure the scene. They gave Donna permission to have her maid, Rosemary Chan, take the children to their friend's house for the rest of the night. They weren't involved and didn't need to be exposed to the parts that came next.

The coroner was second to arrive. I watched as he and his team marched through the house onto the back patio.

Kimmy and I were huddled in the kitchen as everyone else went about their business. The police had begun their interrogations of the remaining guests and, of course, Donna.

On first sight, it looked like maybe Alice had fallen into the pool and drowned. But while we waited, Kimmy and I overheard the coroner say to one of the officers that he'd noticed bruising on

Alice's wrists and neck. His conclusion was that she had been held under water against her will. He needed to take the body to the lab for more testing, but he felt confident about his assessment.

"Well, now she's gone and killed the damn maid," Kimmy spat after hearing the coroner's explanation.

"Kimmy! Shhhh! Don't say that. Someone might hear you!" I peeked over her shoulder to see if anyone on the patio had heard her. They seemed to be preoccupied in their own conversation. "Also, she wasn't a maid, she was a nanny."

"Ha! Semantics. She washed the dishes, Lana."

"Someone was just murdered, can we not bicker about the trivial details of her job description?" I hissed.

She shrugged. "Fine. You started it, but whatever. Hey, do you think the cops will be pissed if I head out to smoke? I'm gettin' kinda antsy sitting around here."

"I thought you quit?"

"Well, I just started back up."

I shook my head. I knew that Kimmy was trying to distract me with her nonchalant demeanor, but that sort of thing never worked on me. "Can't you just wait?"

"You never let me do anything," she returned. "I can't talk about what happened, I can't say anything negative, I can't smoke. Blah blah blah, Lana."

A police officer entered the room, catching the tail end of our conversation. "Is everything all right in here, ladies?"

"Yeah," Kimmy said before I could respond. "Just want to know if I can go for a smoke. This whole situation has got my nerves in a tizzy."

"Actually, the two of you can go on home. We're taking Ms. Feng in to the station for additional questioning."

"Officer, is she being accused of something?" I asked, the palms of my hands beginning to sweat.

"I can't discuss that with you at this time," he replied.

"Because I can tell you that I've known Donna for my entire life, and she is not capable of doing something like this."

"I appreciate your opinion, but this is standard procedure, ma'am."

Ma'am! Who is he calling ma'am?

I was just about to say something when Kimmy pinched my arm. "Let's go, Lana."

We grabbed our things, and I glanced at Donna before heading out the front door. She looked unkempt and small sitting on her couch. She hadn't even looked this torn up when her own husband died. She noticed me as I walked by. "Lana, would you do me a favor?"

The officer sitting with her gazed between the two of us.

"I'm afraid that one of the girls might have left their curling iron on in the upstairs bathroom. Could you go double-check it for me?" Donna looked up at the officer. "Would that be okay?"

The officer nodded. "I suppose that's fine. Make it quick, please."

I told Kimmy I'd meet her outside and ran up the winding staircase to the second-floor bathroom, remembering the first time I'd seen the massive, luxury bath. I'd sneaked into Donna's house hoping to find information on her husband's death. At that time I thought that she might be a killer, though she'd been proven innocent. But now she might actually be one.

I shook the thought out of my head and stepped into the lavish bath, turning on the light. There wasn't a curling iron anywhere in sight. But there was a three inch terra-cotta soldier lying in the sink. I picked it up and inspected it. What the heck was this thing and what was it doing in here?

I didn't understand why Donna had sent me up here, but I imagined it had to be some kind of code. Her kids were too old to play with this sort of toy, and there were no other children in the house. My own summation was that it didn't belong.

I quickly checked under the counter and found a curling iron that hadn't been used in a while. Just in case the cops decided to check on it themselves, I unraveled the cord and placed it on the counter, making it seem as if it had been there all along.

The cop yelled up the stairs. "Hey, is everything okay up there?"

"Yes, on my way, sorry." I slipped the terra-cotta soldier into my purse and hurried back downstairs. Donna eyeballed me as if she knew I'd found what she'd really sent me for. "Darling, was it on?"

"Yes, but don't worry, I took care of it."

"Thank you, Lana, I'll talk to you soon about payment. My apologies for the end of the evening."

"Don't worry," I said. "We can discuss that later."

The cop ushered me out. I found Kimmy pacing in the driveway, puffing on her cigarette. "What the hell was all that about?"

"Nothing, just keep walking."

* * *

Kimmy and I said a quick goodbye and drove off in separate directions, and I kept my finding to myself. Megan wouldn't be home yet—it was only eleven thirty. She'd still be working. I decided to head up to the Zodiac instead of going straight home.

On the way to the bar, I tried calling Adam to let him know what happened, but his phone went straight to voice mail. Adam is a newer addition to my life. He started out as the lead detective in Thomas Feng's murder case, but without intending to, we had taken a strong liking to each other as we kept crossing paths. And now, a handful of months later, he was my boyfriend. What crazy turns life can take when you least expect it. It was safe to say for the both of us that at the time of meeting, the last thing we were seeking was a romantic relationship.

I left a message telling him where I would be. Most likely he was working and it would be a while before he got back to me.

The parking lot of the bar was packed, and I immediately regretted not stopping home first to change my clothes. A qi-pao isn't what you'd normally wear to a place like the Zodiac. It was a very casual bar—jeans and T-shirts were the status quo—and I was going to stick out like a sore thumb. After the night I'd had, though, I didn't really care.

As I walked into the astrologically themed bar, a few eyes glanced my way, but thankfully nobody gawked. I shimmied my way onto a stool at the end of the bar and caught Megan's attention.

"Hey!" She smiled. "I didn't expect to see you in here tonight. How'd the party go?"

"Ugh, you're not going to believe this."

"One minute." She scurried away before I could

say anything else and returned with a mixed drink in hand. "Okay, you need this first. Now tell your story."

I looked suspiciously at the neon-yellow drink she'd brought me.

"It's a Sour Sagittarius, just drink it."

I went through the entire night, the story pouring out of me in a wave of anxiety, from Donna's strange behavior to my conversation with Alice, and everything that happened afterward.

When I was finished, she ran a hand through her hair. "Wow . . . just wow. The woman has finally snapped."

"You think so?"

"Lana, her husband died and she barely batted an eyelash. It's all coming out now. You can't just hold that type of thing in forever."

"True . . ." I chewed on my cocktail straw. "But it's so out of character for her. I mean, violence in general."

"Look, I know you respect this woman, and she does come across as a class act, but the mighty fall, too, ya know?"

"Oh!" I dug my hand into my purse and pulled out the tiny terra-cotta soldier. "I found this in her bathroom sink. She sent me up to her bathroom, but since the police were listening in, she told me there was a curling iron left on and I needed to check it and turn it off."

Megan eyed the solider and took it from my hand. "What the heck is it?"

"No clue." I shrugged. "There wasn't an iron on in the bathroom—there wasn't even one on the counter—and there was nothing there except this.

So I'm assuming she wanted me to take it for whatever reason."

Megan held it closer to her face and turned it over. "What's this line in the middle of it?"

"Huh? What line?" I squinted, trying to see what she was looking at.

"This," she said, handing it back to me.

I ran my finger over the break in the figure. "Hmm . . ." I gripped both ends and pulled. To my surprise it came apart. "Oh my God, Megan . . . it's a thumb drive."

CHAPTER
5

The minute I figured out it was a thumb drive, I wanted to rush out of the bar, run home, and rifle through it on my computer. I didn't think Donna would particularly approve of that, but my curiosity always seems to win these inner battles I have with myself.

Megan, however, made me wait until she got off work so we could snoop together. Reluctantly, I stayed with her until the bar closed, impatiently tapping my fingernails on the bar as I waited for last call.

When we finally got home, Megan turned on the laptop while I took Kikko out for tinkle time and a few good sniffs around her favorite bushes.

Once I was back inside, I found Megan planted at the kitchen table with two beers and a box of wings she'd brought home from the bar. "Okay, let's do this." She slid one of the beer bottles toward me.

I retrieved the thumb drive from my purse and handed it over. She inserted it into the appropriate slot, and a message popped up asking if we wanted to open it.

When we opened the files, I pulled out the chair next to Megan and sat down in stupefied shock.

"Holy . . ." Megan looked at me. "Are you seeing this?"

I nodded in return.

I already knew that Donna Feng wasn't who she said she was. Not entirely, anyway. I had stumbled upon all of Donna's secrets while investigating her husband's murder. There'd been a time when I thought she was the guilty party, and what I found hadn't helped her case in my eyes. While sneaking through some of her husband's personal effects, I had found a hidden envelope with information about Donna's past. Apparently, something had caused Thomas Feng to look into his wife, and he'd hired a private investigator to find out what she was hiding from him. We never did find out why exactly he'd hired the investigator to begin with. Maybe the paranoia of his own double life had gotten to him and he'd begun to see things that weren't there.

As Donna tells it, she was originally from California and had moved out to Cleveland to go to college. But in reality, she and her mother had fled from China when Donna was very young.

Her father had been mixed up in some type of bad business—which Donna had not elaborated on—and Donna's mother made a deal to get the heck out of Dodge before anything tragic happened to her or her daughter. That deal came with a price.

And now, as we sat in front of the computer, reviewing the information we'd found several months before, a chill ran down my spine. Where had this

come from? As far as I knew, the only existing copies of these documents had been in Thomas's possession, and he had hidden them well. I'd held on
to his copies for a short time after the conclusion of
his murder investigation just in case they would be
helpful in some way. But after the murder had been
solved, I'd burned everything we'd found in fear of
the wrong party getting their hands on them.

The files included the finalized report from the
detective agency, Donna's original birth certificate,
the forged certificate saying she was born in the
United States, and candid photos of her meeting
with various people around Cleveland.

Originally I had kept the investigation that
Thomas had conducted a secret, in an attempt to spare
Donna's feelings. The last thing I wanted was for her
to think her husband betrayed her right before his
death, but as time went on, mild concern set in that
somehow it would cause repercussions down the
line if she was kept too much in the dark. As gently
as possible, once she'd had some time to grieve over
the loss of her husband, I'd broken the news to her.
At the time, I'd thought she handled it pretty well.
But seeing her behavior now, I worried that she had
been bottling up all her emotions on the matter.

"What do you think this means?" Megan asked as
she scrolled through some candid photos of Donna.

"I'm not sure. Why was it in the bathroom?"

"Did Donna want you to take this because it was
hers, or do you think it was left for her—maybe by
one of the guests at the party?"

"I have no clue. None of it makes sense. Why was
it in the bathroom, and if she knew it was there, why
would she just leave it?"

"It's possible it was the only place she could ditch it at the time. If the cops were with her and found it . . ."

"This could cause a lot of problems for her. Not only will she be outed for a false identity, but the people she was running from could very possibly find her." I didn't know if anyone would be looking for her after all these years, but if there's one thing I've learned it's that some people can hold a grudge over something that happened decades ago.

"Lana . . . do you think this is why the nanny was killed? What if she was the one who gave this to Donna? Then Donna kills her to keep her quiet. It could be blackmail of some kind."

I shook my head out of frustration. "I don't know. I can't decide what to make of it. At all. My head is just a giant jumble of thoughts."

"Maybe this is why Donna has been on edge this whole time. Maybe she hired Alice because she was forced to and the nanny was holding this over her head the whole time."

"But for what purpose?"

"Who knows?" Megan lifted a chicken wing out of the take-out box and took a bite. "Could be a lot of things."

I thought about the timing of Donna hiring the nanny, and how Donna had insisted the woman move in with her immediately. Was that strange? Did two teenage girls really need that much attention? Or were we making something out of nothing? "I have to talk to Donna as soon as possible," I blurted. "I need to know why she wanted me to take this and where it came from."

"I think what we really need to do is find out who this nanny woman really is. We should also consider talking to the other people who work for Donna . . . or ex-employees maybe?"

I could see the wheels turning at full speed in Megan's brain by the gleam in her eye. If there was anyone who shared in my curiosity, it was her. "Let me talk to Donna before we start sticking our noses into this . . . we could have it all wrong."

Megan shrugged. "Okay, but in this instance, I don't know if you can trust a word that Donna says."

I woke up on Sunday morning feeling as if I hadn't slept all that soundly, what with the many questions I had about the thumb drive and the small matter of seeing a dead body the day before. I couldn't wait to head over to Donna's and start getting some answers. But before I could do that, I had dim sum plans with my parents, my grandmother, and Anna May. It was a weekly tradition that my parents had started once my sister and I had moved out on our own, since it guaranteed them scheduled family time no matter what was going on in our lives.

When the tradition started, I had no clue that I'd soon be managing our family's restaurant, thereby ensuring I saw my mother at least five times a week. Since my grandmother had come to stay with us, though, my mother had taken a backseat at the restaurant and spent less and less time there. See what happens when you do a good job? People start leaving you in charge of things.

In truth, it wasn't as bad as I'd originally thought

it might be. I actually found that I enjoyed running the show. In a former life, I'd had much different plans.

I downed some coffee while I dressed myself and applied makeup. A Lana Lee rule is that you never leave the house without makeup on. If you catch me without my eyeliner, it means that I'm terribly ill.

An hour later, I arrived at Li-Wah's, my family's dim sum restaurant of choice. The restaurant was located in a shopping plaza much like Asia Village, but this one was on the east side of town.

Normally, I was the last to arrive, but since I was so anxious to get things under way and speak with Donna, I beat my family there by five minutes. I think I even surprised the employee who seated me, as most of the employees were well accustomed to how my family and I operated.

I sat at the round table alone watching the dim sum cart circle the room. Being nosy increases my appetite by at least 10 percent.

Finally my sister walked in, spotted me across the room, appeared to gasp, and came walking over.

"Is this the seventh sign of the apocalypse?" Anna May set her Louis Vuitton bag on the table and sat in the seat to the left of me.

Anna May had recently acquired an internship at a fancy-pants law firm, and since had upped her clothing and accessory game. I knew what she made at the restaurant, and considering she didn't work as much because of her schooling, my guess was that she was paying for a lot of this through credit. Being a credit card abuser myself, I knew what a slippery slope she was teetering on. My only hope was that she could secure this job at the law firm. Plus, I had convinced her that a little sister like myself should have a nice Mercedes out of the deal.

"Ha ha," I said. "No, I just happened to get up a little earlier today."

"I can't believe what happened last night," my sister remarked as she turned over her teacup. She refilled my cup before filling her own. "Not to sound selfish, but I'm glad you let us leave early, because there is no way I wanted to be a part of that."

"And I did?"

She placed the teapot back in the center of the table. "I'm not saying that at all. But, you know . . . you tend to enjoy the intrigue of it all."

I snorted, even though I knew what she said was at least partially true. "I would have happily been in my pajamas by nine p.m. if that were an option."

"Do you think Donna did it?"

"How can you even ask me that?"

"Oh, come on . . . at one time you thought she killed her own husband. Don't act like it's a completely unreasonable question."

"Yeah, but that was different."

"You're right, she's actually unhinged now."

My sister had a point about that. Donna did seem to be unraveling, and last night she had been in rare form. But I had to hold on to the hope that it was all a matter of strange coincidence. Then again, did I even believe in coincidence? I'd have to say no.

My parents showed up with my grandmother, and my sister and I pretended like we were talking about something else. I knew that it wouldn't last long since Donna was friends with my mother, but we had to at least try to steer the conversation away from the ordeal that had taken place.

My grandmother, A-ma, sat down next to me and gave me her customary pat on the cheek. Her salt-and-pepper hair was wrapped in a tight bun at the nape of her neck, she wore no makeup, and the only jewelry she ever wore was a gold necklace with a small pendant of the character for "double happiness" that was poking out over her mandarin-collar blouse. She was a simple woman who liked to meditate and pray in the mornings, get in a light aerobic workout, and if the mood struck her she'd play a little mahjong from time to time. Since she'd arrived in the United States, she'd been spending a lot of time with Mr. Zhang, the owner of Asia Village's herbal shop, Wild Sage. Although my mother wasn't a fan of her own mother having a boyfriend, she didn't mind getting back some of her free time.

I didn't really understand what the deal was with my grandmother being here. Originally my parents had gone to Taiwan because A-ma was ill. But through some miracle, she was cured of anything that had been ailing her since she'd left her home.

I had a feeling it had something to do with her being lonely. Even though there was plenty of family over there, I think she felt lost in the mix living with my uncle and his family. My mother hadn't gone into much detail about it when they'd come back from Taiwan, but from the bits I'd gathered, that was my guess.

Now that everyone was present, my sister signaled for the dim sum cart and we started making our selections. My mother was usually in charge of this and requested more food than any of us could ever eat in one sitting. Today's feast included: steamed pork dumplings, fried turnip cakes, fried tofu and vegetables in a black bean sauce, sticky rice, and my favorite—shrimp noodle rolls. I could barely contain myself as the plates were set on the table.

As soon as the server left, we all dug in, passing plates and plucking an item from each dish. My stomach rumbled as I removed my chopsticks from their paper sleeve.

"So, Lana," my father asked. "How did the rest of the party go?"

The cubed tofu slipped from my chopsticks before it reached my mouth. My father wasn't usually the one to initiate snooping. "As you would expect," I said carefully.

"That's a messy business Donna is mixed up in . . ." My father eyed me, waiting for a reaction.

Was he testing me? I knew he didn't like it when I started poking my nose around things.

My mother gave my dad a side eye filled with suspicion. "Donna did not do this."

She said this with so much conviction, I blushed at the thought of thinking anything outside of that statement.

"Of course she didn't do anything to that poor girl," my father responded. "I was just wondering if Lana thought anything about it."

My mother looked between me and my father. "Oh, because she is nosy?"

"Mom!"

She turned back to me and shrugged. "Maybe now that you have a boyfriend, you are too busy."

My cheeks reddened. Before I went on a tirade, I took a deep breath and told myself this could work to my benefit. Let my family think that I was "too busy with my new boyfriend" to get involved in solving anything that had to do with the murder that took place last night. Little would they know that I planned to get knee-deep in this one.

CHAPTER
6

We wrapped up dim sum about half an hour later, and I gave Donna a quick call from my car to ask if I could stop by. She told me the sooner the better, so I drove straight from dim sum to her house in Westlake.

Her maid Rosemary answered the door. She was a woman of little expression, her face showing no emotion, almost in a militant sort of way. Outfitted in a plain black dress and black loafers, she was as drab as they come. Her salt-and-pepper hair was pulled into a bun at the nape of her neck, and she wore no jewelry except a simple gold necklace with a small cross.

She did not bother addressing me, but instead led me to the back of the house opposite where the tragedy had happened. There was an enclosed patio out there, and Donna was sitting alone in silence staring out into the backyard. She had big sunglasses on, and a casual outfit—something I had never seen her in—of black stretch pants and a red fitted T-shirt.

"Rosemary," she said, holding up a hand without turning to face us. "Will you bring us some iced tea and a few black bean cakes?"

"Yes, madam." Rosemary bowed her head slightly and returned to the kitchen.

"Have a seat, my dear." Donna gestured to the padded wicker chair directly across from her. "You'll have to excuse the way I look today. I woke up without the slightest desire to put myself together."

"What exactly happened after we left?" I asked, avoiding the subject of her appearance. I knew a woman like Donna would not want me to pacify her with compliments.

She adjusted her sunglasses, her focus on the yard just beyond the screened walls of the patio. "In a roundabout way, they accused me of killing Alice, of course. Which I clearly did not do." She waved a dismissive hand. "They couldn't prove anything, and when my lawyer arrived and reminded them they had nothing to hold me on, they had to let me go. They weren't entirely happy about it, but there is literally nothing tying me to that poor girl's murder. Not one thing."

I thought about the thumb drive in my purse. *Not one thing* . . . that the police knew about.

Rosemary came back to the patio and placed a tray with two slender glasses of iced tea and a plate filled with almond wafers, black bean cakes, and egg tarts.

When she left and was out of earshot, Donna continued. "The whole situation is an absolute mess, Lana. I am so beside myself. As if I needed another thing to go wrong in this house."

I took the glass of iced tea closer to me and sipped

from the straw. It was chrysanthemum tea, one of my favorites. "Donna . . . why did you send me up to the bathroom before I left?"

She gasped and leaned forward in her seat, finally looking at me. "I thought we understood each other. You did take that little soldier, didn't you?"

"Yes, I just wanted to be sure that's what you meant." I produced it from my purse and showed her that it was safe and sound. "Where did it come from?"

"I don't know. Someone left it on the vanity in my bedroom, sometime during the party I suppose," Donna said, reaching for it. "Imagine my surprise when I opened the files."

"So why was it in the bathroom?" I asked.

Donna sighed, flipping the soldier over in her hands. "I was intending to flush it down the toilet. But then I heard the screams downstairs and it jolted me. I was concerned the girls were causing more trouble, and I dropped it in the sink without giving it another thought. I had no idea what would come next."

"I see. And nothing else was with it? Not a note or anything?"

"No, it was just standing upright on my vanity. It was the strangest thing. Before I even knew what was on it, it gave me chills."

I found it interesting that Alice was murdered on the same night that Donna happened to find a thumb drive containing all of her best-kept secrets. The connection wasn't lost on me, but I didn't want to say too much. I wanted to hear what Donna thought, so I stayed silent, giving her the opportunity to speak.

"Lana, we have to find out where this came from.

I think that Alice's death was a message to me . . . a threat." Donna looked frenzied as she said the words aloud. "I need your help. No one can know about this. No one."

I found myself speechless—which, if you know me, is a rare occurrence—but I truly didn't know what to say. My first instinct was to believe that Alice was the one who left Donna the thumb drive, and then Donna killed her and planned to get rid of the evidence. But the suggestion that Alice's death had been meant as a warning to Donna was an interesting alternative theory.

I readjusted myself in the chair. What I needed to ask would not be pleasant. "I know you don't like to talk about it, but I need to know a little bit more about what happened with your father back in China. I know you told me he was a bad man. But exactly how bad was he?"

She stared off into the middle distance, presumably reliving the buried memories of her past. Softly, she began to tell her story. "I was only six years old when we left for the United States. My father had been involved with a triad that extorted and laundered money. Of course, he never admitted to it, but my mother knew anyway. She would overhear conversations he had with some of his gang members. I shudder to think of the men I saw in my house. They were nice enough to me, but I always knew there was something dangerous about them.

"Anyhow, in the process of his involvement, he crossed paths with a rival triad who felt their turf was being taken advantage of by my father and his group. Threats began, and I noticed a change in my mother as time went on. When we left the house, we always hurried to our destination, and she was constantly looking over her shoulder as if someone was following us. She jumped at every sound in the house, and checked the doors and windows regularly throughout the day. To this day, I don't know the extent of what she knew.

"One day we came home from the market, and a disheveled man was sitting at the dining room table, almost as if he belonged there. My mother sent me to my room. I could see the fear in her eyes. She told me to shut the door and not come out.

"After the man left, my mother came to tell me that we were leaving. She had a bag of money and passports along with some other false documents to help us change our identities. I asked about my father, but she said we would never have to worry about him again.

"The next morning, we left with only what we could carry. My mother told me that my father had died and we needed to be far away. She warned me that I could never speak of anything that really happened. I was to tell anyone who asked that I was born in California and that my father was killed in a car accident, leaving only the two of us to fend for ourselves. We would explain our money by saying that it was a settlement by the person who killed my father.

"Once we arrived in San Francisco, she hired a tutor to help me master the English language and remove any remnants of an accent. It was important to her that no one knew where we came from. She made it very clear that if anyone found out what she'd done, they would come for us out of revenge."

She paused, and I took the silence as time to

gather my thoughts. This was a lot more involved than I'd originally thought.

"So what is it that your mother did . . . what did she talk about with that man?"

Donna inhaled deeply. "We have never discussed this at length. She said he offered her safety. My guess is that she made a deal with him to hand over my father in exchange for an escape from the country. But she will never discuss it with me, and if I dare bring it up, a scolding is inevitable. She often reminds me that we are not those people anymore."

"Donna . . . I don't know what to say."

"There's nothing to say. Nothing I do now can change what happened, or take away who I truly am. All I can do is protect my family. Now can you see why I think Alice's death was meant as a message to me? This is how they operate. Who will be next? I've already contacted my mother just in case she's in danger. I asked if she's received any type of threats, but so far nothing out of the ordinary has happened. She is making plans to move again. I wish that I could be there with her in California to help, but if I left now, something bad could happen.

"Please, Lana . . . will you help me?"

Instead of responding to her request for help, I asked, "How did you end up hiring Alice?"

"She came highly recommended to me by a good friend of mine, Brenda Choi. She knew that I was scouting for someone to deal with the girls and handle some extra tasks around the house. Rosemary made it perfectly clear she would only do so much when I hired her. And watching the girls is not part of our agreement.

"Alice was willing to work for room, board, and a

reasonable salary comparable to other nannies I had interviewed. Brenda decided to let her go because she felt her kids were too old for a nanny and Alice had nowhere to go. I figured, *What perfect timing.*"

I didn't want to tell her that I thought her own children were too old for this much supervision; it wasn't any of my business. Plus, I knew that Donna had been overwhelmed with everything since her husband's murder. "What exactly did you know about her?" I asked.

"Are you asking me because of general curiosity, or because you plan to help me with this situation? And why does any of this matter anyway?"

I couldn't admit to her that I thought Alice was implicated in a different way than she was suggesting. "So far, in my experience, I've found it's best to consider every angle."

"That's a very good point, Lana. See? This is exactly why I'd want your help with this sort of thing. Besides, I can trust absolutely no one else with this. No one can find out about this, not even the police. This could jeopardize the safety of my entire family."

Looking at the desperation in her face, I couldn't help but feel myself caving. It was Donna, after all, whom I'd known my whole life, and who—despite everything—I couldn't help but trust. And I truly was the only one who knew her secret. I inhaled deeply. "Yes, of course, I'll help, Donna. I'll do whatever I can."

She flopped back in her chair, throwing her hands up. "Well that, my dear, is a giant relief. I know if anyone can help figure this out, it's you."

I sipped my tea wondering if that were true.

Would I be able to figure this out? Especially when I still had doubts of my own? "We're going to have to consider all the guests at your party as suspects. Do you think that someone maybe took advantage of the situation?"

"What do you mean?"

"Everyone witnessed . . . the outburst. Do you think any of your friends could have used it as their opportunity to get even with you? How well do you know all of your guests? Is there anyone who would have a way to get this type of information on you?"

Donna blushed. "I am so ashamed of myself for the way I acted. I was trying really hard to force myself into having a good time. Truth is, this birthday devastated me."

My mother taught me when I was very young to never question a woman's age. So I always guessed in terms of five-year increments. I had placed Donna to be somewhere around early to mid-fifties. "I can understand that. My sister is not a fan of her birthdays, either."

"No, I don't mean for that reason," she replied. "I mean because this was my first birthday without Thomas." She ended the sentence on a long sigh without offering more explanation.

I understood well enough and decided to bring her back around to the topic of her guests. "I'll need a list of everyone who was here. And what affiliations they have with one another and you. I know it's a lot, but I'm sure that the police have asked you for something similar?"

"They have," she said, nodding.

A lightbulb turned on in my head. "What about the surveillance cameras you have around the house? You know, the ones that caught me snooping around your house a few months ago."

"They're only focused on certain areas of the house. The police confiscated the recordings and are reviewing them."

My stomach dropped. I wondered what they would see on the tapes and if it would incriminate Donna further or let her off the hook.

"While you finish working on the list, could you start me out with a couple of names? Anyone that you think could be capable of doing something like this. Anyone that might have something against you. Even if it seems petty."

"Of course. I'll have it to you by tomorrow. I'm totally washing my hands of any public involvement with Asia Village for the time being so I have extra time on my hands. Ian is already worried about the bad publicity this will bring to the plaza."

I rolled my eyes. Ian Sung was the property manager and Donna's partner. He was the active one of the two and saw to the daily function of the Asian shopping center while Donna took the backseat and handled the other small rental properties that she and Thomas had owned together. At first I'd had a hard time imagining Donna as a landlady, but I quickly learned that she "had people for that."

We wrapped up our conversation, and she gave me a couple of names I could start looking into before she walked me out to the front door. "Oh, Lana, I am so relieved that you're going to help me with this. I just knew that you'd believe me and come through. You've always been loyal to the Feng family, and it will be greatly rewarded." She gently squeezed my arm.

"Like I said, I'll help however I can," I said, stepping onto the front steps. As she shut the door behind me, I let out a deep sigh. I really hoped that Donna was as innocent as she claimed to be.

CHAPTER
7

When I got home from Donna's, I felt that my brain had been overstimulated for the day. She had given me info on a woman named Denise Jung and said they'd had a falling-out at a charity event when Donna told the woman that she'd done a terrible job on the planning committee. Donna was not ashamed to admit that she'd told the woman her choices for catering and room setup were some of the worst she'd ever seen in her life. Apparently Denise had a chip on her shoulder ever since.

Though it was petty, I'd told Donna to provide me with anything she could think of.

The other name she gave me was that of Anastasia Wong. The two women had a screaming match when Donna insulted Anastasia's children's behavior at the Cleveland Asian Festival back in May. Once Donna made the comment that Anastasia's children acted much like barn animals, Anastasia took a jab at Donna's parenting and how Jill and Jessica behaved in public forums. Ms. Chang had broken up the verbal warfare and Donna hadn't spoken to Anastasia in person since, but she had extended a party invite to her as an olive branch. She was almost certain that Anastasia hadn't been at the party that evening, but couldn't be completely positive. She gave me the contact information for this woman, and it was my job to call her and ask if she'd attended.

Megan was home and greeted me with a somber smile. "How'd it go?" She was sprawled on the couch flipping through a fashion magazine.

Kikko wiggled her tail at my arrival and hopped off the couch to greet me.

"Not well," I told her. "You're never going to believe what I'm about to tell you."

Before hunkering down to give Megan the full scoop, I went to the fridge and pulled out a beer. I needed something to calm my nerves. Once I situated myself on the couch, I went into full detail about my conversation with Donna and the particulars of her childhood.

"Wow," Megan said, her mouth hanging open. "So that's the full story?"

"The fullest story we're going to get," I said. "Her mother has kept the rest from her, and from the way Donna tells it, she'll take it to the grave if it's the last thing she does."

"Do you think her mother is in danger, too?"

"It's hard to say. I mean, we need the proof that this is the actual situation happening. Right now, we know next to nothing."

"How are we going to find out?"

I shrugged. "Donna gave me two names of people that might be suspicious. She said she'd need more time to think on it, so she's going to get back to me tomorrow."

"Who would have thought any of this was real? I mean, did you ever think in your wildest dreams that we'd know someone who had a secret identity and had to hide from gangsters?"

I shook my head and chugged my beer. "Not on my most creative day."

CHAPTER
8

Asia Village is not what you'd expect to find in the suburbs of Cleveland. Nestled in the city of Fairview Park is a group of buildings designed to look like pagodas. As you come through the red entry gate with its twin golden dragons, and enter the plaza doors, you're greeted by beautiful skylights shining on a lantern-covered ceiling, a koi pond filled with healthy fish ready to be fed, and cobblestone walkways that lead to an Asian shopping paradise. There's a wide selection of themed stores carrying clothing, trinkets, cosmetics, books, and much more. Aside from that, the plaza houses our family's restaurant, a karaoke bar—that I absolutely refuse to sing in—a grocery store, and a hair salon.

On my way into the shopping plaza, Kimmy caught up with me from the parking lot. "So, I've been thinking . . ." She took one last drag from her cigarette and put it out in the ashtray outside the front doors. "What if the other maid did it?"

Clearly Kimmy was skipping the pleasantries

this morning. I opened the doors, and as we stepped into the air-conditioned plaza I could feel the hair on my neck stand up from the contrast in temperature. "Huh?"

"That lady . . . Rosemary or whatever her name is . . . maybe she's the one who killed Alice. You know, to get rid of the competition."

"Shhhh." I did a quick check to see if anyone was nearby, but thankfully it was just the two of us. Kimmy was the type of person that didn't need a microphone to be heard from far distances. "I doubt it was Rosemary," I told her. "From what I understand, they weren't in competition with each other for anything. Rosemary handled completely different functions."

"Yeah, but if she was willing to live there and take care of the girls, don't you think that Alice could have easily replaced Rosemary in the long run?"

I hadn't thought of that. And now that Kimmy brought it up, it sure seemed like a good angle. I would have to remember to add it to my list. "We shouldn't be talking about this. The police have it covered."

Kimmy let out a curt laugh. "Okay, Lee, whatever you say. Let's not pretend you don't try to channel your inner Veronica Mars when something goes sideways around here."

"I do not," I lied—with a straight face, I might add. Bully for me. It wasn't that I didn't trust Kimmy; I just never liked to let on to others that I was investigating anything, ever. The fewer people who knew what I was getting into, the better.

"Like I said, you're not fooling anyone. If you don't want my help, that's fine. I've got things to do

anyway, but I'm telling you, look into Rosemary."
She turned to unlock the gate to her family's store,
China Cinema and Song, and I said goodbye before
continuing on to Ho-Lee Noodle House.

Our restaurant sat next to my new favorite shop,
Shanghai Donuts. The sweet smell of baking dough
filled my nostrils as I passed by. The storefront it
resided in had held a variety of businesses that never
seemed to last long. My mother and her friends regarded the space as cursed beyond repair, but so far,
Shanghai Donuts was going strong.

I caught sight of Ruth Wu, one of the owners, in
the window and gave her a bright smile before I unlocked the double doors to the restaurant. Since the
doughnut shop had moved in, I'd been indulging a
little too frequently in my favorite pastry of choice.
To make myself feel better, I took Kikko on extra-
long walks.

Walking through the darkened dining area, I ma-
neuvered myself through the rows of black lacquered
tables to the back of the room where the panel of
light switches hung on the wall next to the kitchen's
swinging doors. Slowly the room came to life. I continued on through the kitchen and headed through
another swinging door to the back room that served
as a break area. The room was small and held a
couch that was most likely older than myself, a TV
set from my youth, and a beat-up wooden coffee
table. In one corner there was a small kitchenette-
style table, and opposite that corner was my office—
really, something reminiscent of a broom closet.

The desk and chair seemed oversized for the
room, but just managed to fit with space on one side
for me to shimmy around and sit down. There were

a few filing cabinets and two guest chairs should I need to reprimand anyone in private. That never happened; usually the only visitor I had was when Megan would stop by. Occasionally my sister would corner me in the office and nearly nag me to death, but since she'd taken this internship at the law firm, I'd received fewer lectures from her.

I reviewed my Monday morning list of to-do items before heading back out into the dining area to straighten up before our first customers of the day arrived. As I was entering the room, Peter showed up at the door and waved for me to let him in.

"Morning," he mumbled as he slunk past me. Peter wasn't much of a morning person, either, so we worked well together. "Dude, I already know today is going to be annoying." He groaned.

I followed him to the kitchen. "I'm sure it won't be all that bad," I said, attempting some optimism.

He wasn't convinced. "Yeah, right. The Matrons are going to be all over this Donna thing. And mark my words, Ian will probably come in here at some point today to complain to you. Everyone in the plaza knows that we were catering the party Saturday night, and as soon as they have the chance to question you, you'd better believe there will be a string of people marching in."

"Well, I guess you're going to be busy in the kitchen cooking up all this delicious food for everyone."

Peter snorted in return as he turned on the cooking equipment. "Yeah, man."

"You're extra grumpy today. What's your deal?" I asked, leaning against the stainless-steel sink bins.

"Nothing, it's just I had to listen to Kimmy talk about her theories on Donna all night. She wants me to try to get close to the twins to see if they know anything."

"Really?"

"Yeah, and I'm not doin' it. They may be half blood and stuff, but there's no way I'm going to try to make friends with that family. They haven't exactly been the best to me or my mother."

"It's the situation. It's awkward for everybody," I said.

"And I totally get that. I'm fine with the way things are. I just don't wanna talk about it."

"I wonder why Kimmy is so interested in this situation?"

"Gee, I wonder," he said, giving me a pointed look.

"This has something to do with me?" I asked.

"That's what I think."

I didn't know what to say to that other than, "I'll try to talk with her."

"Yeah, well, do it quick, because a man can only take so much speculation."

The Mahjong Matrons filed in precisely at nine a.m. as they did every morning. The four widowed women were our most loyal customers and also the Asia Village authorities on gossiping. If something was going on, they knew about it.

Helen, Wendy, Opal, and Pearl stuck to their usual seating arrangements. Opal liked to sit by the window because she was keen on observing what went on in the plaza. Her sister, Pearl, sat opposite her, and the other two liked to sit on the end because they enjoyed the freedom of being able to get up if something dire was happening. They also felt those were the best eavesdropping spots.

I smiled pleasantly at the ladies and noted how sometimes my life felt a little like an episode of Mr. Rogers. That same cardigan . . . every day.

Once they were situated, I went into the kitchen and placed their order with Peter. Really all I had to say was that they had arrived. They ordered the same thing every morning without fail. I prepared their tea and hurried back out into the dining area.

All four of them were sitting gingerly on the edge of their seats. I swear Helen was kind of bouncing when I returned.

"So," Helen started as I set down the teapot. "Can you tell us what happened at the party?"

The others nodded eagerly.

I hugged the tray to my chest and studied the four sets of eyes that stared back at me in anticipation fit for a Christmas morning. "I don't think there's much to tell other than what everyone already knows. Alice Kam was found in the pool, the police are accusing Donna, and Donna is adamant that she did not do it. They're investigating . . . blah blah." I tried my best to act nonchalant about the whole thing, but I didn't think it was working. If you get the Matrons too riled up, they tend to go into hyperdrive and rumors fly faster than a 747.

Pearl leaned toward me and whispered, "Yes, but do *you* think she did it?"

Truth be told, I hadn't decided on that yet. And I felt really guilty about it. I could hardly explain my thought process to anyone outside of Megan, because no one knew the details of Donna's former life but me . . . and, well, whoever had left Donna that thumb drive. My reply to them was, "I'm sure that it will all get straightened out soon."

The two sisters eyed each other and nodded as if I had confirmed their suspicions.

Wendy spoke up next. "I have heard many things while at the beauty shop. Ms. Chang's housekeeper said that she heard from some girl who is friends with Alice that things were getting very bad at the Feng house."

"Bad in what way?" Opal asked, barely above a whisper.

Wendy made a gesture with her hand to insinuate that Donna was hitting the bottle pretty heavy.

The other three looked down at the table and shook their heads.

"Do you happen to know what this girl's name is?" I asked Wendy.

"Not at the moment, but I am sure I can find out for you."

"Thanks, I'd really appreciate it." I started to back away from the table before they could ask me any other questions.

But before I could walk away, Helen said, "You be careful, Lana, Donna could be a very dangerous woman."

I thought about that statement for most of the morning as I went about my duties on autopilot. When Nancy came in at eleven for the split shift she often worked, I retired to my office to handle some paperwork before the lunch rush officially started.

With a few minutes to spare, I pulled from my purse the sheet of paper that had Anastasia Wong's phone number on it. I kept my fingers crossed and dialed the number.

"Hello?" a woman barked into the phone.

"Hi, is this Anastasia Wong?" I asked using my customer service voice.

"Yes, who is this?"

"My name is Lana Lee, I'm a friend of Donna Feng's."

Silence.

"I was calling some of the guests from her birthday party to—"

"Well, you called the wrong person!" she yelled into the phone. "You tell that foul good-for-nothing woman that I ripped up her invitation and let my cat use it as kitty litter. I would never think of going to her party after the way she insulted me."

Even though she couldn't see me, my face was turning red. "I'm sorry to have bothered you, Ms. Wong."

"As you should be. You shouldn't be doing her any favors. That miserable woman . . . I heard about what happened on the news and I am doubly relieved that I wasn't there. Now if you'll excuse me, you interrupted a very important meeting."

She hung up without giving me the chance to say goodbye. I let out the breath that I was holding. Talk about intense.

I scribbled a note next to her name that she was not present at the party and went back to totaling receipts from the night before. When I was halfway through my stack, Donna called my cell phone.

"Hi, Lana, I have that list prepared for you. I've also taken the liberty of jotting down a few notes on why I think specific people might be guilty. I thought that would help steer you in the right direction. But truly, I think this is a waste of time. You know my feelings on this subject."

"I know, and thank you for entertaining this, Donna, I appreciate that. I'll swing by after work and pick it up."

We said our goodbyes, and I sat for a moment staring at my blank phone screen. Yeah, *steer me in the right direction* . . . any direction away from her.

After work, I stopped by China Cinema and Song to visit with Kimmy and advise her to lay off the whole Feng case. She protested a little, as I suspected she would, but when I told her that Peter was concerned about her safety, she mellowed and agreed to stop speculating. Of course, that wasn't his real reasoning—well, maybe partially, but I didn't want to say that she was actually just getting on his nerves. Kimmy tends to fight fire with fire. And I knew if I told her the truth, she'd dig deeper into what had happened to Alice Kam just to spite Peter.

When I got home that evening, Megan had already left for work, so I leisurely walked Kikko around the apartment complex while I contemplated what steps I needed to take. By the time we got back to the apartment, I had come up with a list of starting points, and I now had Donna's list of guests and suspects as well.

However, I was disappointed to find that she had hardly helped after all. She had starred and highlighted the names of the two women she had already mentioned to me the previous day. The only difference was that she had added their husbands' names in parentheses. There was also a note about Brenda Choi's husband. She'd written down that the husbands had not been fans of Thomas and might like to see her suffer now that she was a widow. I didn't know if that was valid reasoning, but I've heard of people killing for less, so I wasn't going to exclude them.

The fact that Donna had told me she would take my request seriously, yet didn't, really perturbed me. Here I had thought she'd provide me with juicy tidbits on the society women she hung around with. But this list she'd given me was almost no help at all. I found it also slightly suspicious and didn't know if I should take that into account. In the event that Donna believed her own story, it was possible that she was going to have a one-track mind about this.

Regardless of her reasoning or what I thought was her reasoning, I had to keep pushing forward as best I could. Next to the list of guests, I had my trusty investigation notebook opened to a fresh page. The five-subject spiral notebook was kept hidden under my mattress, and I only brought it out for occasions such as these. Writing down my thoughts as I went along helped keep me organized and on point. I tend to drift and spiral otherwise.

In the notebook, I jotted down the names Brenda Choi, Anastasia Wong, and Denise Jung and made notes that their husbands hadn't exactly gotten along with Thomas Feng. I tried to mentally match the names with faces, but I really didn't recognize who any of these people might be. In parentheses, I put a note next to Anastasia's name saying that I had already spoken with her and she hadn't even come to the party. Donna hadn't mentioned being suspicious of Brenda since they were friendly, and had only suggested her husband. But I was leery of Brenda considering it had been her idea for Donna to employ Alice. So she went on the list.

I made a note that I wanted to talk to Ms. Chang's housekeeper: the "friend" of Alice's who supposedly dished out the juicy details. I also made a note to find out if there was any validity to the claim that Donna had a drinking problem. She did seem to be drinking quite a bit at the party, but it was her birthday. I couldn't base anything off that if I wanted to be fair.

Kikko barked abruptly, startling me and causing me to jump in my seat. I watched as she beelined for the door and sniffed at the door crack. A moment later, there was a light knock at the door.

Who the heck could that be? I shuffled to the door and peeked out the peephole. It was Adam. Even though we had been dating for a few months, I still got butterflies every time I saw him. I opened the door, and his large, muscular frame filled the doorway. He scooped me up with one arm and kissed me as if he'd just come back from war.

As he pulled away to smile at me, I noticed that his reddish-brown hair had been freshly cut. I returned the smile and then nuzzled the side of his neck, inhaling the cologne that he always wore . . . he smelled of sandalwood and cinnamon.

With his free hand, he closed the door behind him and carried me away from the threshold. He only put me down when Kikko began to whine. "Well, hey there, young lady," he cooed as he bent down to give Kikko a pat on the head. "Missed me, too, did you?"

"What are you doing here?" I asked.

He stood upright his full six feet two inches and rubbed my shoulders. "I just left the station and thought I'd swing by and see if you wanted to have dinner. Are you busy?" His green eyes drifted over to the dining room table where my notebook was wide open for the world to see.

"No, no, not busy." I hurried over to the table and shut the notebook.

"Lana . . . what is that?"

My cheeks flushed. The jig was up. "Nothing."

"You're a terrible liar." He laughed heartily, his eyes crinkling with the gesture.

Not too long ago, we'd agreed that we wouldn't keep things from each other. And though I'd been open about everything else, I still felt strange admitting my detecting activities to him. I decided to give in. "It's a notebook I keep . . . with information in it."

"What kind of information?"

"Oh, you know, about certain key events that have taken place around here."

I watched as his jaw muscles clenched. That was usually the symbol of a lecture on its way.

"I was hoping that you wouldn't get involved in this whole thing with Donna Feng. If you get caught poking your nose around, I can't help you this time. I don't have any friends in the Westlake Police Department."

"Well, I won't get caught snooping then." I lifted my chin. "I am getting better at this, you know."

"Uh-huh."

"I'll go get ready. I'll just be a minute." I rushed into my bedroom and sat on my vanity stool to touch up my makeup.

I was pleasantly surprised with his reaction. A few months ago, he would have completely flipped out on me and given me a lecture on how I'm not in law enforcement and therefore should leave the investigating in the capable hands of the professionals. But we'd been through a lot together in the last few months, and I think he finally understood why I could not just let these things go.

I made a pit stop in the bathroom to fix my hair before heading back out into the dining area. I found him intently reading my investigation notebook.

"Okay, I'm ready!" I said, scanning the room for my purse.

"Lana . . . honey . . ."

"Hmmm?" I turned my back to him and continued to search.

"You wrote in here that I'm a jerk-face . . ."

"What?" A nervous giggle escaped. "That must have been the first time we met. You were kind of harsh, you know."

"A couple pages later you call me an a—"

"Found it!" I grabbed my purse off the couch. "Let's go. I'm starving." I grabbed his hand and pulled him out the door before he could read any more of my notebook.

CHAPTER
9

By the time I got back from dinner with Adam, I was so exhausted, I passed out without even taking another passing glance at my notebook. It took every bit of energy I had left just to shower, throw my pajamas on, and stumble into bed.

I slept like the dead—okay, maybe a bad choice of words considering what I was currently investigating—but it was worth it when I woke up the next morning feeling refreshed and alert.

Megan was still in bed and I didn't want to disturb her since I knew she had closed out the bar the night before, so I left a Post-it note on her door telling her to call me as soon as she got up. We needed to talk.

The morning passed as usual. The Mahjong Matrons had acquired the name of Ms. Chang's housekeeper's friend: Evie something or other. And I also learned that the housekeeper's name was Susan Han. I added them to my mental list of people I needed to talk with.

Around eleven thirty, Peter told me that Megan was on the phone, so I slipped into my office to take the call.

"I'm guessing this is about the case?" she asked when I picked up.

I started with Kimmy's angle on the housekeeper and then continued on with what I'd learned from the Mahjong Matrons. "What do you think?"

"Wait a minute, is Kimmy getting involved? I love you to death, Lana, but I can't work on this with that girl. I have my limits."

"No, no, nothing like that. She just wanted to pass it on to me. I already talked to her for Peter because he's sick of hearing about her theories."

"Imagine that."

"Focus."

"Right, sorry. As much as I don't care for the girl, I have to say, she has a point. Rosemary has worked for Donna for a long time, and it's very likely she could know her story, even if by accident. You should ask Donna if that's a possibility, but yeah, look into her anyway. It can't hurt. What's her last name? I'll do a quick search for her online."

"Chan, I think. Yeah, that sounds right, Rosemary Chan."

"Okay, and what else, are we going to look into all of these people from Donna's list? Because that's a lot."

"I wish I knew these people better, or who was still at the party at what times. If any of these people left early, then they don't necessarily matter, though I guess someone could have sneaked back in . . ."

"Did Donna specify anything on her list?"

I told her about the starred names. "Everything is

listed in my notebook. It's in the usual hiding spot. That's about all the help she gave me."

"I feel like I need to severely catch up with everything. Closing every night this week has not been working out for me."

"I know. Do you know if they're getting close to replacing Robin? This process is taking forever."

"There are two people they're considering. One guy, he's pretty cute and I think he'd do well . . . and then some girl who I'm not too excited about. I don't think she'll last."

"Well, hopefully they hire someone new soon because I really need your help on this."

"I'll do what I can. I don't have to go in until six, so I can check these people out online and I'll make notes for you to look at when you get home."

"Thanks, I'll probably miss you again. I'm supposed to get together with Rina for drinks after work, but I really want to talk with Penny—after all, she was there that night, too."

"You think maybe she saw something at the party?"

"It's possible, but I haven't gotten a chance to really talk to her. She was quick to leave the party without saying anything to anyone. I'm sure she doesn't want to get herself involved."

"Well, I'm sure the cops have questioned her already. So if she does know anything of use, she would have passed it along to them at least."

"True. Okay, well, it's just about noon, I'd better get back out there before Nancy has my head on a platter for leaving her alone during lunch rush."

We said our goodbyes and I went back to my duties as the other Lana.

* * *

A few hours after lunch, Ian walked in. Though he looked well put together in his expensive Italian suit and French burnished leather shoes, I could tell by the expression on his face that he was frazzled and not feeling as assured as someone might first assume. As I assessed his demeanor, I considered how odd it was that he was just stopping by the restaurant now. I had expected to see him first thing on Monday morning, ranting and raving, as was his usual style.

I was in the middle of wiping down a recently vacated table, so I set down my rag and sanitizing cleanser before going to greet him at the hostess station.

He evaluated the dining area with an air of importance. His eyes fell on me, and his expression softened a tad as he tried to read my face. Everyone who knew me at all knew that's where my emotions could be clearly read. "Lana, I'd like to speak with you in private, if you have the time."

"Sure." I signaled to Nancy that I would be in the back.

Ian followed behind me as I led him into the kitchen. Peter turned to acknowledge us but didn't bother saying anything. He raised an eyebrow at me and gave Ian a curt nod as we passed through.

Peter, like most of Asia Village, and Adam, knew that Ian had the hots for me. At times it made things uncomfortable for me because the feelings were not mutual, but mostly I tried to act like it wasn't happening. Ian was indeed an attractive man, but something about him had always put me off. I couldn't quite put my finger on it, but there was a vibe that came off him that told me to stay away.

Despite the fact that I was now with Adam, Ian continued from time to time to insert himself into my life more than necessary. And though it annoyed Adam to no end, he was not intimidated by it and knew that I'd never act on any of Ian's attempts to win me over.

Once we were in my office and the door was shut, Ian relaxed.

He unbuttoned his suit jacket as he sat down. "I'm sure you must have wondered where I was yesterday."

I sat down in my swivel chair and folded my hands in front of me on the desk. "Actually, I did."

He raised an eyebrow. "You did?"

"Yes, in a professional capacity."

He slouched in his seat. "Oh."

"You wanted to talk about something?"

"Well, yesterday, I spent a majority of the day doing damage control."

"Because of the murder?" I asked.

"Why else, Lana?"

"Well, what's happening? It's not like I'm in the loop on this one."

"Things are not looking good for Donna. And this plaza is too closely associated with the Feng name. It's going to cause problems. A reporter actually suggested that the murder of this Alice woman and Thomas Feng's death is some sort of conspiracy."

"What?"

"They think there is some type of connection between the two murders. One of the more popular theories is that Thomas was having an affair with this woman before he died and that Donna found out about it. This then prompted her to strategically plant this woman in her house as an employee in order to kill her. Another more sensational theory is that this woman was working in connection with Charles An as his contact to the outside world and trying to ruin what remains of the Feng estate."

Goose bumps ran up and down my arms. Charles An had been the man responsible for Thomas Feng's death and was currently serving life in prison. He had also held me at gunpoint. I didn't like to think about him. "Are you being serious? That's the most ridiculous thing I've heard all day. That sounds like a plot from a crime show. These people need to tone down their imaginations."

"That's what I assured them," Ian replied. "Of course, the most logical is that Donna has been under severe stress since the murder of her husband and simply lost her mind, leading her to take it out on the help."

I leaned forward, trying to read the expression on his face. "Is that what you truly believe?"

He teetered his head back and forth as if weighing his answer carefully. The fact that he had to think about it at all was not a good sign. "I will admit, I've seen Donna in a better state of mind. In recent weeks, she has completely stepped back from any responsibilities that have to do with the plaza. She won't return half my calls. And the ones she does return, well, she acts as if she has no idea what I'm talking about."

"She's just under a lot of stress," I said, becoming a little defensive. "She is so occupied with keeping herself busy that she hasn't fully dealt with what happened. She hasn't really given herself enough time to grieve." And it was true. Donna was running all over town bending over backward for several charities and associations. I suspected the reason why she was steering clear of the plaza had something to do with how much her husband had loved it. It was probably a painful memory for her.

"Well, it's going to put this place in danger. People are starting to think some type of gang is involved. And frankly, Lana, that is the last thing we need around here."

I gasped. "Why would they think that?" Never mind that it was a possibility; Ian didn't have to know that. No one knew that . . . except me, Donna, and two people who were already dead: Thomas and Alice.

"You know how people start rumors. The Fengs have a lot of money, there are secrets in the family, seemingly shady dealings . . ."

I drummed my fingers on the desktop, absorbing everything that Ian had told me. This seemed to be spreading faster than I thought it would. Probably due to the fact that her husband had been murdered just a few months ago. "So why are you telling me all of this?"

"Because I know you, Lana. And I know that you're most likely already involved with this on your own accord, if Donna hasn't asked you yet."

I didn't confirm his statement.

"I'm here to tell you that you need to work this fast. Before it gets ugly."

We stared at each other, and I don't know if it's because we didn't want to face facts about what Donna could be capable of in her current mental state, or because what else was there to really say? This wasn't a good situation any way you spun it.

I didn't have any more time to think about it because Nancy knocked on my office door. "Excuse me, Lana, but someone is here to see you."

"Who is it? Can you tell them to come back?"

"I don't think so. He really wants to speak with you."

I groaned. Looking at Ian, I said, "I'll be right back."

Nancy had already returned to the dining area, so I didn't get another chance to ask who was waiting for me.

I stepped out into the dining room and scanned the area. At the hostess station stood a man a little over six feet tall with his back facing me. His dirty-blond hair was styled in a messy tousle. As he turned slightly to look at something, I studied his profile: square jaw, high cheekbones, full lips posed in a casual smirk.

My stomach clenched as he turned fully in my direction and I stared back at his pale-blue eyes. It was the man who shall not be named. The man who broke my heart in a thousand tiny pieces and sent me on a shopping spree that made even MasterCard cringe. It was Warren Matthews, ex-jerk-face extraordinaire.

His smirk turned into a smile, and I swallowed the lump that began to form in my throat. Collecting my nerves as best I could, I returned the smile with a shaky lip quiver and walked with a straightened back through the dining room up to the front.

He was dressed in a navy-blue suit and plain white dress shirt. His tie consisted of diagonal stripes in varying shades of blue.

"Hi," he said casually, as if we'd just spoken the day before. In reality, it had been over a year since we'd said two words to each other.

"Hi," I returned, my voice barely above a whisper. "What are you doing here?"

"I was in the neighborhood and thought I'd stop by and see how you were."

"I'm doing really well," I said. I could hear the defensiveness in my own voice, and I tried desperately to mean what I was saying. I *was* doing really well. I wasn't lying. Things had never been better. Well, minus the recent murder, of course. So why did I sound like I was faking it?

"I was hoping we could grab a drink. There were some things I wanted to talk to you about." He stuck his hands into his pant pockets and gave me a shrug. "Maybe catch up?"

I relaxed my shoulders, took a deep breath. "I don't think that's a good idea."

His head drooped, and he bit on his lower lip. "Look, I know you probably don't want to see me . . . or talk to me for that matter. But I'd really like to sit down with you and explain, if that's possible."

Another deep breath. "There's nothing to explain. Really. I'm over it."

"Over what?" a voice asked from behind me.

It was Ian. I guess he got bored of waiting in my office.

"Nothing," I replied.

Warren cleared his throat. He acknowledged Ian and stuck out a hand. "Hi, I'm Warren."

Ian regarded my posture, scrutinized Warren with a condescending once-over, and didn't return the gesture. "Pleasure."

Warren shrugged and let his hand fall. "Yeah, sure." He turned back to me. "Just think about it, okay? Maybe we can talk tomorrow or something. I clearly caught you off guard."

"You think?"

He nodded slowly. "Okay, well, I'll give you time to think."

I didn't respond.

"It was nice to see you, Lana. You look good." He looked at me thoughtfully and turned, walking out the door.

My body released all the tension it had been holding. I put my hands on the top of the lectern to steady myself. I started to count to ten.

Ian put a hand on my shoulder. "What the hell was that about?"

"I'll tell you later." I took some more deep breaths and headed back for my office without giving any further explanation. I guess Donna wasn't the only one whose past was coming back to haunt her.

CHAPTER
10

"He actually came into your work?" Megan shouted into my ear. "He's got some kind of nerve to pull a stunt like that."

After I made it back into my office and took a few more deep breaths, I called Megan right away to tell her about my encounter with Warren. Within seconds, she'd become riled with the news. My heart was still pounding, and the palms of my hands were slick with sweat. "I thought I was going to die right there," I admitted to her.

"Well, good on you for keeping it together. I can't believe that jerk had the audacity to come to your restaurant and act like catching up was just another day."

"He's always been super casual like that, though."

"No excuse," Megan returned. "He is the biggest jerk in the universe. Hands down."

"I know." I could still remember how it felt when I'd seen him Christmas shopping hand in hand with another girl. I'd felt like my entire existence with him had been a lie. They hadn't noticed me and so I followed behind them, hoping that I'd seen it all wrong. But I hadn't. He seemed so familiar and comfortable with her, and I often wondered if he said the same things to her as he did to me. Instead of confronting him then and there and risking a huge embarrassing scene that I didn't want to put myself through, I'd phoned him later that evening and called him out on his two-timing ways. That's when I learned the sad reality that I had actually been the *other* woman.

Weeks had gone by, months even, and I hadn't been able to shake that horrible feeling in my gut. I couldn't even put it into words. Was it shame? Was it panic? A mixture of the two? I felt so stupid for having believed every word that had come out of his mouth. And as I thought about it now, all the pain and upset I had felt at the time came rushing back.

"You're not going to talk with him, right?" Megan asked. "*Right?*"

I paused. "I don't know yet. I haven't decided."

"You don't know yet? What do you mean you don't know yet?"

"Megan, this could be my chance to say the things I never got to say. To let him know how he made me feel."

"I don't think it's going to make a difference. Really, Lana. I mean, he's going to apologize and act like he's so sorry for what he did. But in reality, is he? Then he gets away with it. If you forgive him, then he wins. He gets a free pass."

"Maybe . . . I don't know. I feel like it's more for me than it is for him."

"Do you even care about him anymore? I mean seriously, you have Adam now, and he's amazing and wonderful and thinks the world of you. Why waste your time on this? He's taken enough of your time and energy."

I shook my head as if to remove the thoughts from my mind. "It doesn't matter. I can't think about this right now anyway. We have bigger things to worry about." I told her about my conversation with Ian.

"Damn . . . when it rains it pours, huh?"

"You can say that again." I reminded her that I was meeting with Rina in a little while and would talk with Penny if I could while I was at the Bamboo Lounge. "Did you find anything interesting in your Internet searches today?"

"Not really. I'm still looking. These people don't seem very interesting. There's a lot of charity work recognition, but nothing juicy that we'd care about. I still made some notes for you, though. Check them out when you get home."

We hung up for the second time that day and I attempted to go back to work as if my mind weren't spinning with all that had happened in the last few hours.

Ever since Rina had put down roots in Cleveland, she had become one of my closest friends. We'd met in an unconventional sort of way—at her sister and brother-in-law's funeral—and became friends shortly after. I'd even helped solve their double murder. Since that time, Rina and I had taken up the tradition of having drinks every Tuesday after work. Even though we saw each other every day, we didn't always have the chance to talk at length.

The plaza's karaoke bar, the Bamboo Lounge,

was our weekly meeting place of choice and re-
quired the least amount of effort on our parts. After
all, we were always at the Village anyhow.

Normally we sat at a booth, but since I wanted to
question the lounge's owner, Penny Cho, I suggested
we sit at the bar. It was still early for the posh place,
and so we pretty much had the run of it. The lights
were dimmed, and a few workers tended to the small
stage where people would be singing in a few hours.

Penny brought us two cocktails. A Blushing
Dragon for me, and a Mai Tai for Rina. I thought
maybe letting a drink's worth pass before I attempted any type of pointed conversation was a
good idea.

"Are you okay today, Lana?" Rina asked as she
studied me. "You seem kind of tense."

Here and there, I had talked to Rina about my
past relationship at our weekly chats. Mostly it was
to bring up the differences between Warren and
Adam, and also to note some of the challenges it had
brought up in recovering from trust issues. Adam
and I both had them . . . for different reasons, but we
did understand each other. Adam had been incredibly patient with me and vice versa while we'd gotten our feet wet again.

I didn't know that I felt like talking about it at
this particular moment, because I needed to keep
my head about me in regard to what was happening with Donna. And if there was one thing I was
known for, it was spiraling out of control when it
came to my previous relationship with Warren.

I returned her concern with a simple, "Nothing,
I'm fine."

"As if I believe that for one minute."

"I'm just tired," I lied. "Long day and all. How are things going with you? How's the shop?"

She shrugged. "Everything is going pretty good, although it's been a bit slow in the summer months. I'm still trying to come up with a gimmick to get people to come in. I'd participate more at the night market if it weren't so hot out. A lot of this makeup doesn't do well in these temperatures."

"What about makeovers or something? Hire a makeup artist and have them do summer make-overs. You could feature bright-colored eye-shadow palettes and shimmering bronzers."

"Hey, that's not a bad idea," she replied. She sipped her drink daintily through her straw and thought it over. "I'd have to find someone, of course. Someone who can work for cheap."

"Maybe talk to Jasmine over at the salon. She might have a friend who could help out."

"That's another great idea, Lana." She continued to study me, suspicion in her eyes. "But why am I getting the feeling that you're trying to keep the subject off you."

"Really, I'm fine," I told her again.

Penny came over to check on us.

"Hey, Penny," Rina said. "Does Lana look fine to you?"

Penny focused in on me, tilting her head to the side as she assessed whether or not I was "fine." "Hmmm, she does appear to have extra-dark circles under her eyes today."

"Hello, I'm right here," I said, looking between the two of them. "I just have a lot on my mind recently." I figured this would be my perfect segue into talking about Donna's situation.

"Uh-oh," Rina replied. "I know what that means."

"What do you mean by that?" I asked innocently.

"I should have known that's what's been bothering you."

Penny regarded Rina with confusion. "Huh?"

"It's this whole thing with Donna Feng, isn't it?" Rina asked.

I nodded. "It is."

"Don't even think about it, Lana Lee," Rina said.

Penny crossed her arms over her chest. "Donna is a menace if you ask me. I like her well enough, but I feel like a dark cloud just follows her wherever she goes. If I didn't need the extra cash, I wouldn't have even agreed to bartend the party."

"Do either of you remember anything odd happening at the party that night?" I asked.

Rina shook her head. "No, not really. I did notice she seemed to be drinking quite a bit, but other than that, everything seemed totally ordinary."

Penny leaned against the bar and thought. "I did notice a woman in a blue dress sneak up the stairs at one point in the evening."

"Around what time?"

"Not sure," Penny replied. "I slipped inside really quick to find a broom and dustpan because I'd broken a glass behind the bar. I happened to notice the woman rushing up the stairs, but I figured it had something to do with getting to a bathroom quickly."

There was a much closer bathroom downstairs, so unless this woman needed the utmost privacy, I couldn't see why she wouldn't just use the nearest one. "Was this before or after Donna's outburst?"

"I'm pretty sure it was after."

"And you didn't recognize the woman?"

"I think I've seen her somewhere before. Maybe she shops here or something. She's got shoulder-length black hair, maybe about your height . . . super skinny."

I made a mental note about this mysterious woman. It made me wonder about the home surveillance tapes that had been confiscated by the police and if they had found anything of importance on them.

"Lana." Rina sounded queued up for a lecture. "You need to let the police handle this. Things could get messy with Donna involved, and you don't want to associate yourself with her in case she's guilty."

"Do you really think she's capable of drowning someone like that?" I asked. I, myself, had tried several times to picture Donna holding Alice's head underwater, and I just couldn't make it work.

"I've never seen anyone get quite that mad at something like their kids messing around. And the way she yelled at that poor girl." Rina shook her head. "She definitely had malice in her eyes. I can tell you that."

Penny straightened and regarded both of us. "If you ask my opinion, I'd stay away from the whole thing. I wouldn't be surprised if Donna Feng ends up being involved in this somehow. All I know is her best bet is to plead insanity."

CHAPTER
11

-- -- -- -- -- -- -- --

That night when I got home, I went over Megan's notes. She hadn't found anything of interest on Donna's socialite friends. My phone rang while I was searching the Internet for background information on Alice. It was Adam, and for some reason, I didn't feel like talking to him. Maybe because then I'd have to tell him about my day and I didn't want to lie about my encounter with Warren. I decided it would be best to deal with it the following day.

I continued my search looking over Alice's social media accounts, her friend lists, and any generic information that came up on her. There wasn't a lot to find, and I found that in itself to be suspicious. For a young woman in today's society, it was uncommon not to share where she was from or include pictures of family. Most of what Alice posted was articles on childcare, photos of flowers, and the occasional meme. After going back a few months, I got bored and decided to give up on that direction for the time being.

Next, I went over the list of starred names again and did another search on them, too. Nothing special. Though their names appeared in articles about charities and random acts of kindness provided to the city, there was nothing juicy or interesting that might raise an eyebrow.

With the minimum information I had, where to begin seemed to be my biggest problem. I settled on getting in touch with the woman who had recommended Alice to Donna. From the way Donna had made it sound, Alice had worked for the Choi family for a long time and lived in their house throughout her employment. So there was a chance they'd gained background information on her through natural conversation.

It wasn't yet nine o'clock, but I figured it'd be okay to call Donna since it was business-related. I needed to put my plan into action right away.

"Lana, have you found anything?" Donna asked, her voice a little more high-pitched than normal.

"Hardly," I admitted. "None of these people seem to be very forthcoming on social media. But I have another plan. I need you to back up the story I want to use, though."

"What do you mean, dear?"

"Well, I was trying to find a way to talk with these people without seeming suspicious. I thought maybe I could say that you found something at your house that might have belonged to one of these people and I'm trying to figure out who. Then once I have a foot in the door, I could get them talking a little bit."

"Lana, that sounds like a brilliant idea. And yes, I'll back you up on it. What are you going to say was found?"

"How about an earring?" I suggested.

"Perfect. I think that would work out just fine. Especially with my group of friends. All the women there would be absolutely devastated to lose a piece of jewelry. It would buy you just enough time to grab their attention."

"Have you heard anything about the surveillance tapes yet?" I asked.

"They didn't find anything of importance. No wayward meetings or strangulations. Just people coming in and out of the back patio area. The camera in the back doesn't really show all areas of the pool, it's mostly focused on the door."

I let out a heavy sigh.

"Chin up, my dear," Donna said. "I'm sure you'll get to the bottom of it. Let me know how everything pans out with your earring plan."

We hung up, and I readied myself for bed. I was disappointed in the camera not providing something more useful, but at least now that I had my starting point, I could relax. Kikko and I snuggled under the covers, and I fell asleep before my head even hit the pillow. The day had really worn me out.

The following morning, I woke with my brain going at hyperspeed. With Anna May now working her internship at the fancy law firm she hoped would eventually employ her, I was a person down at the restaurant. Most days that wasn't an issue—summer business proved to be slow more often than not, and Nancy and I could easily handle the flow of customers. But it wasn't beneficial for my investigative duties.

I caved and decided to call my mother claiming that I had a doctor's appointment that I needed to get to. I asked her if she'd mind coming in for a few hours to cover with Nancy just in case things got busy.

My mother, of course, had said yes. She was a sucker for a doctor's appointment. When she arrived at the restaurant, she had my grandmother in tow. "A-ma wanted to come eat."

My grandmother smiled up at me, and I saw a twinkle in her eye. Right then I knew she hadn't actually come to eat; she really wanted to visit with Mr. Zhang at the herbal shop.

"Thanks so much for covering for me, Mom. I really appreciate it."

"Yah, no problem, Lana." She sized me up. "This is a checkup, yes? Or are you sick again?"

"No, I'm not sick again." In actuality, I hadn't been sick in over a year, but she insisted all the time that I must be ill. It was probably all these fake doctor's appointments I kept going to. "Just a regular checkup."

"Okay. You look too skinny. Maybe Mommy should check on you more and make sure you are eating enough."

"I'm eating fine, Mother."

"Eating doughnuts does not count. You need to eat good food."

Before she could go on a tangent about my eating habits, I scurried into the back and grabbed my purse out of the office. On my way back out, Peter said, "Be careful, dude."

"What do you mean?" I asked.

"I know you, Lana. And I know the closest you've

come to seeing a doctor is when the paramedics checked you out after the night market at the beginning of summer."

"Okay, fair," I admitted. "I'll be careful." I left before anyone could lecture me on anything else.

The nice thing about living in a city like Cleveland is that everything is roughly twenty minutes away. Accordingly, I arrived at the Choi household about twenty minutes later.

They lived in a ritzy development community with oversized Colonials that made me wonder how many family members had to live inside for the place not to feel empty. The Choi property was beautiful with its meticulously cared-for landscaping and picturesque ponds.

I'd selected one of the fancier earrings in my jewelry collection to take with me as my cover story. It was a rhinestone chandelier earring that looked nice enough to possibly belong to one of Donna's friends.

It was an overly warm and sunny day with not a cloud in the sky. So I shouldn't have been surprised that the maid who answered the door told me Brenda Choi could be found lying out by the pool. She led me through the expansive home, and I took a moment to appreciate the polished wood flooring and vaulted ceilings.

The backyard wasn't as big as I would have imagined it to be, but the view of a pond made up for the lack of land. The cemented patio area was large enough for a table with four chairs and a few plastic chaises for lounging poolside.

Brenda was sprawled out on one of the chaises wearing a floppy straw hat, sunglasses, and a blue two-piece bathing suit. She broke her attention away from the book she was reading to assess me. "Hello . . ." she said pleasantly.

"Hi, I'm Lana Lee . . . I'm not sure if you remember me from Donna Feng's birthday party."

She shifted in the chaise, hoisting herself up and throwing her legs over the side to get up. She stood and shook my hand. "Yes, I remember you from the party. You're the girl that runs that charming noodle shop. What brings you by?"

I plucked the earring from my purse. I had placed it inside a tiny ziplock bag, much like the ones that Adam carried around with him for evidence. "I was wondering if this happened to be yours? Donna found it in between the couch cushions after the party and isn't sure who it belonged to."

Brenda inspected the earring. "No, that isn't mine." She studied my face. "That's awfully nice of you to run Donna's errands for her."

"Well, she is a family friend, and with everything she has going on, I thought it was the least I could do."

"Yes, that whole thing is quite a shame, isn't it?"

As the words came out of her mouth, it dawned on me that I recognized this woman. She was the woman in the blue dress who was gossiping with the other ladies at the party. If my memory served correctly, she had been the one to say she hoped Donna didn't do anything she would regret. It was also likely that she was the woman Penny saw rushing upstairs: Her slender body and hairstyle matched what Penny had described to me at the Bamboo Lounge.

"It really is," I answered. "I can hardly believe that Donna would do something so horrible, though."

Brenda gestured to a chair at the table. "What have you learned about the investigation, anything?"

I had a sneaking suspicion that this woman was an equivalent to one of the Mahjong Matrons. She was probably the head gossiper among her socialite friends and would share everything I said to her today with the rest of her group.

Once we were seated across from each other, she offered me some cucumber water from a carafe covered in condensation. I hate cucumbers, but to be polite, I accepted. Ah, the things I do in the line of duty.

"I don't know much actually," I said. "The police are reviewing the surveillance tapes from around Donna's property, but I don't think anything has turned up yet. And they have nothing to prove that Donna is guilty."

"That poor woman," she said, shaking her head sympathetically. "I've had my concerns that she would snap one day. As much as I admire her resilience, no woman is that well put together. And I believe she proved that to be true with her little outburst at the party."

It was amazing to me how many people were ready to believe that Donna was capable of wrongdoing. Not that I could entirely eliminate myself from that group, so maybe I shouldn't judge.

I decided to turn the conversation away from that and focus on getting the information I'd originally come for. "From what I understand, it was you that recommended Alice to Donna."

"Yes, and I feel terrible about it." She raised a

hand to her chest and sighed. "I can't help but think I'm partially responsible for that girl's unfortunate death. I know in reality, it has nothing to do with me, but what if she had gone to work for someone else? She might still be alive today."

"Perhaps," I said noncommittally. "But then again, we don't know why she was murdered, or what actually happened . . . *or* who this girl was affiliated with."

"What do you mean?"

"Well, what can you tell me about Alice? Do you know anything about her past?"

"Her past?" Brenda looked confused.

"Yeah, you know, maybe she was mixed up in something and this has nothing to do with Donna at all. I'm sure you've considered the possibility what with you and Donna having been friends for so long. I know you say that Donna has become unhinged, but there has to be a part of you that believes she's innocent."

"It's true, Donna has been a close friend of mine for many years, but Alice was a good girl with a solid track record. I could hardly say a word against her. She took excellent care of my kids, and it's hard to believe that she would be involved in anything . . . unsavory."

"And the only reason you decided to get rid of her is because your kids are too old for a full-time nanny, correct?"

There was a slight pause. "Well, yes and no."

"I don't know what you mean by that," I said.

"Alice proposed the idea to me."

"She did?"

"Yes, she knew her time was coming to a close,

and she suggested that one of my friends might benefit from her services. Alice was well aware of the circle that I run in and knew there was money to be made. She happened to bring up Donna's name, and I said I would speak with her on Alice's behalf."

Alarm bells were going off in my head. I had so many questions that I wanted to ask, but all I said was, "I see."

Brenda gazed out toward the pool. "I could hardly object. After all, Donna needs all the help she can get. What's a widow and two fatherless teenagers to do in a house that size? And that maid of hers . . . she is a militant nightmare. I figured Alice would do some good around there."

"Speaking of, do you know Rosemary well?"

The woman chuckled. "Just in passing. The times I've been to Donna's to play mahjong have shown me enough. Matter of fact, I have to wonder about *her* sometimes. Who knows, maybe it was Rosemary that finally snapped."

She stopped there and left the insinuation hanging in the air. It felt so pointed that I couldn't help but feel in my gut that this woman was hiding something. I just didn't know what. I had to agree with Donna, though: This woman definitely deserved a suspicious star next to her name.

CHAPTER
12

Since I was nearby, I stopped at Donna's house to update her on what I'd learned from Brenda Choi.

Rosemary answered the door appearing less than enthused at my arrival. "Ms. Feng is in the bath."

"Would it be all right if I waited for her? It's kind of important."

She pursed her lips. "Very well. You may wait in the sitting room." She opened the door wider to let me in and led me into the sitting room. "Would you like some tea?"

"Sure, that would be nice," I responded politely.

While I waited, I dug my phone out of my purse and noticed I had another missed call from Adam. Crap. I'd forgotten to call him back. I sent him a quick text message telling him I'd call him as soon as I left Donna's, so he didn't send the troops searching for me.

When Rosemary returned, she set a tea service tray delicately on the coffee table and then proceeded to pour a cup for me.

"Thank you," I said, picking up the cup from the tray.

She bowed her head and turned to leave. "Rosemary . . ."

Pausing in mid-step, she did not turn, but replied, "Yes?"

"I was wondering if I could ask you a few questions about Alice?"

She was silent for a moment, and I thought she would continue on her way without bothering to acknowledge me any further. But she finally turned and gave me a stern frown. "Why would you be curious about such a matter?"

I assumed that she had no idea that I was investigating things for Donna, but I'd hoped she would be a little forthcoming in the spirit of casual conversation. "I suppose I'm just curious about her is all. In the short time that she worked here, did you get to know her well?"

She straightened her back and lifted her chin. "It is not my duty to converse with the other help in a personal manner. I choose to keep things very professional. I did not entertain small talk." She gave me a pointed look.

"I see," I said, deflated. "So you don't happen to know if she was mixed up in anything shady?"

"Shady?"

"Yeah, you know, crooked."

Rosemary folded her hands in front of herself and lifted her chin even higher than before. "No, Miss Lee, I do not know if she was shady, as you say. But I will tell you this: Donna Feng is a commendable woman and a fair and kind employer. These bad happenings do not concern her."

"Did I hear my name?" Donna shouted from the spiral staircase. "Rosemary, who's here?"

Rosemary, clearly not one to raise her voice, spun on her heel and marched out into the hallway to inform Donna of my arrival.

I leaned back against the stiff sofa and sipped my tea.

Donna entered the room in a summery silk robe covered in cherry blossoms, her hair gathered on top of her head in a matching silk wrap. "Lana, darling, if I had known you were coming, I wouldn't have piddled around for so long."

"It's okay," I responded. "I just got here maybe ten minutes ago."

"Has Rosemary been taking care of you?" she asked, noting the teapot. "Would you like something to eat? I can have her whip something up real quick."

"No, no. I won't be long, I have to get back to work. I only stopped by to fill you in on some things."

Donna nodded at Rosemary, and Rosemary disappeared down the hallway toward the kitchen. Donna entered the sitting room and sat in the chair adjacent to me. She crossed her legs gingerly and adjusted her robe to cover them. "Now, what is this about? You have my full attention."

I told her about my interaction with Brenda Choi, making sure to allow time for her to soak in the information.

She sank into her chair, lifting a hand to her head. "I don't understand. Alice wanted to work for me all along?"

"Brenda claimed your name simply came up because Alice knew that she ran in a wealthy social circle. There's a slim possibility that's true, but add in the fact that Alice asked for you by name, and the mysterious thumb drive, and I'm not so sure."

"Why wouldn't Brenda tell me this to begin with? She made it seem like it was all her idea."

Donna's expression told me that she felt betrayed, and I couldn't blame her considering the circumstances.

I sighed. "Well, my guess is that maybe she didn't think anything of it at the time. She probably thought it was an innocent suggestion. Brenda said she knew you needed help with the children." I left out the other things she'd said about Donna to spare her feelings.

"Well, yes . . . of course . . . the children." Donna seemed to drift off, and she wasn't sharing with me where her mind had gone.

"Donna . . . there's something else Brenda said that kind of struck me as odd."

"More?"

"Yeah, she insinuated that Rosemary . . ." I stopped. I didn't want to even say the words out loud. Especially because I feared that if Rosemary heard me, she might come in here and smack me with a wooden spoon.

"Lana . . . don't worry, you can tell me anything."

I leaned forward and lowered my voice. "She suggested that Rosemary had something to do with it. That maybe she snapped . . ."

"Oh, you have got to be kidding me." Donna threw her hands up. "Has everyone completely lost their minds?"

I shrugged. "Is there anything that would give that impression to Brenda or anyone else?"

Donna glanced toward the entryway to make sure that Rosemary wasn't anywhere nearby. "No, of course not. Yes, she can be a little rough around the edges, but she would never resort to any kind of violence. It would be too undignified for her nature."

"Do you know how they got along?"

"Who, dear?"

"Rosemary and Alice."

"Fine, I'm sure."

"You're sure?" I asked. "That doesn't sound sure to me . . ."

"Well, I don't really know, I suppose. They always seemed cordial in front of me."

"I tried to ask Rosemary a little about her involvement with Alice, and she wouldn't tell me anything. She said it's not her place to make friends with the other staff."

"That's silly," Donna said with a dry laugh. "Rosemary! Can you come in here, please?"

I shrank in my seat, regretting my decision to mention it at all.

A few moments later, Rosemary came striding into the sitting room. "Yes, madam?"

"Rosemary, how did you get along with Alice? Did you ever have any trouble with her?"

"No, madam, no trouble. We were civil with each other." She slid her eyes toward me in accusation.

I felt my cheeks redden.

"And did you happen to notice anything strange about this young woman?" Donna asked.

"No, madam."

"Thank you, that will be all, Rosemary."

Rosemary took a step forward. "Madam, if I may . . ."

"Yes, of course, what is it?"

"It is only my duty to keep the house clean, see to the laundry, and prepare meals as needed. I hardly had any reason to associate with Alice, and I did not engage in friendly chitchat."

"Never?" Donna asked.

"No, madam."

"Okay. Well, thank you again, Rosemary."

"Yes, madam," she said with a slight bow and turned to leave.

As she turned the corner, I notice her give me the stink eye before going out of view.

"Well, there you have it," Donna said, shifting her body back toward me. "They hardly even talked."

I tilted my head in confusion. "You don't think that Rosemary is a little on the cold side?"

"She's just extremely professional, and very good at her job, I might add," Donna said with satisfaction. "I hate the fact that Brenda Choi could even have the nerve to suggest something so ridiculous. No, Lana, don't even waste your precious time on this line of questioning. It won't lead anywhere productive."

"What about the fact she said Alice wanted to be placed in your house. Doesn't that worry you?"

"Lana, if Alice Kam wanted to blackmail me, I highly doubt that she would have just up and left that thumb drive for me to find without saying anything further. Don't you agree? It would be a shoddy attempt, if you ask me. Though I do find the circumstances of this new information strange, I'm not sure this is the right angle, either. I truly believe this was a message meant for me. I'm sorry, my dear, but I can't see it any other way."

I left shortly after, feeling disappointed, and

slightly more suspicious of Donna's maid. It didn't help that as I got into my car, I noticed her watching me from the second-story window.

Points for me, I remembered to call Adam on my way back to the restaurant.

"I'm glad you didn't try to pull that doctor's appointment story with me," he said after I told him where I'd been. "I have to admit, I was a little worried when you didn't call me back last night."

Adam had a not-too-nice history with a significant other not responding in a timely manner, so it was something I could understand, and I felt guilty about it. But I didn't want to tell him about Warren's sudden reappearance. At the same time, it wasn't something I could keep from him, either. "I know, I'm sorry, yesterday was one heck of a day."

"You can tell Donna that the police are more than capable of handling the situation, you know," he said. "This isn't your responsibility, and shame on her for even thinking to involve you in this."

"Believe me, she's aware. And, it's not that anyway," I said.

"Well, what is it? Did something happen at work yesterday?"

I hated how he always seemed to know when something was up. There was very little I could get by him. "It's no big deal."

"Usually when people say that, it's a big deal . . . or going to make me extremely unhappy." He sighed. "Tell me."

I held my breath. "You know my ex . . . the one who added trust issues to my mental baggage list?"

"Yeah, Will or something right?"

"Warren," I corrected him.

"Okay, Warren. And?"

"He came into the noodle shop yesterday." I cringed as I waited to hear his response.

"Okay . . . well, we'll go with option two . . . I'm unhappy, but it's not that big of a deal. So, what's the deal, then?"

"Really there's no deal. He wanted to apologize and explain himself. But he doesn't want to do it at the restaurant. He wants us to talk away from there."

"I can understand that," he said plainly.

"You can?"

"Of course. He doesn't want to be at your place of employment while he tries to sweet-talk his way back into your life."

"Adam."

"Lana."

"First of all, he's not going to win his way back into my life. There's no amount of sweet talk that could make that happen."

"I didn't say there was . . . I just said that's most likely his plan."

"Are you mad?"

"Not at you, sweetheart," he said, softening his tone. "I don't like the idea of this guy even trying to get one ounce of your attention though. Did you tell him you were dating a big bad detective that carries a gun?"

I could hear the smile in his voice, and I laughed. "No, I thought that might be bragging a bit."

"A little bragging never hurt anybody," he replied. "Look, I trust you, so you do what you feel is right. I prefer you don't meet him anywhere privately, but if you do, please tell me when you plan on meeting with him, and then when it's over. Is that a deal?"

"Yes, that's fair," I said, pulling into the plaza parking lot. I exhaled and felt a weight lift off my shoulders. "I haven't decided either way yet, though."

"Okay, well, take your time. Whatever you decide is okay with me."

"Thanks, Adam."

"Besides, if he hurts you in any way, shape, or form, I'll just break his kneecaps."

We laughed together as we hung up, but I knew that Adam wasn't kidding.

CHAPTER
13

When I entered the restaurant, I was surprised to find Megan sitting with my mother and grandmother at a booth near the back. Nancy stood at the edge of the table, holding a tray, and the other three women were seated comfortably in the booth, laughing and eating an assortment of appetizers.

My mother was facing the door and noticed me walking in. She waved me over as she yelled across the restaurant. "Laaa-na! Come eat! Come eat!"

The few customers we had all turned to see who she was talking to. This was not a rare occurrence. More often than not, my mother yelled to me from across restaurants, stores, parking lots, and even quieter places like libraries and movie theaters. You'd think by now I wouldn't be so embarrassed, but as I walked over to the table of women, I felt my cheeks warming.

"Mom, you don't have to yell," I groaned.

"Ai-ya, no one cares, Lana. This is Mommy's restaurant. I can do anything I want."

Megan winked at me. "Hey there, roomie, how was your doctor's appointment?"

"Oh, just fine," I said.

My grandmother scooted over and I sat down next her, resting my purse on my lap. She smiled at me and tapped her plate. "Eat. Eat."

The table was covered in plates. I had yet to eat anything and my stomach grumbled. "I don't want to leave Nancy to work by herself now that I'm back."

Nancy batted my shoulder. "No, you eat something. It is not very busy this afternoon."

Without any more argument, I grabbed a teriyaki stick, a spring roll, and plucked some shrimp lo mein off the various dishes.

Megan laughed at me as I bit into my spring roll. "Doctor's appointments make you pretty hungry, huh?"

"You have no idea."

"I tell Lana all the time, she does not eat enough," my mother said matter-of-factly. She eyed Megan. "You also do not eat enough. Maybe I should cook for you both and bring food for your apartment. You cannot always eat pizza and doughnuts."

"We're fine, Mom." I made sure to give her my serious face even though I knew that more than likely she would start delivering care packages of random Chinese food. I decided to change the subject and make use of her being here. "Mom . . . what do you know about Donna's maid, Rosemary?"

"She's okay," my mother said. She was now focused back on her plate of noodles.

"Do you think she's kind of mean?" I asked.

"Why do you ask this?" My mother eyed me. "What happened?"

"Nothing happened. I was just curious. This whole thing with Donna has made me wonder if maybe something was going on in that house. I thought maybe Rosemary might be jealous of Alice or something."

"I thought you told Daddy you were not going to be nosy this time," my mother scolded.

"I'm not being nosy . . . sorta . . . mostly. I'm mostly not being nosy."

"This is not your business. Donna picks good people to work for her. You do not have to worry about this."

I sighed. My mother was not nearly as fun as the Mahjong Matrons. Maybe they would have some enlightening things to tell me.

We finished eating, and my mother told me it was time for her and my grandmother to head off to bingo. My grandmother thoroughly enjoyed it because she could follow along with her minimum English.

A-ma was all smiles, her silver front teeth sparkling in the restaurant lighting. "Lana, you come."

I waved my hand no and smiled apologetically. "No, A-ma, you go. Have fun."

"Lana," my mother sang. "A-ma wants you to come. You should come with us. It will be nice to have more family. Anna May will come, too."

I groaned. If there was anything I disliked, it was bingo. "Mother . . . I have to work." I swept my arm out as if displaying the restaurant.

"You will hurt A-ma's feelings," my mother returned. "You can come after work. We like to play all day. This is no problem."

"Anna May's not going to go. She's got too much going on."

My mother batted her hand, dismissing my protests. "She will go. You worry about you. We will see you later, okay? Be a nice girl."

Through clenched teeth, I wished them good luck as they left and willed the universe to swallow me whole before five o'clock. After I was done throwing my mental tantrum, I sent Nancy on a break and headed up to the hostess podium with Megan. All the tables had cleared out except for two businesswomen who looked to be deep in conversation.

"So . . ." Megan said, keeping an eye on the businesswomen while I faced the door. "What happened?"

"Well, I'm stuck going to bingo with my family tonight. That's what happened."

Megan chuckled. "No, that's not what I meant. I meant about the case and your progress."

"Oh, that." I shook the thoughts of bingo out of my mind. "I hate to admit that Kimmy might have been right about Rosemary. But I also have my reservations about it."

"Why's that?"

I told her about my encounter with Brenda Choi and how she seemed to be putting the idea in my head. Not to mention the fact that Alice had suggested she wanted to work for Donna.

"Well, here's something more interesting. I hit some pay dirt on Alice's social media."

"You did?"

"Yup, I've been sifting through her junk since I woke up today," she said. "Does the name Bryce Blackwell mean anything to you?

She was being coy about it, but I wasn't following. "No, should it?"

"Yes. He was the DJ at Donna's party. Do you remember him at all?"

"Not really. He stopped me on his way out to ask where Donna was because he needed to be paid, but that was about all the interaction we had. Why, what's the big deal with him?"

"Apparently he was Alice's boyfriend for a while."

"What? But I checked her social media, and I didn't find anything like that."

"Yeah. Like I said, I was sifting through her junk for a while. I went way back. It was at least seven months ago. Then all of a sudden their posts stopped being about each other."

"It kind of fits together now. I think Donna told me that Alice recommended him, too."

"Okay, call me crazy, but would you recommend your ex-boyfriend to work your current employer's party?"

I snorted. "No ex-boyfriend of mine, I can tell you that."

"So maybe he couldn't let go or something. She tried to be friends with him, does nice things for him like get him jobs, he mistakes her kindness for wanting to get back together, and when she says no, he takes her for a swim."

I sighed. "You've been watching too many dramas again."

"It's totally plausible and you know it. This might not have anything to do with the thumb drive at all."

"Yeah, but then where did it come from?"

She shrugged. "That might be a bad coincidence. Given Donna's history, I think we both already know that someone might be coming for revenge. If anyone from Donna's father's past found out who she was, it could put the whole Feng family in danger."

"This is true." I weighed the likelihood of these two instances happening at the same time and not being connected.

"If it all tied together, I hate to say it out loud, but I think one of our suspects might end up being a hit man."

The term *hit man* stayed with me long after Megan left the restaurant. It followed me through taking care of customers, totaling out receipts, and finalizing the bank deposit. I didn't even want to consider it as an option. Like Megan said, it had been in the back of my mind this entire time, but I wanted it to stay there. Far away from any other thoughts I had about what really happened that night.

It seemed to make more sense the more it crept to the forefront of my mind. The only person who had this information on Donna was already dead. Thomas Feng had hired a private investigator to obtain the information, and that was the only open trail as far as I knew, other than myself. And since we had destroyed everything Thomas had acquired from the PI in fear of someone else finding it, I couldn't see how this thumb drive could exist.

So because it did, in fact, exist, where else could this unknown person have gotten the information? All that I could come up with was that they were connected to the original situation with Donna and her mother. An angry relative, or maybe a mob associate of Donna's father looking for revenge. Here's Donna Feng in her nice, new shiny life, living it up without a care in the world. Sure, her husband was murdered, but had it stopped her from having a cushioned life? I didn't like to admit it, but it had barely slowed her down. Suppose this person had found out who Donna really was and had been spying on her, watching her almost flawless life unfold while they suffered painful memories of Donna's father "accidentally" being killed. Revenge could be a powerful motivator, and if Donna's theory was correct, it would make sense that this person would want to take out those around her first—that was usually the best way to hurt people.

My mind spiraled out of control with these thoughts as I left Asia Village for the day. The only thing that made sense to me was that on top of talking to the people already on my list, I needed to find the PI that Thomas hired and confront them. Maybe they could lead me in the right direction.

CHAPTER
14

- - - - - - - - - - - - - - -

My original plan was to go home and relax until it was time to leave for bingo, but that didn't happen. After walking Kikko around the apartment complex, I called Donna and asked if she could check the thumb drive for the name of the investigation company that Thomas had used to dig up her checkered past. She told me it was called Price Investigations, and the documents had been signed with L. Shepard. We hung up and I did a search online. They were located downtown on Euclid Avenue. I jotted down the address, and then began a search for Bryce Blackwell.

He had his own website and it appeared that he worked solo. That made things easier. I wouldn't have to go through a company or receptionist to talk with him. I filled out the contact page and said that I was interested in hiring him for a party, asking for an in-person meeting.

Then I sat down with my notebook and quickly

wrote down everything I had learned throughout the day and what my plan of action should be.

My first order of business was to get a better grasp on Rosemary and if she was really someone to consider. Right now, there were some factors leading me that way, but I didn't feel 100 percent committed to it. Just because she came off as a cold woman didn't necessarily mean she had it in her to drown someone. But I would be a fool not to dig a little deeper.

I also needed to understand why Alice would specifically ask for Donna. Was it a coincidence? Had she only asked because she knew that Donna was in need of extra help around the house? Brenda did mention that Alice knew all about her circle of friends. Maybe she had heard Brenda talking about Donna in passing. I made a note to get clarification on that fact.

And who *was* Alice anyway? Would I be able to find out anything new about her through this Bryce person?

I spent a few moments speculating that Alice was some type of undercover, stealthy ninja sent from China to expose Donna for who she really was. And then began a manhunt that would inevitably end in Donna's death. But Donna, being vigilant in protecting her family, got rid of Alice before anything further could come of it. However, if that was the case, then Alice's death might also mean that someone else would come to take her place in getting revenge on Donna.

I grumbled. And here *I* was, accusing Megan of watching too many dramas.

I scribbled out the idea and started anew with the

consideration that Bryce might have actually killed Alice as Megan had suggested earlier. But maybe for different reasons. Maybe Bryce and Alice were the ones working together to blackmail Donna. But that would also lead me back to Donna being the killer to protect herself.

While I considered that fact, I also came to the realization that it might not be the best idea to have an in-person meeting with Bryce if he were, in the fact, the killer, but talking over the phone wasn't going to cut it. I would just have to be careful.

I stared at my page of scribbles and hated every word. I didn't like any of my options, yet there they were.

Anna May texted to let me know she was heading to the bingo hall and provided the address. I shut off my laptop, stuffed my notebook back under my mattress, and put on my "Lana the daughter" hat. It was going to be an interesting evening.

If there were such a thing as professional bingo, my mother would definitely be the best player there ever was. I found her, A-ma, and Anna May sitting at a folding banquet table toward the back of the narrow room. Several rows of tables and plastic chairs filled the hall and faced a small stage where an announcer stood with a microphone to call the numbers.

The seat between my mother and my grandmother was empty and I silently scolded my sister for leaving it open. She knew that sitting next to my mother would mean scrutiny over how you played. Betty Lee did not mess around when it came to stamping numbers.

I greeted my family with a mumble of hellos and sat down in the vacant chair. Sprawled out in front of my mother were nine jumbo sheets with four cards on each page of randomly placed numbers. To the left of her were three different bingo daubers—she liked to coordinate with the colored border of the pages.

My sister reached her arm over my grandmother and handed me two sheets and a purple dauber. "Here, I got these for you. I thought you might like three because I know how you are about numbers, but Mom said you're too slow."

I inhaled a calming breath and thanked my sister for the pages, organizing them in front of me.

My mother handed me a can of Coke and held out a bag of chips. "Do you want this?"

"I'll get my hands all greasy," I said.

She took them back and put them on the opposite side of her. "You are right, and you are already slow."

A-ma grinned at me and pointed to her own bingo sheets. "A-ma feels lucky!"

I laughed and wished her luck.

The announcer alerted the crowd that we would begin in a few minutes and that anyone walking around should return their seats. The sounds of shuffling and chairs scraping on the linoleum echoed through the hall.

As the announcer began to call the numbers, I started to think this would be a good distraction for me. Lately it seemed all I did was work or solve murders. I needed a break from the seriousness of everyday life. I stamped the numbers I had with renewed enthusiasm. Maybe I would get lucky and win some money tonight.

But as I continued on, my mind—like it tends to do—began to wander back to the mystery of what was really happening. Could I trust Donna? Was she playing me to her advantage? She knew that I was a loyal family friend, and I had already been keeping her secret. And if she were taking advantage of me, what would I need to uncover to find out? Did I want to uncover it?

Because I had become lost in my thoughts, I didn't realize that my hand was frozen in midair and I had been staring into nothingness.

You'd better believe my mother noticed, though. She lightly smacked my arm. "Ai-ya, why are you dreaming? You missed many numbers." My mother quickly stamped my pages for me as I brought myself back to the present moment.

She gasped. "You have bingo, you have bingo." She grabbed my arm and shot it up in the air. "*Bingo!*"

I stared at the diagonal row on my paper. Hey, look at that. At least I was winning with something.

When I got home that night, I was two hundred dollars richer. Though my mother wanted to celebrate with a late-night dinner, I politely declined and told her that I was tired from the long day. Reluctantly, she let me go home, knowing that I had to open the restaurant in the morning. To celebrate, I pulled some pizza out of the fridge and shared my crust with Kikko. I continued to flesh out scenarios one after the other until it was time for bed. Unfortunately most of them revolved around ways that Donna could be lying to me in order to protect herself. How far would she go to keep her family safe?

Once I'd officially exhausted myself, I crawled into my queen-sized bed while Kikko burrowed herself underneath the blankets. I went to sleep wishing that some type of answer would come to me in my dreams.

CHAPTER
15

-- -- -- -- -- --

I woke up five minutes before my alarm went off. I lay there anyway, wondering what this day would bring to me. When the buzzer sounded, I forced myself out of bed, shuffled out to the coffeemaker, and pressed the START button.

Kikko came padding out to see what I was doing. Her curly tail wagged as she waited patiently for me to let her out for morning tinkle time.

After I finished my morning routine, I set off for work feeling hopeful that I would learn something extremely beneficial to Donna's predicament.

I sped through the regular duties of preparing the restaurant for opening. I always made it a point to check each table's place setting, straighten chairs, wipe down the menus if they needed it, and make sure that there was no shortage of silverware or chopsticks.

The hands on the clock had barely moved and with time to spare, I went back to my office to check my email and social media until Peter arrived. To my surprise, I had an email response from Bryce Blackwell. I hadn't expected him to get back to me quite so fast. He said he could meet with me during early-evening hours any day between Monday and Thursday. I responded asking if he was available later this evening. Why not get it out of the way as quick as possible?

Peter sent a text message letting me know he was at the front door, and I hurried through the restaurant to let him in.

"Oh good, I thought you fell asleep back there," he joked as he walked in.

"Just catching up on some emails." I locked the door behind him and followed him into the kitchen. "How are things with Kimmy?"

"Better. She's calmed down about the whole thing mostly. In a way, I think she lost interest in it."

"Good." And I meant it. The less she tried to get involved, the better. Just because I had a habit of sticking my nose where it didn't belong didn't mean it wasn't better if others stayed out of it.

The time began to fly by after he arrived and before I knew it, I was unlocking the doors and waiting for the Mahjong Matrons to march in. Without fail, they came in and greeted me with a polite nod as they headed to their usual booth.

I headed for the kitchen to prep their tea, and when I came back, I had a line of questioning prepped for them.

"So, ladies," I said as I set their teapot down. "What can you tell me about Brenda Choi?"

Helen's face lit up as if she'd just been told she won the lottery. "The true question is, What can't we tell you about her?"

"Brenda is a very interesting woman," Opal added.

Wendy nodded in agreement. "Brenda thinks she is better than most people. She is always saying how she feels sorry for everyone else and that she wishes to help them."

That seemed to track with what I'd overheard her saying at Donna's party and also what she'd said to me while I was at her house.

Pearl continued for Wendy. "But . . . she is not so lucky herself."

"Oh?" I was intrigued. "And why's that?"

"Her life is very messy," Helen replied. "Her husband is a cheater, and her children are thieves."

"Really?" I looked among the four women, unable to hide my surprise.

"Yes, really," Pearl confirmed. "She even hired someone to follow her husband so she could catch him cheating on her."

"Hired someone?" I asked. "What do you mean? Like a private detective?"

Helen nodded. "Yes. And she hired people to cover her children's bad deeds as well. Money can help you cover many things."

I thought about the possibility of Brenda also using Price Investigations and what that connection could potentially mean. If the timing lined up, there was a slim possibility she'd run into Thomas at the detective agency; it could have even come as a recommendation. Still, would Thomas really tell her what he was up to? And how would she get a copy of the files from his investigation?

"How do you know all of this?" I asked.

"Lana, you know we hear many things. All one

has to do is listen carefully and much will be revealed to you," Opal said.

The bell in the kitchen sounded, signaling that their food was ready. I excused myself and retrieved their food from Peter.

When I returned to the dining area, I noticed that someone had come in and was waiting by the hostess station. Upon further inspection, I realized that it was Warren . . . again.

My stomach sank. I wasn't in the mood to deal with him when I had so many other things on my mind. But isn't that always the way?

I took my time placing each of the Matrons' plates on the table before willing myself to greet my ex at the hostess station. He was dressed in a casual suit with no tie, was clean-shaven, and I could smell his cologne as I approached. It brought back memories of better days, and I winced at the images they created in my mind.

When we made eye contact, he smiled brightly and extended a paper to-go cup. "Hi, I was passing through on my way to meet a client and I thought I'd bring you some coffee. It's just the way you like it, too. Two creams, three sugars."

I hated that he remembered something so mundane as how I take my coffee. "Thanks," I said, hesitating to accept the cup from him. "I don't really drink coffee anymore . . ."

"Oh, come on," he said with a look of disbelief. "You hate me that much you're willing to sacrifice steaming-hot caffeine?"

I debated the answer to that. But before I could say anything else, he continued.

"While I'm here, I thought I'd see if you've made

a decision on whether or not you're willing to sit down and talk with me."

I grabbed the cup from his outstretched hand, set it down on the counter, and folded my arms across my chest. "I still don't know. And I don't know why it matters to you all of a sudden how I feel. It's been well over a year now."

"Aw, come on. Don't be like that. It's always mattered to me how you feel. If you would just let me explain the whole story, then I think you would realize that."

"Why can't you just tell me right here and now? Is it really necessary to drag this out?"

"You're cute when you're stubborn, you know that?"

I gave him the best glare I could muster. "You're not winning any points with your attempts at being charming."

"Who said I'm attempting?"

"Ugh!" I was seconds away from stomping my foot like a toddler. "You're absolutely infuriating, you know that?" Right before I was ready to launch into a tirade, I remembered that the Mahjong Matrons were still in the restaurant and that anything that happened here would easily become gossip fodder. No matter how loyal they were as customers, I was no exception to their gossip mill.

"Forget it," I said in a quieter voice. "We'll talk elsewhere, I suppose. But I don't know when. I'll figure it out and let you know."

He held up his hands. "Okay, that's fair. I'll take what I can get." He looked down at the coffee mug and back up at me, winked, and said, "Enjoy the coffee."

As he was walking out the door, Adam came walking in. The two men looked at each other, some type of silent exchange took place, and then Adam was standing in front of me wondering if anyone was home.

He snapped his fingers to get my attention and I snapped out of my daze.

"Lana, who was that?" he asked, jerking a thumb over his shoulder.

"That was Warren."

Adam turned back around to look through the door. "Oh, it was, was it?"

"Yeah. He stopped by to see if I've made a decision."

"You want me to break his kneecaps? I told you that's an option."

"Maybe later," I said. "What brings you by?"

"Do I need a reason? Maybe I just wanted to see your sweet face." He smiled and kissed me on the forehead. "I actually have a meeting with the chief so I can't stay. Want to have dinner tonight?"

"Sure. I might have a meeting later after work, but aside from that, I don't have any plans."

"What kind of meeting?" he asked.

"Oh no, not with him," I said, meaning Warren. I didn't want to tell Adam about meeting with Bryce Blackwell in case the Matrons should overhear, so I nodded my head toward them and told him I'd text him later.

He stole a kiss before leaving, and I took a deep breath of relief. I felt so much better after seeing Adam for just those few minutes. As I reflected on my life and everything that had been going on, I realized that I was grateful for the many changes that had taken place.

Now there were just these two issues of the past to contend with, and everything would be at peace again.

CHAPTER
16

Sometime after lunch in the early afternoon, Bryce emailed back and said he'd gladly meet me at six p.m.; I could pick the location. Perfect. I responded saying that we should meet at the Zodiac. That way I would be in an environment I was comfortable with *and* Megan would be in the vicinity. I ended the email by giving him my cell phone number in case he needed to reach me before we met up.

Of course, because I had a plan of action and needed to be somewhere, the rest of the day crawled by. I swear at one point in between three and four o'clock, the minute hand went backward.

Then, finally, it was time to leave, and I could tell by the bounce in my step that I was a little past the point of anxious. I swung by the bank on my way to the bar and dropped the cash bag into the overnight deposit slot. I made it half an hour before I was supposed to meet Bryce, which gave me the perfect opportunity to update Megan on my day.

"This guy is absolutely ridiculous. He will not

give up." Megan clenched her jaw. "He's got some nerve showing up at your work twice now. He's lucky I wasn't there."

After she'd brought me a drink, I'd filled her in on Warren's visit and the odd timing of Adam coming in just then.

"If you ask me, Lana, I'd tell him you don't need to hear anything he has to say, and he can go straight to hell."

"I know, I think that's what he ultimately deserves. At the same time, I feel like he has a right to speak his mind. I would want the same courtesy extended to me. Plus, I have a few things I wouldn't mind getting off my chest."

"Yeah, but you also wouldn't treat someone the way he treated you."

"Fair point." I sighed as I took a sip of my cocktail. Today's random mixed drink was a Luscious Leo. I didn't bother asking what was in it, but it was kind of a peachy color and tasted a bit sweeter than how I prefer my alcoholic beverages. "Well, let me tell you about Bryce before he gets here."

We easily chatted away the minutes before Bryce showed up. I will give him points for being punctual. He walked in the door at exactly six p.m. He was dressed in a short-sleeved, slate-gray, button-down shirt with black jeans and had a messenger bag slung across his shoulder.

He wasn't too bad looking of a guy, and I tried to picture him and Alice as a couple. She was a little on the proper side and he was definitely more casual, with dark, shaggy hair that could use a trim and loose-fitting clothes.

I waved, and he paused as recognition set in.

He nodded and headed over. "Are you Lana?" he asked.

I extended a hand. "Yup, that's me."

He took my hand and gave it a weak shake. "Don't I know you?"

I noted that he did have soft hazel eyes and full lips that would be appealing to any woman. His olive skin gave him a Mediterranean look, and I wondered to myself if he might have some Greek in him. "Yes, we met in passing at Donna Feng's birthday party. I did the catering."

"Oh, right on," he said, nodding. He slid onto the stool next to me and removed the messenger bag from his shoulder, placing it on the counter in front of him. "I brought my book with recommended playlists. I'm not sure what you're looking for, but I have a little bit of everything in here. You also have the option of creating your own, but I would need it at least two weeks before the actual event." He passed the book over to me.

I took the book from him and flipped through the pages as if I were interested.

Megan came by to take his drink order. He chose a draft beer and then turned his attention back to me. "Or if you want, you could tell me what kind of vibe you're looking for, and I can put something together. Depends on how in control of the music you want to be."

"I see," I said, pausing on a page to act as if I'd found something I liked. "What did you do for Donna's party?"

Megan returned with the beer and zipped away without acknowledging me.

"Ummm, she wanted a bit of control on the music,

so she picked a list. I can look through my records if you want to do something similar . . . I forget what she chose."

"No, that's okay," I said, closing the book. "So Donna mentioned to me that you came recommended by Alice Kam."

"Yeah . . ."

"That was nice of her," I responded casually. "Did you know Alice well?"

He set his beer glass back down on the bar top. "Why do I have the sudden feeling that you didn't ask me here to hire me for a party?"

I feigned surprise. "What would give you that idea?"

He smirked, picking his beer glass up and taking a long sip. After, he said with amusement, "For one, you don't seem all that interested in anything I have to offer professionally. You flipped through that book faster than anyone else that's ever asked to meet with me."

"Maybe I'm a decisive person."

"Also, you didn't mention what your event was or bother with giving me any details . . . that's usually what people lead with when they're hiring a DJ."

Damn, he had me there. I would have to remember to be more convincing with my backstory in the future. "Okay, fair enough. I'm sorry; you're right, I don't actually need to hire you for a party. I just didn't know if you would talk to me otherwise."

"It all depends on what you want to talk about . . ."

I could tell his guard was up in a way it hadn't been before. I didn't know if it was because I appeared untrustworthy or because he had something to hide. I decided to feel things out as I went along instead of making snap judgments about his character.

"Okay, here's the deal." I shifted in my seat so I could make better eye contact. "I'm sure you've heard about Donna Feng being a main suspect in Alice's murder."

"I have."

"Well, she didn't do it."

"And you know this for a fact?" he asked.

"I know it in my gut." Okay, I was sorta lying. There was a small part of me that still doubted, but I definitely wasn't going to tell him that.

"So what exactly do you need from me?"

"Information." I sighed. "The problem is that none of us really know much about Alice. And since she recommended you, we thought maybe you'd have some details about her and her life that might help us."

"Why would you assume that I knew anything you didn't?"

"You guys dated, right?"

He reached for his beer glass. "Kinda."

From what Megan had told me about their social media posts, they'd been pretty hot and heavy in the beginning. Again, there were two obvious reasons he could be hiding things: because he was guilty, *or* because he was being prideful. It was very possible that she had been the one to end things and move on; perhaps *she* was the one with the ability to remain friendly. And maybe he couldn't reciprocate. Of course, I was just speculating . . . as I often like to do.

"In that time, you must have learned some stuff about her. Who her close friends were, what kind of stuff she was into, if she had any enemies . . . you know, the usual stuff."

He drained his beer glass and signaled Megan for a refill. "She didn't have any enemies that I know of. She never complained about anything, either. She was pretty chill."

Megan swung by with a fresh beer and a new cocktail for me.

Bryce noticed that Megan and I didn't exchange words, and narrowed his eyes. "You come here often, I take it?"

At this point, I figured why lie. "Yeah, the bartender's my best friend."

"Ah," he replied. He took a sip from his new beer glass. "So yeah, she was a cool chick."

"What happened with the two of you?"

"What do you mean?"

"Obviously, the relationship didn't continue . . . so how did it end?"

He shrugged. "She wanted to end things, so we did. We stayed friends. Not much of a story."

Talking to him felt like pulling teeth. "So there was no bad blood between the two of you?"

"Nah, we were all good. Why else would she recommend me for the gig?"

"Did you know anything about her relationship with Brenda Choi?"

"That's the rich lady with the bratty kids?" he asked.

"Yeah, her."

"I think everything was cool with them. Like I said, Alice didn't complain a lot. She said the kids could be a handful sometimes, but it wasn't anything she couldn't handle. I guess they liked to steal stuff and were always getting into trouble."

"Did they ever steal from Alice?"

He shook his head. "Alice was sort of a minimalist and didn't have much. She's not from here. Matter of fact, I don't know where she came from originally. She never really said."

"How's that?"

"Well, she just said she was from around. You know, like she moved a lot and stuff."

"She never said where she lived prior to coming here?" I prodded, having a hard time wrapping my head around that concept.

"Nope. She said that the past didn't matter and she wanted to leave it where it was. That people should try focusing more on the present instead."

"Interesting," I said, taking a sip from my drink.

"Why's that interesting?"

I couldn't tell him that Alice might have been blackmailing Donna with her past life, so I shrugged instead. "I don't know. Just an interesting take on life, I suppose."

He appeared uninterested in my response and continued. "She was always going on about living in the moment and she seemed to get pretty upset if I tried to ask her too many questions. After a while I gave up trying. Why start fights when you don't need to, right?"

"It didn't bother you that the woman you were dating didn't want to share her past?" It still wasn't sitting well with me that anyone would be okay dating someone while knowing zero information about their past.

"Not really. I was just happy to be with her in general. Girls like her don't really go for guys like me." His eyes shifted away from mine, seemingly embarrassed.

"Why do you say that?"

"Well, she was a little on the clean-cut side for one. I felt like she should have been with someone who's got a nine-to-five, wears suits, and drives a sensible sedan. On top of that, I work a lot of nights and weekends, so it's not like we could hang out and go on dates like other couples do."

"So you were in fact a couple then?" I'm not sure why it was important to me, but I wanted him to admit it.

"You know what I mean."

"Not really."

"Anyway . . ." he said, tapping his finger on the bar top. "We ended whatever we had on good terms. Is there anything else you need to know?"

"Did you have any major interactions with her on the night of the party?"

"You're really like a junior detective or something, aren't you?" He laughed to himself.

"As they say, this isn't my first rodeo."

"We made some small talk, but nothing special. It's not like she was actually a guest at the party. I still can't believe that Donna woman went off on her like that. I'd be so embarrassed if that were me."

"Believe me, she's paying for it now."

"Ain't that the truth."

"What about close friends? Do you know if she had any?"

"Not really. Although she did hang out with some other nanny and her friend. I don't remember the chick's name, though. I guess they would have wine nights or whatever. But I don't think that the friendship went beyond that."

"Are you talking about someone named Evie?" I remembered writing the name down in my notebook. The Mahjong Matrons had mentioned her to me. "Does that sound familiar at all?"

He thought for a moment and then shook his head. "No . . . I don't know if that's what it was or not. Like I said, she probably wasn't anybody important."

I pulled out one of my restaurant business cards. "If you happen to think of anything else, or remember this other person's name, would you mind giving me a call?"

He took the card and skimmed it over before sticking it in his back pocket. "Sure. I'm being serious, though, you really are like a private detective. You ever think about doing this professionally?"

"No, and I think if I did, my mother would kill me."

Bryce left shortly after finishing his beer. Since I was already at the bar, I texted Adam and asked if he just wanted to meet me at the Zodiac for some food and drinks. I didn't feel like going anywhere else. He agreed and said he'd see me in half an hour.

In the meantime, I filled Megan in on what I'd learned from Bryce. The bar was starting to fill up, and her opportunities to talk to me became few and far between. Before I realized it, half an hour had passed and Adam walked in.

He greeted me with a kiss and sat down in the same stool as Bryce. "And how's my little troublemaker?"

"Flustered."

He waved to Megan. "And why's that?"

I told him the same story I had told Megan about Bryce. I could tell he was genuinely listening and calculating the information as if he were on duty. He took a minute to consider what I'd said before answering.

"It's odd he's not open to talk about their relationship, almost as if he wants to distance himself from what actually went on with them."

"That's what I thought, too," I said.

Megan came by and dropped off a bottle of beer with Adam, eyeballed my drink, and scurried off to tend to the other patrons.

"But," he added after sipping his beer, "that can be a lot of men. Other than that fact, I don't know if there's anything that makes this guy a suspect. It's pretty flimsy."

As we talked about the situation and various angles, I took a moment to appreciate the fact that this conversation was even happening at all. A few months ago, Adam's main objective was to keep me out of anything of this nature. We'd come a long way in the short time we'd been together.

It also made me contemplate my own situation concerning Warren and whether or not it actually mattered to me to let him speak his piece. Or how important it was for me to even speak my own. That time of my life was gone, and it truly needed to be laid to rest.

On the other hand, as I was learning from Donna's situation, if you don't deal with your past, it's gonna come back and bite you in the bupkiss.

CHAPTER
17

It was hard to believe that it was already Friday morning. Any other Friday, I would be busy preparing myself for an evening at the night market, but with everything that had happened the previous week, I'd canceled our booth until I had more time to focus. I'd been partially concerned that my mother would pitch a fit over me canceling a money-making opportunity, but with what had been going on with Donna, I think it was the furthest thing from her mind. I kept my fingers crossed that she wouldn't suddenly notice.

As I readied myself for work, I reflected on the past week and wondered where the time had gone—and reminded myself of everything that still needed to be done.

I made a quick list of what I wanted to accomplish by the end of the day before I left for work. By the time I made it to Asia Village, I had already tired myself out just from thinking of all I had on my plate.

One of the first things I needed to do was check in with Donna and see if she had any news to relay. I had yet to meet with Ms. Chang's maid, Susan Han, and wondered if Donna could help coordinate that. And hopefully, she could connect me with this Evie person as well. Aside from that, I'd been so busy, I hadn't even gotten the chance to use my earring story on any of the other starred women from Donna's list. *Then* there was still the business of talking with whoever L. Shepard was at Price Investigations.

I would never admit it to her, but the lack of my sister being present at the restaurant really screwed things up. I decided it was time to call in my last resort. Vanessa Wen.

Vanessa Wen is our entirely too bubbly teenage helper. Her parents had asked my mother a while back if Vanessa could help out around the restaurant to learn the value of money and earning your keep. And of course, my mother had said yes, because what better lesson is there for a teenager to learn?

Meanwhile, I was stuck dealing with her most of the time.

I think once you've left your teen years, you always find yourself saying things like, "Man, I didn't act like that at their age." Or "Wow, don't they have it easy?" So really, could my judgments on what Vanessa was actually like be accurate? Probably not, but she still annoyed me.

Megan had told me on several occasions that I needed to practice patience and that Vanessa was a good outlet for that. But what did she know? She worked in a bar, and teenagers weren't allowed in.

But alas, I needed the help and it was summer, so she was available if I needed her. To my surprise, she'd even offered to work any extra hours I threw her way. Once I got in my office, I made a note to call Vanessa around ten a.m. and see if she was available. If I could leave a little after lunch, I could get a lot done with that extra couple of hours.

The morning passed per usual. The Matrons came in and gossiped, my mother called to make sure that everything was running smoothly, and Nancy showed up around eleven.

Vanessa had agreed to come in at one p.m. She strolled through the door at exactly one, chomping on her gum, her head bopping back and forth to whatever she had playing in her earbuds. I thanked her for being a lifesaver.

She removed one earbud as she approached the hostess station. "Hey, Lana! Thanks again for calling me in. There's a concert I want to go to and I could really use the extra money to buy a ticket. They're not cheap and my mom said if I want to go, I have to pay for it myself."

I could hear the noise coming from her earbud. "How loud do you have those on?"

"Pretty loud," she replied. "I basically can't hear anything when I have them in. I feel like that makes things more Zen, you know? Like I'm just moving to the soundtrack of my life and whatever."

"Uh-huh, just don't get hit by a car while you're at it," I warned her.

She rolled her eyes. "Ugh, you sound just like my mom. She's always like, *Pay attention to where you're walking, Vanessa* . . . or like, *You're gonna blow out your eardrums, Vanessa.* But like, whatever, that's totally not gonna happen. I'm super aware of my surroundings, you know?"

I stifled a groan and shimmied from behind the counter to let her squeeze in and put her things away. "I have a lot of errands to run today, but I'll have my cell phone on, so just call me if anything comes up, okay?"

"Totally. But no worries, you know? Me and Nancy got this. We gel so well when we work together." A bubble of laugher escaped. "Gel so well. Ha!"

There was a moment I thought my eyes might roll of their own accord. But I remembered Megan telling me to practice patience. I said my goodbyes to the noodle shop team and headed out to see what I could find out about L. Shepard.

CHAPTER
18

- - - - - - - - - - - - - - - -

Price Investigations was part of an underwhelming building on Euclid Avenue that housed several small businesses. The directory in the tiny lobby told me that I could find the detective agency in suite 102.

The door to the office had a frosted-glass window with a fading decal of the business name and the words LICENSED DETECTIVES below it. I tried the handle, and the door was unlocked. I stepped into the small reception area to find a middle-aged woman with bright auburn hair sitting behind a shabby desk that might have originated in the 1970s. She didn't bother acknowledging me as I walked in. I let the door shut behind me and took a step farther in. The nameplate read: MEREDITH WALKER.

"Hello," I said, bending my head down to get her attention.

"What can I do for you, dearie?" she asked without taking her eyes off the computer screen.

"I was wondering if there is an L. Shepard that works here?"

Her eyes flitted upward at me so fast I wasn't sure it happened. "Yeah, who's askin'?"

"My name is Lana Lee. I had some questions I wanted to ask . . . them."

"We charge by the hour, sweetie."

"Damnit, Meredith!" a booming voice shouted from one of the closed office doors. "Who's there?"

"Lana Lee!" she yelled back. "I told her she's gotta pay."

There was some rustling behind the door, and then it swung open abruptly. A tall, skinny man in a baby-blue wrinkled dress shirt and khaki pants stepped out and gave me a car salesman sort of smile. "Well, hello there, young lady. You'll have to forgive my receptionist's lack of enthusiasm. I keep her around because my wife makes me."

"Watch it, Eddie," Meredith replied.

He rolled his eyes and stepped around Meredith's desk to shake my hand. "I'm Eddie Price, pleasure to make your acquaintance. What can I do for you? Have a cheating boyfriend you need us to follow?"

I shook the hand he offered. "If only you'd asked me that a year ago," I joked. "Actually I'm here to speak to an L. Shepard. They worked on a case a few months back and I wanted to inquire about it."

"Oh sure, that's Lydia. She's my best gal. Well, she's my only gal, really." His eyes slid toward Meredith.

She groaned in return.

Lydia? It was a woman? I hadn't expected that. "Is she here? I'd really like to talk with her, if that's possible."

"Sure thing, that's her office right there," he said, pointing to the door next to his own. "She should be hiding in there." He turned to knock on the door. "Lydia! You in there?"

A muffled "*Yeah, hang on*" came from the other side.

He turned back and smiled, showing all his teeth. "You can have a seat if you'd like. Want some coffee? Meredith should be the one to ask you that question, but she's involved in an extremely important game of solitaire."

Meredith finally glanced up. Her mauve lipstick clashed with her hair, and her mascara was a bit on the chunky side. "Do you want some coffee, dearie?"

"No, thank you," I responded politely.

She swiveled in her chair to face Eddie and crossed her arms. "See? She didn't want any coffee."

He threw his hands up in the air. "Every day! Every day with you, woman."

The door behind him opened and a young woman, maybe in her early thirties, with jet-black hair and olive skin stepped out. She was dressed in a loose-fitting black T-shirt, gray skinny jeans, and black dress boots. "What's all the yellin' about out here? I'm trying to do some paperwork."

"This young lady would like to talk to you," Eddie said, jerking his head in my direction.

She seemed to just notice that I was standing there, looked me up and down, and said, "Boyfriend trouble?"

"Actually no," I said. I assumed that was a frequent occurrence around here. "I'm here to talk to you about a case you worked on several months ago."

"I'm sorry, but you'll have to make an appointment." She pointed to Meredith. "Our receptionist can help you."

"It's about Donna Feng," I told her. "Well . . . Thomas Feng was actually the one that hired you, but—"

"Feng, you say?" She gave me another once-over. "You the other woman?"

"What?" I gawked at her. "No! I'm a friend of the family."

"Come into my office." She spun on her heel and walked back through the door she'd come out of.

I smiled politely at Eddie and followed Lydia into her office.

"Shut the door," she said, shimmying behind her desk.

Her office was similar to mine in that there was absolutely no room to move around and truly resembled something more fitting for a utility closet. There were no frills to be found. Her desk was black metal, covered in papers, a landline phone, and a laptop. She had some filing cabinets on top of which were various reference books. There were two black leather chairs that looked like they might have been around since before both of us were born.

"Have a seat. Did they offer you coffee?"

"Yeah, they did, thank you."

"Best you don't drink any. It's kinda crappy." She smirked. "Anyways, sorry about trying to send you away, I thought you might be a dissatisfied customer or something. I've had to deal with that a time or two and it's not a pleasant ordeal."

I laughed. "No, nothing like that. I was hoping you could enlighten me on the Feng case. Do you remember it?"

"How couldn't I? The guy was murdered shortly afterward. I assumed his wife figured out what he was up to and took matters into her own hands. Surprised to hear it was an old friend. Wait a minute," she said, eyeballing me. "Are you the girl that was in the paper? The guy who killed Thomas Feng held you at gunpoint or something like that, right?"

"Yup, that's me." I blushed.

"You got lucky, chickadee." She leaned back in her chair and gently rocked back and forth. "He's not out of jail, is he?"

"No, he's still in. As far as I know, he'll be in there for life."

"Good," she said. "Watch your back if he ever gets parole. You never know with these people. Everyone's always looking for revenge."

I didn't want to think about it. Every now and again, the thought would cross my mind. Would they let him out for good behavior? He was older, so maybe someone down the line would show him sympathy. Either way, though, I knew he had years ahead of him before that option would even be considered. The court case hadn't gone well for him.

"So, you said you had some questions?"

"Yeah, I was wondering . . . how were you able to find this information on Donna Feng? From what she told me, there shouldn't be anybody who can get access to it. Her mother sacrificed quite a bit to make sure it all stayed hidden."

Lydia nodded in understanding. "Well, all I can tell you is that it pays to have friends in weird places. I know some interesting people. There's a local guy who knows another guy who handles falsifying international documents—birth certificates and so on. He was the one who led me on the path to figuring out that her current documents were fake to begin with. Once I managed that, it just took a little bit of digging to figure out the rest."

"But a regular person wouldn't be able to find this stuff out, right?" I asked.

"Someone like you?" Lydia shook her head. "No, you'd have to have a lot of connections."

"Like mob connections?"

"Do you have mob connections?" She leaned forward.

"No," I replied. "I'm just trying to figure out how someone could find this stuff out." I told her the story of what had happened with Donna and Alice, the thumb drive of information, and how I was the only one alive—other than Megan—who knew Donna's secret.

Lydia listened to everything I had to say, nodding at the appropriate intervals, and making "hmm" sounds every few minutes. When I finished, she closed her eyes and rubbed her temples.

"Look, you seem like a nice girl and all," she said. "But this really isn't in your pay grade, you know?"

I felt my ego's feathers getting ruffled, and I straightened in my chair. "I'm capable of handling it. This isn't the first time I've . . . assisted on something like this."

"Miss Lee—"

"Lana," I corrected her.

"Lana . . . that's all well and fine. I've known a few armchair detectives in my day, but if the Chinese mob is somehow involved in this, you're not prepared to handle it. Trust me on that one."

"Well, we're not sure," I said. "It's a possibility, but it could also be one of the people that I mentioned."

"There's no way any of those people could get that information. A couple of housewives, a DJ, and a nanny? Not a chance."

I sighed. Maybe she was right. Maybe I was out of my league. "Okay, well, what do you think about the whole Alice thing? Do you think she was involved? Do you think Donna could be guilty? Do you think she was the one with the thumb drive?" The questions came out of my mouth as rapid as gunfire. I could feel everything I'd been contemplating starting to bubble up in a panic.

"Whoa, whoa, whoa," Lydia said, holding up her hands. "Calm down, sister."

"Right, sorry," I said, taking a deep breath.

"I can't answer any of those questions. It's not my case," she said. "But if you want to hire me to help you . . . we can talk payment. It's not cheap, but if you wanted me to look into matters, then I'd be willing to give it a shot."

I knew I didn't have the kind of money it took to hire a private investigator. I was still shoveling my way out of credit card debt. But I knew someone who did have plenty of money. I just didn't know if she'd be willing to spend it. "It's a possibility," I told Lydia. "Could you put together something and I can show Ms. Feng? She may be willing to pay for this."

"Sure, I can type up a contract and have it to you by tomorrow," she said. "I don't know that this woman will go for it considering my past relationship with her now deceased husband. But if you think she's an open-minded sort of person, I'm not opposed to the whole thing."

"Thank you," I said. "I appreciate it."

"Not a problem. I'm here to help." She smiled

reassuringly. "But I will give you this one piece of advice. You need to stay out of it. If the mafia is involved, you're not going to be the only one in danger."

"I know," I told her as I stood up to leave.

"No, I don't think you do, Lana." She stood up with me and shimmied around her desk. "If they're involved, then your family, friends, and anybody you're close with would be in danger, too."

CHAPTER
19

I had only been at Price Investigations for an hour, but within that hour, the content of conversation was enough to completely rattle me. Over the past several months, I have often put myself in danger, but I have never jeopardized the safety of my family or friends. I couldn't live with myself if something happened to Megan, or my sister. My parents. My poor grandmother who hadn't even been in this country for very long. I thought about Adam and considered that out of everyone, he was the best prepared to handle himself. But he had to know the danger was there. I needed to tell him the truth. I just hoped that he would be willing and able to keep that information to himself.

I sat in my car for a couple of minutes, sipping the cold coffee in my travel mug and trying to bring my blood pressure down. On the way to the parking lot, I had already decided my next stop would be Donna's house. I hoped that she would be willing to hire

Lydia. In this situation, I felt that hiring a professional was our best course of action.

About twenty minutes later, I pulled into Donna's driveway next to a car that I didn't recognize. It was an old burgundy sedan with a giant dent in the passenger's-side door and old rusty plates. I couldn't imagine that being anybody Donna knew; all her friends drove luxury cars.

I rang the doorbell and a few seconds later, Rosemary opened the door and pressed her lips together upon seeing me. "Good afternoon, Miss Lee," she said. "Ms. Feng is currently conducting business, you can wait for her in the sitting room if you'd like."

"Who's here?" I asked, glancing back at the sedan.

"One of the vendors she hired from the party," Rosemary said, stepping off to the side to allow me entry.

"Oh." I walked into the foyer, and she shut the door behind me. "She shouldn't be much longer, I presume."

I followed her into the sitting room, and she gestured for me to have a seat. "Would you like any tea?"

"Maybe just a glass of water."

She bowed her head and left in the direction of the kitchen.

I sat down on the love seat, my eyes trained on the stairs, wondering which vendor it could be. I knew that Donna had payments left to settle, but I didn't think that any of these people would make house calls.

Rosemary returned with a glass of water and a small plate of lemons and limes. "Here you are, miss."

"Thank you." I took the glass from her as she set the plate of fruit slices on the coffee table in front of me. "Rosemary, can I ask you a question?"

"If you are here to further inquire about my relationship with Alice, I have nothing more to tell you. I have spoken quite enough on the subject."

"No, I actually wanted to ask you about Donna."

She looked away from me, and the expression on her face told me that she did not approve of this line of questioning, either. But she didn't leave, so I figured that was my cue to go ahead and ask my question.

"I was just wondering. Does she seem all right to you lately?" I asked. "I mean, I've heard that she is coming a bit unhinged, and if anyone would know something like that, it would be you."

"Wise women never entertain gossip, Miss Lee," Rosemary said plainly.

"I can understand that, but with everything that has happened recently, I wanted to be sure that she is actually okay."

"Madam Feng has been through quite an ordeal. I imagine that many people would act out in more severe ways than her. But as you can see, she is generally levelheaded. Aside from her outburst at the birthday party, she has remained put together as always."

"So she wasn't constantly yelling at Alice? And she hasn't been drinking in excess?" I asked.

Rosemary glared at me. "Where have you heard such things?"

"Alice mentioned it to a friend of hers, and it spread."

She nodded curtly. "I see. Well, you can be assured

that while madam has been indulging in a nightcap more frequently than is, perhaps, usual, she has always been a fair employer. If Alice was handling a situation poorly with the girls, it was within madam's right to scold her."

As she said these things, it felt like sugarcoating the situation to me. So Donna was drinking more than usual and she did at one point or another "scold" Alice. But what was the severity of the situation? I didn't think I would hear the real truth from Rosemary. If nothing else, she seemed loyal to Donna. But unfortunately for her, that just made me consider her being a murderer as even more likely. It seemed possible she would do anything to protect Donna from harm—perhaps including killing someone.

"Did you want to ask any other questions, Miss Lee? I have work that needs to be done."

"No, that was it. Sorry to keep you from your duties."

She bowed her head and left the room without saying anything.

I was fidgety so I pulled my phone out of my purse and texted Adam asking if he was free later that night. I had to fill him in on what was going on, but I didn't mention anything about it now or he'd call me right away and make me tell him over the phone.

A couple of minutes went by before he responded, telling me that he was in fact available, and that we could meet at my apartment later that evening.

I sipped my water, feeling the impatience inside me grow. I still wanted to talk with the housekeeper, Susan Han, whom Alice had supposedly divulged all this information to. Fifteen minutes went by, and I heard a man's voice coming down the stairs.

"And that was all she had?" the man asked.

It was a voice that I recognized, but I couldn't quite place it.

"Yes, that's everything," Donna replied. "It wasn't much, was it?"

A pair of legs appeared on the stairs, and as the man descended, I realized who it was. It was Bryce Blackwell.

CHAPTER
20

"Lana, darling!" Donna exclaimed as she descended the stairs and I came into view. "What on earth are you doing here? I hope I haven't kept you waiting long."

It was the first time in days that I had seen her resembling her old self. She was dressed in a beige Donna Karan skirt suit and matching heels. Her hair was done in the customary French bun she preferred, and her makeup was flawless as ever.

When Bryce realized it was me, he shrank back a little as if he hoped to meld into the wall of the hallway. But we both knew that wasn't going to happen. He was holding a medium-sized packing box. He appeared sheepish and I was more than curious—and suspicious—as to why he'd made a personal visit to Donna. Didn't these people send invoices?

I smiled pleasantly, fixing my eyes on Bryce. "Not at all. I wanted to stop by and go over some details with you on our project."

Donna's face lit up. "Oh well, that's wonderful."

She turned to Bryce. "Is there anything more I can help you with?"

"No, this helps a lot." He held up the box. "And thanks for the check."

"Of course. After all, you need to be paid for your services. I'm only sorry it took me this long."

He glanced at me. "Not a problem. I know you have a lot going on."

They said their goodbyes in the foyer and I kept my place in the threshold to the sitting room. "It's nice to see you again, Bryce," I said.

He looked over his shoulder and gave me a nod. "Yeah, you too."

Donna shut the door as he stepped out onto the stoop and turned around, clasping her hands together in excitement. "Okay, what do you have for me? Some good news would be wonderful right about now."

"What was he doing here?" I asked.

"Oh, let me just tell you he is the sweetest young man." She joined me at the threshold and ushered me back into the sitting room. "He was Alice's fiancé and wanted some of her personal items as a memento. I didn't know what to do with them, and since the police had already gone through her things, I figured I'd give them to him."

"What?" I didn't even bother hiding my surprise. "He was Alice's fiancé?"

"Yes, I was just as surprised as you, my dear. She never mentioned it to me. Perhaps she just wanted to keep things professional."

"And you don't find any of this odd?" I asked.

"Well, no. Why would I?"

I told her about my meeting with Bryce and how he had been more than reluctant to admit that he had any involvement with Alice at all.

Donna took in the information but did not react as I expected her to. "My dear, I can tell you after talking with him that there is no way he would even be a suspect. He truly loved that girl, and there isn't a violent bone in his body."

I was incredulous. In all the years I had known Donna Feng, I had never taken her for a sucker. And now here she was saying the most naive things to me that I'd ever heard come out of her mouth.

"Never mind all of that, Lana," she said coolly. "What did you come to tell me?"

Trying to pull myself back together, I told her what had taken place at Price Investigations. I relayed that Lydia warned of the potential danger my snooping around could cause and how no one without unusual connections would be able to find the information that involved Donna's past.

"Well, see, there you have it. There's no way that Bryce could be involved. He's hardly anyone with the means to blackmail me."

"Yes, but what if he killed Alice?"

"Darling, no. I am telling you, the two are connected. Whoever left me that thumb drive is who killed Alice. And that was not Bryce. No, this is much more sinister."

"Then that's not a good possibility, either. And it also eliminates any of the housewives that you've starred."

"Not necessarily." Donna shook her head. "Their affiliations could be something to question. We need to get background checks on who these people really are, or if they have any unsavory associations. I am confident this is the right direction."

I wanted to groan in frustration, but I didn't want to let on how aggravated I really was. If these women did have contacts of that nature, was Donna really willing to risk my involvement?

I took a deep breath. "I think we should consider hiring Lydia Shepard to take this over, Donna. I don't know if this is something I should be involved with anymore. Not if the danger is this great."

Donna tapped her chin. "I don't know how I feel about this woman. After all, she did try to help expose me to my husband. I only hid what I needed to hide from him to keep him safe."

"She was just doing her job. It wasn't anything personal."

"That might be so, but what an unpleasant job it is. And she could have very easily seen the information I was hiding and realized on her own why it needed to stay hidden. But no, she proceeded, and if Thomas hadn't been killed by someone else, and continued to seek out answers behind my back, what would have happened then? Our whole family could have been in danger."

"I understand that, but Lydia has the tools to get this done. I'm just a restaurant manager."

"Nonsense, you are not *just* a restaurant manager, Lana. You are an intelligent girl with a strong head on her shoulders and the ability to suss this whole thing out for me. No, we will proceed as planned. Once you find out who could be involved, then we'll decide what steps to take next. Nothing bad is going to happen to you as long as you don't approach anyone with what we've found. No one even knows what we're up to. Let's keep it that way."

I rolled my shoulders, half ready to walk out the door and tell her that she was on her own. But I had known her too long, and maybe I had let my conversation with Lydia color my judgment too much. Would Donna really risk putting me in grave danger? Besides, she was right about one thing. No one knew what we were up to, and it's not like I was planning on confronting this person myself. All I needed to do was find out who was responsible. "Well, if that's really how you feel, I need to talk to Ms. Chang's housekeeper. Can you help me with that?"

"Say no more. I'll put in a call. I have her address in my contacts. Let me get that for you, and you can be on your way." She rose from her seat and hurried off to get her address book.

I leaned my head back against the love seat and tried not to hyperventilate. I really hoped that we were doing the right thing.

Donna was able to get a hold of Ms. Chang, who said it would be no problem if I stopped by and spoke to Susan. She didn't understand exactly why I was coming, but she and Donna had been friends for so long, she didn't question much when it came to her. Ms. Chang was satisfied with Donna's short explanation about me trying to track someone down that was friends with her maid.

I left the Feng house with the address and set it into my GPS. Ms. Chang lived in Rocky River, which was about a ten-minute drive from where I was. She was a wealthy housewife with one young son who was still in elementary school and an older daughter who was getting ready to graduate from high school.

Traffic was heavy as the workday was coming to a close, and I imagined a lot of people were heading home in excitement, ready to begin their weekend. I, on the other hand, felt as if it was just another day. Considering the current circumstances, the only thing I was looking forward to was the fact that I didn't have to open the restaurant in the morning.

When I pulled up to the Chang home, I double-checked the address to make sure I had the correct place. This was the grandest home I had visited by far. Part of me could hardly believe that this house—mini mansion, whatever you wanted to call it—was in the city of Rocky River. It sat against the shore of Lake Erie and took up half an acre of land. Now, mind you, I am making that up based on what I think an acre of land would consist of. Point is, the place was big.

The two-story brick home was an architectural masterpiece with big beautiful windows and an arched overhang at the front entrance. The driveway was a roundabout and allowed me to turn my car so I could face the exit. I parked next to their three-car garage and composed myself before getting out.

As I exited the car, one of the garage doors opened, and I was greeted by Ms. Chang and her two children, who promptly stepped into their own car. Ms. Chang came to the entrance of the garage and smiled pleasantly. "Hello, Miss Lee, it's nice to see you again. You did a lovely job at the party. I may have to hire you for one of our soirees in the future. Those teriyaki sticks were absolutely amazing."

I bowed my head in appreciation. "Thank you for saying so. I'll be sure to pass the compliment along to Peter."

She was dressed in knee-length khaki shorts and a paisley tank top. "You'll have to excuse me, we were just on our way out to the park." She turned to leave.

"Ms. Chang, before you go, I want to thank you so much for letting me talk with Susan today. I really appreciate it."

She turned back around. "It's no problem. Donna mentioned something about trying to track down a friend of Susan's. I hope there's nothing illicit going on."

"Oh no, nothing like that," I said, shaking my head emphatically to reassure her. "Just trying to figure out who might have been friends with Alice Kam. Donna has been going back and forth on whether to submit a memorial piece about her in the paper, but doesn't know much about her." Okay, I was lying again. But who would it hurt?

Ms. Chang sighed. "Oh, that poor thing. Even while in the midst of all these problems, she is still thinking of others. She is a stand-up woman indeed."

Her response gave me a sense of relief. "It's nice to hear someone say so," I replied.

"Well, if you ask me, this whole nonsense about her losing her mind is just the most absurd thing I've heard in a long time. Donna is a woman of class. She'd never entertain such behavior."

"Unfortunately, not everyone feels that way."

She snorted, her nose turned up in disdain. "You send them my way, Miss Lee. I'll set the record straight."

I grinned. I was beginning to really like Ms. Chang.

One of the kids honked the horn, and the noise startled both of us. Ms. Chang laughed at her own skittishness. "My word, these children are impatient today. I'd best be on my way." She turned back toward the car. "Have a nice chat with Susan."

I waved them off and made my way to the front door. The doorbell chimed loudly in a nice melody that went on for about fifteen seconds, but I couldn't imagine listening to it every time someone stopped by.

A small woman about my age with her long hair gathered at the nape of her neck opened the door. She was dressed in a blush-colored, short-sleeved blouse that was tucked into her plain black, knee-length skirt. Her shoes were respectable black flats, and she looked comfortable and conservative. In a way, she reminded me of Anna May.

She smiled at me, but I could see the question in her expression. "Can I help you?"

"Hi, I'm Lana Lee, do you happen to be Susan Han?"

"Oh yes, come in," she said, stepping off to the side. "Ms. Chang told me that you were coming by, but I didn't realize that it would be this soon."

"If I'm disturbing you, I can come back at another time."

"Not at all. Please, come in."

I walked in and literally gasped out loud. I have seen some fabulous houses in my recent adventures, but this took the cake. The foyer itself might have been the size of my entire apartment. And was that an elevator I saw?

Susan noticed my expression and chuckled. "It's

something, isn't it?" She gestured for me to follow her.

"That's one way to put it." My eyes roamed over the crown molding that bordered every room, the flawless blond hardwood floors, and the elegant Victorian-style furniture.

Susan led me through a living room, past a wood-paneled study that someone had left the door ajar to, through the dining room, and finally into the kitchen. The white cabinets went up to the ceiling and met a delicate crown molding more intricate than what was in the other rooms. A marble-topped island in the center of the room was surrounded by eight leather stools. The floors were the same blond wood, and the walls around the sink were glossy ceramic tiles.

Against the far wall of the kitchen were large French doors that led out onto a deck. I could see Lake Erie through the thin lace curtains.

She opened what I thought was a giant pantry door, but it turned out to be a refrigerator. "Would you like something to drink? We have a little bit of everything."

"Water would be fine."

She pulled out two bottles of Evian and pointed to the French doors with one of them. "Let's go out onto the back deck and talk. It's so beautiful outside, and I've been cooped up in the house all day."

I followed her out onto the deck. If my jaw hadn't already dropped when I entered the home, it definitely would have hit the floor now. The deck we were standing on had stairs leading down a level. I made my way down the stone steps onto an even larger deck made up of the same stone as the stairs.

There was a long table with seating for twelve, six chaise lounges, a firepit made out of bricks, and two large tables with umbrellas near a fence that separated the property from the lake's shore. I could for sure fit my entire apartment in this massive space.

Susan led me to one of the covered tables and pulled a chair out for me to sit.

"What, no pool?" I asked her sarcastically.

"Oh yes, there is, but it's inside on the lower level."

"Oh."

She laughed. "You get used to it after a while. I've been here for a couple of years, and it doesn't shock me as much as it did when I first started. Prior to moving in with the Chang family, I was living in a shoebox of a studio apartment over in Lakewood."

"I can't imagine living in a place like this," I admitted, thinking about the modest ranch that had been my childhood home.

She passed me one of the water bottles. "Being a maid can have its perks if you do it right."

"Do you also take care of the children?" I asked.

"Here and there. Mostly I just clean and take care of the meals. Ms. Chang likes to be very hands-on with her children. They've actually all stepped out for some type of outing, so we have the place to ourselves."

"Yeah, I ran into them on my way in. She seems like a really nice woman."

"She is. I love working for her." She leaned back in her chair and looked out onto the water. "You know, this is my favorite place to be. I could sit out here for hours and watch the lake."

"It is nice and peaceful," I said, sharing in the

first tranquil moment I'd experienced all day. For a few minutes, we sat like that gazing out onto the water, and I imagined what it would be like to live a life of leisure, spending my days on a chaise overlooking Lake Erie with my nose in a book.

She sipped from her water bottle and turned her attention back to me. "But you didn't come here to ask me what it's like to be a maid for a wealthy family."

"No, I came to ask you about Alice Kam. I was hoping you could tell me something about her."

Her expression saddened. "I was sorry to hear about what happened to her. She was such a nice girl."

"It seems that everyone thought highly of her," I replied. "I haven't found a person yet who would speak ill of her."

"She never gave people a reason to."

"What about Bryce Blackwell?"

"Who?" she asked.

"Her fiancé."

Her eyebrows crinkled together. "She wasn't engaged to anybody as far as I knew."

Well, wasn't that interesting? I knew that guy was lying about something.

Susan snapped her fingers. "Oh, Bryce . . . yeah, I remember him . . . the DJ. She didn't talk about him too much. But he was her boyfriend a little while back, I do know that much."

"Do you remember why things ended between them?"

"No, not really, she didn't talk about it with me. I don't know that she talked about it to anyone, really. She could be very private about her personal life.

Although we kind of lost track of each other over the few months before she was . . ."

"It's okay, you don't have to say."

She gave me an apologetic smile. "It's hard to think about knowing that something like that happened to someone you know. That's stuff you see in crime shows and on the news."

"Trust me, I can understand," I said. "I heard a rumor that she told you she was having problems with Donna Feng. Something about Donna drinking excessively and constantly berating her."

She tilted her head, thinking it over. "She did mention once that Donna was becoming increasingly difficult. But she expressed concern about it rather than it coming across as a complaint. Where did you hear that from?"

"It was a thirdhand story I heard from some ladies at the plaza."

"Ah, like a game of 'telephone.'"

"Exactly," I said, laughing. "They heard it from someone who heard it from you who heard it from Alice, and there you have it."

"Hm, the only person I'd talk to about that sort of thing was our mutual friend, Evie."

"Oh yeah, I meant to ask you about her. I've heard her name a couple of times in passing. Were the two of them close?" I asked.

"As close as I ever saw Alice get with anyone. They actually started spending more time together in recent months."

"Would you mind putting me in contact with her?"

"No problem. I have one of her cards in my purse. I'll grab it on your way out," she said.

We talked for a little while longer, and she told me the little she knew about Alice. She hadn't lived in Cleveland long, and her first job in the city had been with Brenda Choi. The only boyfriend or romantic interest she'd heard even a peep about was Bryce. But once they broke things off, Susan had forgotten all about him because Alice never brought him up. She expressed a little surprise at the fact that Alice had recommended Bryce for Donna's party, but attributed it to Alice being a nice person.

On my way out, she stopped in a small mudroom off to the side of the main entrance and dug through her handbag. "I know I have one in here somewhere." She started to remove her wallet, a compact, a cluster of receipts . . . it was like the clown car of purses. "Ah-ha! Here is it." She handed me the card. "Just tell her that you're friends with me."

"Thanks, I really appreciate this," I said. I noted how not one time had she even asked me why I was inquiring, and I was grateful for the fact I didn't have to explain myself or come up with some ridiculous story that only partially made sense.

I took the card from her and looked it over. "Wait, this is a business card for Yvette Howard. This is the party planner Donna used for her birthday."

"Oh yeah . . . that's her, Yvette Howard. Evie is her nickname."

CHAPTER
21

So Evie and Yvette were the same person. And Yvette had been the party planner. How convenient. It appeared as though Alice was charitable to more than just Bryce in her recommendations. Donna hadn't mentioned to me that Evie/Yvette was chosen as a referral from Alice. But the party planner situation had never come up in our conversations. The night of the party, I had thought it was a little odd that Donna had chosen to hire a party planner to begin with, because party planning and organization was her own specialty. But I had dismissed it, figuring it had something to do with her recent mental capacity. Who doesn't need help every now and then?

As I pulled away from the Chang house, I considered whether or not *I* had the mental capacity to check in with the other housewife that Donna had starred on her list, Denise Jung. I decided I did not. I headed home instead and hoped that Megan hadn't yet left for her shift at the bar.

I made it home in time to catch her still getting ready for work. I found her in her room, putting the finishing touches on her makeup. Kikko was beside her on the floor, nibbling on the head of her favorite stuffed duck, and she barely paid me any attention as I walked in.

"It's nice to actually run into you at home," Megan laughed. "I feel like we've barely seen each other this past week."

"That's because we've haven't." I plopped down on her bed and put my head in my hands. "I've about had it with this whole thing. The minute I think I'm getting somewhere, I find out that I'm completely wrong."

"Sorry I haven't been much help. The extra shifts at the bar have been sucking up a lot of time. Do you know I didn't even wake up until two p.m. today? I haven't slept that late since we were in college."

"Wow, that is a record for you."

"I had just enough time to make it to the gym, eat, do a load of dishes, and start getting ready for work. By the way, it's your turn to grocery shop this weekend. I can't do it."

"That's fine. Adam is coming over tonight, but I'm off tomorrow. I'll swing by the store tomorrow. Do you have a list of things you want?"

"On the fridge," she said. "There's also some money in an envelope with it."

"Are you working all weekend?" I asked.

She groaned. "Yes, unfortunately. I'm there almost all day tomorrow. There's another person coming in for an interview, and I told Shane he has to make a decision at some point. I keep threatening to quit, but he never believes me. I can't keep picking up the slack like this. The others aren't offering to help. They all have some excuse—kids, school, whatever." She touched up the corner of her eyeliner. "The whole thing is ridiculous. I've seen lemonade stands run by five-year-olds function better than this."

"I'll try to come in tomorrow night, have a couple of drinks. I wouldn't mind it after the week I've had."

"So tell me what happened. I have about twenty minutes before I have to head out."

I followed Megan into the bathroom as she did her hair and told her about everything that had gone on throughout the day. By the end of the story, she was as flummoxed as I was.

"I can't believe she's not willing to hire this Lydia woman. If anything, that would help so much. I mean, the woman already knows the backstory, it's not like you'd have to bother explaining it all over again to her."

"What's worse is that if Lydia is right, and the mob is involved, you could be in danger, too. Donna doesn't seem to be worried about that fact, though."

"I'm not worried about it that much, either," Megan said, readjusting a bobby pin. "It's not the first time we've taken a risk. And we're careful. Besides, on the slim chance the mob was involved, we'd probably be dead already."

"Gee, that's comforting," I said. "I'm gonna have to tell Adam. I can't keep him in the dark about Donna anymore. If something does end up happening, then he needs to be prepared."

She turned away from the mirror and gave me a

sympathetic look. "I can see his reaction already. He is just going to love this."

After Megan left for work, I thought I might take a quick nap. I felt completely drained and would be useless in entertaining Adam if I didn't get some sleep. Kikko and I curled up on the couch together, and I listened to the sound of her snorting breaths to help fall asleep. It turned out I didn't need as much help as I thought because the last thing I remembered was resting my head on the couch's decorative pillow. Then waking up to the sounds of someone pounding on the front door.

Kikko sprang to attention and barked her whole scuttle to the door. She sniffed the crack and whined while her curlicue tail wagged at high speed. The sun had begun to set and the living room was dim. I was groggy, and it took me a moment to understand where I was.

The pounding on the door continued. "Okay, okay," I yelled. "Hold on a minute."

I hobbled to the entry, my left leg sore from the position I had been lying in, and pressed myself against the door to look through the peephole. It was Adam.

A moment of panic rushed through me. What time was it?

I flung the door open, and the look of frustration on his face was clear by the setting of his jaw. His lips were sucked into his mouth, and his brows hung low over his eyes. "Lana . . . you're going to give me a heart attack one of these days. I've been calling you for over an hour."

Standing to the side, I ushered him in and shut the door. "I'm sorry, I think my ringer is off. I fell asleep and forgot to set an alarm."

Kikko pawed at his legs, and he knelt down to give her a good back scratch. "I saw your car in the lot, so I knew you had to be here. You sleep like the dead."

"You're not the first person to tell me that," I said, stumbling into the kitchen. "Do you want some coffee?"

"If you're going to make it anyway, sure, I'll have a cup." He went to sit on the couch and Kikko followed him, resting her front paws on his lap as he sat down. "I take it you had a busy day."

"I did. Busier than I would have liked." I scooped out the appropriate amount of coffee, filled the water reservoir, and turned the pot on before joining him in the living room.

Kikko appeared unwilling to move from her position in the middle of the couch, so I sat on the other side.

"How was your day?" I asked.

"Usual stuff," he replied.

Since the beginning of our relationship, Adam had never been very forthcoming about his work or what was happening with his cases. For the most part, he liked to leave his job at the station. But I also suspected that he didn't want to discuss it too deeply with me, in particular.

"I'm more interested in hearing about your day. I was surprised that you weren't working at the night market tonight. I was planning on stopping by and surprising you."

"With everything going on, I thought it might be

good to cancel for a week. With any luck, we can get back to normal by next weekend."

"So what happened?"

The coffeemaker beeped, signaling that the coffee was done. I got up, prepared two cups, and brought them back to the couch.

Once we were situated, I went through the painstaking task of repeating the story of my day, yet again. Our conversation was a lot longer than mine and Megan's because I had to explain the backstory on Donna Feng. I swore him to secrecy, and if I thought it would do any good, I would have asked him to pinkie-swear. He did, however, agree that he would not utter a word about this to anyone.

He took a few minutes to absorb all of the information. "So, none of your day involved Warren?"

My eyebrows lifted. "That's what you have to say after everything I told you?"

"A man has to wonder." He smirked playfully, sipping from his coffee mug and resting his free hand on my leg. "Lana, I'm teasing."

"This is serious, Adam."

"I agree," he replied. "It also explains a lot of Donna's behavior. I always knew there was something that woman was hiding. I just couldn't figure out what it was."

"Well, now you know."

"And she refuses to hire this private detective?"

"She doesn't think it's necessary," I said. "I can't decide what I think. I keep going back and forth between the options of mild danger and severe danger. What do you think?"

"You already know my feelings on everything

you end up getting involved in," he sighed. "But we've already come to the conclusion that I can't stop you from anything."

"So, as a professional, what do you think?"

He took a moment to mull it over. "I think we should grab some dinner and then watch a movie. Maybe have a few drinks, see where the night takes us." He nuzzled my neck playfully.

I couldn't understand his lackadaisical manner. This was completely unlike him. Every other conversation we'd had resulted in him being too serious and me trying to make jokes as if I were auditioning for a stand-up comedy routine. I pushed him back gently. I decided to be blunt. "Adam, what's gotten into you? Are you just making light of this because you're not taking what I have to say seriously?"

He leaned forward and set his coffee cup on the table in front of him. "Look, doll face, I honestly don't know what to think of this whole thing. Do I think you're in danger? Yes. Do I think that Donna is selfish in asking you to help her figure this out instead of going to a professional? Yes. But currently, I don't know what to do with this information and I don't have all the facts. I need time to think about it and weigh the options.

"So in the meantime, I think we should go to dinner, have some drinks, and enjoy a nice evening as a regular couple. Once I've had some time, I can give you a more concrete answer, okay?"

"Okay," I said, still uncertain about his response.

"Lana, you should know by now that I don't like to speculate or jump to conclusions."

"I know, but—"

"No buts," he said firmly. "You go get ready, let's go someplace fancy tonight. While you're freshening up, I'll take Kikko out for a walk. Sound good?"

"Okay," I replied. "If you're sure."

"Trust me," he said, kissing my forehead. "I'm sure. A nice steak dinner always helps put things into perspective."

CHAPTER
22

Adam and I went to Red Steakhouse on Prospect Avenue near East Fourth Street and enjoyed two juicy steaks surrounded by jazz music and soft lighting. It was a nice, balmy night, so we stopped for drinks across the way at Flannery's Pub and had a few cocktails on the patio.

We spent our time out talking about everything except the ordeal with Donna. It felt good to have a conversation about regular stuff. I filled him in on Anna May's adventures at her new internship and how she was starting to fall for one of the partners. Then we talked about things we'd read recently and what movies we should go see in the coming weeks. He suggested a beach picnic, and I reminisced about our recent getaway to Put-In-Bay. It seemed like ages ago that the two of us had escaped for the weekend, and I longed for the relaxation of the cozy little cottage that we'd stayed in.

The night passed quickly, and even though I'd napped earlier, I could feel myself getting sleepy again. Adam called an Uber, and we headed back to North Olmsted.

He stayed the night with me, and we fell asleep almost as soon as we got back to the apartment. I was dreaming about being in high school again with my old boss from my previous office job as my math teacher when the bell sounded and jarred me awake. Only it wasn't a school bell ringing, it was my phone.

Adam stirred next to me. I reached for the phone, my eyes groggy with sleep, and squinted to read the screen. It was Donna.

I thought about letting it go to voice mail, but it was really late and I had a pit in my stomach that told me something was wrong. So I answered. "Donna?"

"Lana." Her voice was gravelly and she didn't sound at all like herself.

I sat up in the bed, my pulse beginning to quicken. "Donna, what's wrong?"

"Lana, I'm at the hospital. There's been a situation at the house." She coughed heavily.

"What happened?"

"There was a bad fire that started downstairs— half the house caught on fire. I was able to get the girls out fine, but we're all suffering from smoke inhalation."

"What about Rosemary?" I asked. "Is she okay?"

"Fortunately, she'd already left for the day," she told me. "Listen, I didn't want to alarm you, but I am lying in this hospital bed just sick about the whole thing. I'm positive this is another message for me."

"Were there signs of a break-in? Do you know anything?"

Adam put a hand on my arm. He was sitting up and listening to my conversation. I leaned in his direction and held the phone close to his ear so he could hear Donna, too.

"Not that I'm aware of. I passed out for a little, and the girls are still sick from the smoke as well, so the nurse told the police that now is not the time to talk with us. They'll be back in the morning. We're not even entirely sure what caused the fire yet."

I felt silly asking considering what they had just gone through, but formality's sake, I posed the question anyway. "Are you guys okay for the most part?"

"Jill and Jessica seem to be coughing quite a bit more than myself, but we're going to be okay. They're taking good care of us here."

"Is there anything that I can do? Do you want me to come there in the morning? I can be there first thing."

"No, dear, I appreciate that, but it's not necessary. However, there is something else that I would like you to do."

"Okay . . ."

"I think I underestimated what we're dealing with here. I didn't think anything else would happen so quickly after Alice's murder. I should have listened to you . . . we need to hire Lydia Shepard to help. Can you take care of it?"

Adam and I glanced at each other, and he nodded in approval. "Of course. I'll get in touch with her first thing in the morning."

"Oh, but Lana, I will only trust this woman under one condition."

"What's that?"

"She has to allow you to be involved in every step. I would handle it myself, but I think I might wring the woman's neck if I have to be in her presence for too long." She began to cough heavily; it sounded as if she were choking.

"Donna, why don't you try to get some sleep? We can talk about the particulars tomorrow after you've had time to rest."

"You're right, dear," she said through a coughing fit. "Talk to you then."

She hung up before I could say goodbye.

Adam wrapped an arm around my shoulders and pulled me closer to him. I rested my head on his chest and sighed.

The rest of the night I slept fitfully. To my dismay, I was up before nine o'clock on a Saturday morning. I found that type of behavior to be sacrilegious. Slipping out of bed, Kikko and I ventured out into the kitchen, where I readied the coffeepot and took her out to tinkle.

After I'd gotten off the phone with Donna, I'd wanted to check the Internet for information on the fire. But Adam told me that they would probably have limited knowledge at the time and it wasn't worth stressing myself out over it. Instead, he'd insisted on me going back to sleep and leaving everything for the morning. I'd lain there for a long while with his arm draped over me, heavy and slick with sweat from his warm body. Moving him had been impossible: Every time I tried, he'd grunt and hold me tighter. I finally gave up and counted to one hundred, hoping that the numeric focus would calm my mind. I must have been sleepier than I thought, though, since I couldn't remember anything past seventeen.

When Kikko was satisfied with her potty adventures, we headed back to the apartment and straight for the coffeemaker. I poured myself a cup, added cream and sugar, and just stood in front of the coffee machine while I took my first sips.

Megan's door was closed and I knew she'd be sleeping for quite some time. I'd heard her come in around three thirty that morning.

I settled myself on the couch while Kikko stuck her nose in her food bowl and enjoyed some breakfast. I watched her eat and thought about the day ahead.

If anything, I felt a lot of relief now that Donna was willing to get Lydia involved. I didn't know how Lydia would feel when I told her that Donna wanted me to work with her on the case. Hell, *I* didn't know how I felt about the whole thing.

But even though I was comforted that a professional was getting involved with the particulars, there was still the situation of the house fire to contend with. The whole thing made me nervous. It crossed my mind that Bryce had been over there earlier that day, and I wondered if his real intention was to get another look around the house before lighting the place up like a campfire. But I assumed that he hadn't been left unattended in the home, so I doubted that he'd had time to plant anything there . . . like a bomb that was set to go off while the family was sleeping.

No, it was more likely that he returned to the home sometime that night, and his visit earlier had only been meant as an opportunity to scope the place out.

I heard a bedroom door open and craned my neck

to look down the hallway. Adam came stumbling out, scratching at the scruff on this face that had grown overnight.

"Why are you up already?" he asked. He didn't bother asking if I'd made coffee, just went straight into the kitchen and helped himself to a cup.

"I couldn't sleep anymore," I told him. "I was up most of the night."

"I know," he said, joining me on the couch. "I could feel you trying to squirm free."

"I just want this over with," I said, leaning on his shoulder. "What if Donna hadn't been able to get the girls out in time? Or what if she herself hadn't made it out?"

"Believe me, I know." He sipped his coffee. "Maybe you'd better stay at my place."

I lifted my head up. "But I've never stayed at your place."

The reason had never been clear to me, but Adam wasn't fond of me spending the night at his apartment. He preferred staying here, and since I liked being home surrounded by my things, I didn't mind or complain. I'd hardly even been there in the months since we'd started dating. Only a few times did we stop through his place so he could grab something, or occasionally I'd swing by for pizza and a movie.

"Well, maybe it's time," he said. "I don't know. It's such a guy's place. I never have things to eat other than the basics, there's nothing girlie there for you, and half the time I run out of toilet paper. You wouldn't last an hour without toilet paper."

I rolled my eyes. "I'm not that bad."

"Do you want Megan to weigh in on that?" he said, laughing.

"Speaking of which, what will she do? I can't just leave her here by herself."

"We need to get her a boyfriend with a crappy apartment, too," he quipped.

I playfully smacked his chest. "Come on."

He shrugged. "She could come stay with me, too. I don't know how she feels about sleeping on a leather couch."

I thought it over. "Do you think we've reached that point? That someone might come here next?"

"It depends on if this person knows that you're involved or not."

I told him my theory about Bryce being the one who'd set the fire. If Bryce was the guilty party, then he would definitely know I was up to something.

Adam drank his coffee and contemplated the idea. "I don't know, Lana. Anything to do with this guy could just be a coincidence."

"Yeah, but what about the fact that Alice's own friends never heard of this supposed engagement?" I asked.

"If she was a private person, then it's possible that she wouldn't have mentioned it. Didn't you tell me both Bryce and that Susan woman said she kept things to herself?"

I gawked at him. "Yeah, but what woman do you know who doesn't tell her friends someone proposed to her? I'm convinced he's lying. I feel like he only told Donna that story so he could get to Alice's stuff. I have no idea what he would want from her . . . maybe he was searching for the thumb drive. As far as he would know, it would still be in her possession."

"It's thin, Lana. Very thin."

"Thin or not, it's something we need to consider at this point."

"And you're absolutely going to believe a hundred percent that this Susan Han woman was telling you the truth and she'd never heard anything about an engagement?"

"Sorta," I said, suddenly doubting my willingness to believe her. Maybe it was the conservative manner of her clothing and the fact that she reminded me of my sister. Now that I thought about it, I really couldn't say why I believed everything she'd said. "Do you think she wasn't telling the truth?"

"In most cases, when I interview people, they lie about something small. Sometimes it's relevant and sometimes it's not. But without being there myself, I couldn't tell you for sure. You have to be good at reading someone's tells."

"Can you teach me about that?" I asked. "How to read tells and stuff?"

He chuckled and gave me a wink over his coffee mug. "I'll think about it. In the meantime, let's get ahold of this Lydia person. She's going to need to be brought up to speed pretty quickly."

CHAPTER
23

I called Price Investigations and Meredith answered the phone. She told me that Lydia didn't come into the office on Saturdays, but she'd put a call through to her and let her know that I was interested in talking to her.

In the meantime, I dragged Adam to the grocery store. It was still kind of funny to do domestic-type things with him. When we'd first started dating, it was hard to imagine him doing anything besides being a detective or sitting on a barstool. He always seemed so serious to me in the beginning, but as we'd gotten to know each other more and had become closer, he'd loosened up a lot and I'd become familiar with his softer and more relaxed side.

After we finished at the grocery store, we stopped for gas on our way back to the apartment. He helped me carry in the grocery bags, and when we entered the apartment, we found Megan sitting at the kitchen table scrolling on her iPad and eating a bagel.

"Oh good, you guys went to the store. I just ate

the last one," she said, holding up the bagel slice in her hand.

Since Adam and I had yet to eat, I'd bought stuff to make French toast, and while the two of them sat at the kitchen table, I fried egg-battered bread and scrambled some eggs. As we ate, I filled Megan in on what had happened at Donna's house the night before.

Once we'd finished breakfast, Adam told me he had to check in at the station, but had the day off so he'd be back in a little while.

"I think I'm going to head to Denise Jung's house and see if I can learn anything from her. Donna starred her name on the list she gave me, and she's my last open link aside from Yvette Howard."

"If I came with you, that would probably be suspicious," he said. "Call me when you're done."

We said our goodbyes and he headed out the door.

Megan finished her cup of coffee and set it in the sink. "So now what?"

I sank in the chair and wrapped my hands around my coffee mug. "Honestly, I don't know. All I can think to do is keep going until I hear back from Lydia. I have a gross feeling about this Bryce guy that I can't shake."

"Not about Rosemary?" she asked.

"I don't know. I've thought about that, too. But I feel like her loyalty would be to Donna, not against her. If Alice's death were an isolated incident, I would be more likely to believe that Rosemary had some involvement. But this fire was clearly targeting Donna. And I don't see Rosemary doing that."

"But we don't know that to be one hundred percent true. Maybe she's a pissed-off employee."

"Donna insists that the person who left the thumb drive is the same one who killed Alice . . . and is responsible for this fire."

"Yeah, but so what about what Donna thinks? We still don't know for sure that Alice isn't the one who left the thumb drive. We don't know conclusively that Donna isn't the one responsible for all of this, and we don't know what lengths someone like Rosemary Chan would go to on any level." She leaned against the kitchen sink. "By the way, have you ever asked Donna if Rosemary knows her secret? Even that little bit of information would help us greatly."

"No, I just assumed that she didn't. Donna said that the only person who knows is me, and Thomas . . . well, okay, and Lydia."

"Yeah, but now Adam also knows . . . and so do I. And Donna doesn't know that."

"So?"

"So, that means that Donna doesn't know everything. How does she know that Rosemary didn't accidentally stumble upon what Thomas was doing? Or how does Donna even know that Thomas didn't tell Rosemary himself? Maybe he thought Rosemary already knew."

"True. I suppose those are all realistic scenarios."

"Lana, I know you want to go by whatever Donna is saying and believe it to be the whole truth and nothing but. I get that. But don't forget what we're always saying to ourselves. We have to be objective."

It was well into the afternoon, and I hadn't heard anything from Lydia. I decided to call the number that Susan Han had given me for Yvette Howard. I got her voice mail and left a message telling her who I was and that Susan had sent me her way. I left my cell phone number and told her to call me back anytime she got the chance.

With nothing else to do at the moment, I decided to head over to Denise Jung's house and use my earring story.

Denise answered the door herself. I was surprised because it seemed everyone else had someone to do that for them. I was also surprised to find that she was the other woman at the party that Brenda Choi had been gossiping with.

"Can I help you?" She glared down her nose at me, which really wasn't hard considering there was a step up into the house. She barricaded the door with her body, her arm outstretched against the frame, clearly stating with body language that she would not be inviting me in.

I tried to straighten my back and hold firm on my position. She wouldn't get rid of me that easily. "I was stopping by to see if you'd lost an earring the night of Donna's birthday party." I began to dig in my purse for the baggie containing the earring.

"I don't believe I lost anything that night," she replied coldly. "I would have noticed right away."

She didn't even give me the chance to pull it out and show her. "Okay, do you know anybody it might have belonged to?" I asked. I was grasping and she knew it.

"How would I know whose earring it was? I don't go around looking at everyone's accessories. What is the real reason you're here? I don't appreciate people who waste my time."

Immediately, my cheeks were hot with embarrassment. I think in different circumstances, I would have been furious, but in this instance, I felt like a child being scolded.

"Well?" She crossed her arms over her chest. "I don't have all day."

"Okay, truth is, I was wondering if you happened to know anything about Alice Kam or if you saw anything suspicious the night of Donna's party."

"What do you mean, *anything suspicious*? What kind of question is that to ask someone?"

"If you saw something—"

"Is this you trying to stick your nose in other people's business again? I read about you in the paper. I know you've meddled in people's private affairs before."

I blanched. *Meddled? I helped solved the case, you rude*—I pushed down the profanities that were threatening to bubble up. "The police aren't getting anywhere with what they know. Donna is a family friend, and I thought she was yours, too. I'm only trying to help."

"If that's what you want to call it." She shifted her weight. "The only thing that stuck out to me that night was the fact that Donna completely lost it on that innocent girl. And now I've heard she had some kind of house fire on top of it. I wouldn't be surprised if that batty woman lit the damn thing herself. Probably wants to collect the insurance money or take attention away from the real crime that happened there."

I couldn't help but find myself completely appalled by this woman's reaction. And she was supposed to be one of Donna's friends? "Do you really believe that?" I sounded like a child who'd just heard that Santa Claus wasn't real.

She stuck out her chin. "Yes, I do believe it. Ever since she lost Thomas, she has been slowly falling apart. Piece by piece, she's become totally erratic. Every time I see her she has a drink in her hand. I wouldn't be surprised if she was completely intoxicated at her birthday party. Probably doesn't even remember killing her nanny. If I were that Rosemary woman, I'd watch myself. She could be next on the chopping block."

I couldn't listen to this anymore. "How can you call yourself Donna's friend and think these terrible things about her at the same time?"

"I would use the term *friend* loosely. Besides, with her current state of affairs it's not that far a stretch. Now, if you'll excuse me, I have more important things that I need to do with my time than talk about Donna Feng."

Without waiting for me to respond, she slammed the door in my face.

I stood there for a moment, completely stunned by the conversation I'd just had. Maybe I should have left the rest for Lydia to handle after all.

I returned home and spent some quality time with Kikko. We walked all over the apartment complex while I replayed everything Denise had said. I needed to find out more about her and what her deal was. Was she always this angry? Did she and Donna have bad blood? I remembered seeing her at the party and she seemed to be all smiles. Then again, the times that I had seen her she was with her gossiping circle. Who knows what she was smiling about at the time?

I also thought about what she'd said in regard to the fire. Could it be a possibility that Donna set the house fire herself to take attention away from what happened with Alice? It would solidify her story that someone was after her. But I was the only one who knew her theory on that. The police didn't know anything about the thumb drive or that Donna thought Alice's murder was a threat against her own life. She had only told them that she was innocent and there was nothing more she could do to help them fill in the blanks. And they couldn't actually pin anything on her because no one had seen anything except for the argument near the pool.

I wondered how the investigation was going for them. It was a shame that Adam didn't know anyone at the Westlake Police Department. The man seemed to have friends everywhere. Of course, this one time when I really needed him to know someone, he didn't.

When I got back to my apartment, I found I had a missed call from Lydia. Finally.

I called her back right away.

"So she agreed to let me investigate, huh?" Lydia asked after I'd filled her in on Donna's new request. "I have to admit, I'm a little surprised. I didn't think she'd want anything to do with me."

"Yeah, she caved," I said. "Did you hear about the house fire?"

"Saw it on the news this morning. Figured that had something to do with it."

"I think the fact that her kids were put in danger helped motivate her into making the decision. Donna is not a woman who gives in easily."

"I didn't get that impression, either, but I can see it happening in this case," she replied. "I don't have kids myself, but if I did, I'd be a bear for sure. You have kids?"

"Nope, but I'm sure I'd be the same, too."

"I'll draw up the paperwork. Can you stop by the office tomorrow around lunchtime? I'm assuming she won't be coming into my office anytime soon."

"Yeah, I could probably swing it," I said. "But she has one stipulation I need to mention before I let you go."

Lydia chuckled. "Of course she does. She's too rich not to. What is it?"

"She wants me to be involved in the investigation."

"Sorry, come again?"

"She wants us to work together."

"Oh no, sorry, chickadee, I don't work with civilians and I doubt my boss man would be okay with it, either. I'm licensed, you're not . . . if something happened to you . . ."

"Look, I know it's not ideal, and believe me, I'd rather give this whole thing over to you considering the circumstances. But it was the only way she would agree to hiring you. If you don't go along with it, she might back out. She's very protective over this situation, and she's not very trusting of you, as we both know. It's really just a formality if you think about it. I'd take the backseat anyway."

There was silence on the other end.

"Lydia? Are you still there?" I wasn't sure if she'd hung up on me or not.

"Yeah, I'm still here. I'm weighing my options."

"Do you want a day to think it over?" I suggested. Maybe she just needed time to warm up to the idea.

"I'll tell ya what. Let me talk it over with Eddie first. If he says it's cool, then it's cool with me, I guess."

"Okay, that's fair."

"I'll be in touch."

When we hung up, I flopped backward on the couch. Kikko, sensing my frustration, put a paw on my leg and grunted.

"Today stinks," I said as I scratched behind her ears.

I don't know why I was so worried about Lydia's decision. Either way, I wasn't getting out of the case. If Lydia said yes, I'd still have to be involved. But by not giving me an answer, she'd made me feel like there was just another loose end to deal with.

Saturday evening should be spent either doing something incredibly fun, or doing something very relaxing. It should not be spent talking about murder suspects with your significant other while you binge-eat cheesy popcorn and doughnut holes.

We'd decided against going out after all, and thought it would be a better idea to veg out on the couch. The only problem was, I was having a hard time getting my mind to calm down.

"You're going to make yourself sick eating all that," Adam warned.

I shoved another handful of popcorn into my

mouth. "I eat or I shop when I'm stressed, you know that. And since I'm still letting my credit cards cool off, eating will have to do."

"We haven't even started the movie yet. Or ordered the pizza."

"Well, whose idea was it to bring over a whole bag of doughnut holes?" I asked.

He gave me sheepish grin. "I thought you would share them with me."

I clutched the bag closer to my chest. "I haven't decided yet."

Kikko sat diligently at my feet, waiting for the moment I would undoubtedly drop something for her to snack on.

"You have to stop worrying about this case so much," he said, rubbing my shoulder. "There's nothing more you can do about it tonight. Let's try to enjoy the evening and relax."

"I just don't know how someone's friend could say stuff like that. And I don't know what to do if Yvette doesn't get back to me. I thought for sure name-dropping Susan Han would be an easy foot in the door and she would call me back right away."

"Does she have an office?" he asked. "Somewhere you can corner her?"

"No, she works from home, and I didn't ask Susan where she lives. I suppose I could try contacting her again tomorrow and asking."

"If the PI gets back to you, then maybe you can just pawn it off on her. She'll be able to track this Yvette woman with no problems."

"Yeah, that's true." I pulled another doughnut hole out of the bag and popped it into my mouth. "But you know what awful thought I had?"

"What?"

"What if Donna really did do it? And what if I'm doing all of this for nothing? I mean, I don't want to believe that. But . . . ugh." I reached for the popcorn.

Adam took the bowl away from me. "Okay, if you keep eating all this junk, you're going to make me sick in the process."

Kikko and I both followed the bowl with our eyes.

"Now that I've had time to think about it, I've come up with some scenarios," he continued.

"And when were you going to tell me about them?"

He chuckled. "I'm telling you now."

"I'm ready," I said, using my fingers to close the imaginary zipper over my lips.

"Most likely, Donna is right: The thumb drive and Alice are connected. It would be too odd for both events to happen on the same night and have nothing to do with each other."

I nodded in agreement.

"So I think that eliminates the boyfriend. Unless they were working together to blackmail Donna and something went south between the two of them."

"Yeah, but what about him coming to Donna's house the same day that her house mysteriously catches on fire? You don't think that's weird?"

"Too obvious," Adam said, discrediting it without too much thought. "If he was planning on setting her house on fire, he would not have showed up the same day. But you do have to find out why he was there, and somehow get to the truth about his and Alice's relationship. There's something that doesn't add up there."

"Then we're back to the hit-man scenario?"

"Maybe . . . I dislike that idea the most out of them all. If that's the case, a PI isn't going to cut it. We need to get proper authorities involved if it comes to that."

I didn't even want to think about that. "What about Denise?" I asked. "What do you think about her?"

He tilted his head. "I think she's too openly angry to be guilty. If she had something to hide, I think she'd do a better job of actually acting like Donna's friend."

"That's a good point." I had to admit, it actually made me feel better that he thought so. "And what about Rosemary? Do you have any feelings about her?"

"I do in a way. She's definitely someone to look out for. It's even possible she started the fire as a way to take attention off the situation with Donna. If anyone, I would have the PI search into that woman's past and see if anything strange comes up. This all could be her attempt to protect her employer."

He was right. With Lydia's resources, we might be able to learn more about Rosemary. We would be able to learn more about *everything* if we were lucky. I started to panic again thinking about whether or not Lydia would take the case. There was always the option of using a different PI, but Lydia having the background knowledge on Donna made things so much easier. Plus I didn't know how Donna would feel about getting another person involved in her backstory.

Adam got up from the couch and stretched his arms.

"What are you doing?"

He turned to look at me. "I'm getting my cell phone from the kitchen and ordering our pizza. We are going to relax whether you like it or not. Besides, it's time to stop thinking about hit men and killer housekeepers for the night."

CHAPTER
24

Adam and I woke up at a reasonable time on Sunday considering we'd stayed up into the early morning having a *Supernatural* marathon. By the time we finished, the whole bag of doughnut holes was gone and only two slices of pizza were left. Let's just say that Kikko wasn't the only one who had to waddle to bed that night.

He left after sucking down a cup of coffee, and I readied myself for dim sum with my family. I am always in the mood for dim sum, which should say something about how crazy it was that I wasn't feeling it today. If I could just sit and eat without being disturbed, it might be a different story, but with my family there, well, conversation was bound to happen.

I kept to myself for most of the lunch, letting my sister take the attention off me. She was so busy talking about her new internship and how much she loved one of the partners, Henry Andrews, and how smart he was, how charming he was, and how *still*

single he was, that my family didn't even notice that
I was more on the quiet side than usual.

When we left, my grandmother patted me on my
cheek and gave me a look that told me she had noticed my silent behavior. Before we parted ways, she
squeezed my hand three times and winked.

I got in my car and checked my phone. No missed
calls from Lydia. Granted, it was a Sunday; maybe
she hadn't gotten the chance to talk to her boss yet.
My impatience was getting the best of me.

Donna and her daughters had been released from
the hospital and were staying at the Hilton downtown while their house was being worked on. To my
surprise, my mother had not brought up anything to
do with Donna while at dim sum. I couldn't help but
wonder if my sister's interest in a successful lawyer
who happened to be a partner at a major law firm
had anything to do with it.

I decided to give Donna a call.

"Hello, Lana," she said, still not sounding quite
like herself. "How are things? Anything new to report?"

I filled her in about the conversation I'd had with
Lydia, but decided to skip telling her about Denise
and the things she had said about Donna. I figured
she didn't need that kind of negativity in her life
right now. She had enough.

Donna was quiet for a moment and then said, "If
she declines my terms, offer her double the usual
rate."

"Double?" I asked, incredulous.

"Yes, double," Donna said with resolve. "I've
found that money can be an excellent motivator in
getting people to say yes in these types of situations.

And I have the money, so why not use it to my benefit?"

"If you're sure that's what you want me to do."

"Lana, someone is after me, they killed my nanny, set my house on fire, and I'm now living out of a Hilton with my two teenage daughters. Yes, I'm sure."

"Have you talked to Rosemary?" I asked.

"Yes, of course . . . why do you ask?"

"You don't think . . ." I couldn't bring myself to say it out loud.

"Do I think what?"

"That maybe she had something to do with the fire?"

"That's absolutely absurd!" Her voice rose and then she coughed. "Rosemary would never do such a thing. What have these people been filling your head with, my dear?"

"I have to consider all angles. I know it's hard. I'm sure that Lydia will want to do the same thing."

She groaned and coughed.

"How are you feeling?" I asked when she was done with her coughing fit.

"Better. My throat still burns and my lungs are sore, but it's less painful than it was that first night. I'm just grateful that we're all okay. This could have turned out much worse."

"Did the fire department say what caused the fire?"

"Something about faulty wiring in the kitchen. I'm having an electrician come to the house tomorrow morning. I barely understood what the fire marshal said to me, it was all very technical."

"Faulty wiring in the kitchen?"

"Yes, they said that's where it started. He asked if I noticed the lights flickering or had problems getting the appliances to work correctly. But as far as I know, Rosemary has had no issues in the kitchen. She would have told me the minute there was one."

"I see."

"Lana, I am telling you, don't get any crazy ideas in your head. Rosemary had nothing to do with this. If there's any one thing I can be sure of, it's that she would never betray me."

I found it interesting that Donna felt it necessary to say this. Clearly she understood that my mind was furthering thoughts on Rosemary's guilt given that the fire started in the kitchen—the area of the house that Rosemary worked in the most.

We hung up after I told her that I'd be in touch once I heard from Lydia.

Megan had to work yet again, and I was beginning to worry they'd never find anyone. She was grumpy, tired, and overworked. To help pick up the slack, I cleaned the entire apartment when I got home. After I'd finished stuffing the dishwasher with everything that had piled up over the weekend, I sat down at the kitchen table with my notebook and Kikko at my feet.

Normally at this stage in the game, I had certain feelings about who I thought would be the likeliest suspect and I would home in on that person, but for whatever reason, that was not happening.

It bothered me that I had not met or spoken with Evie since I'd learned of her existence. Because she had been the one to pass along information from Alice to the rest of the gossip community, I felt she was an important part of my missing puzzle pieces.

I still didn't know what I felt about Rosemary, but it certainly seemed like something was amiss there. Until I had clear confirmation that she was not at all involved, I wouldn't be able to let it go and feel mentally sound about it.

On top of that, the situation with Alice's ex-boyfriend, fiancé, whatever he was, still gnawed at me. I made a note that I should try to talk to him again.

Then there was the idea of Brenda Choi and Denise Jung to contend with. It crossed my mind that they could even be in on it together and they were covering for each other by making Donna look like the crazy one.

And of course, there was the possibility that Donna truly was crazy.

I wrote *hit man* on a fresh piece of paper and circled it with a question mark. I still didn't want to think that this was a possibility, but how could I ignore it considering Donna's history and the fact that her mother had found it necessary to run to another country and change their identities?

The rest of the day passed uneventfully. I felt discouraged and disappointed with my lack of progress. Close to bedtime, I decided to forget about the day and just focus on preparing myself for the dread that is Monday. I picked out clothes, spent extra time pampering my face with a mask, toner, and night creams. I inspected the bags that had formed under my eyes, and then flopped into bed with the hope that tomorrow would produce better results.

CHAPTER
25

Monday morning seemed to drag on for what felt like seventeen hours. The only customers we had all morning were the Mahjong Matrons and two take-out orders.

I thought for sure the Matrons would have some juicy comments to add about the recent house fire, but to my surprise they only expressed deep concern for Donna and her children. I suspected that because the children were involved in the equation, it took the luster out of gossiping. Still, I can't say that I hadn't thought they'd give me some ideas to mull over and add to my list of suspicions.

Nothing at all exciting happened until around eleven thirty after Nancy showed up. I slipped into my office to prepare a bank deposit when my cell phone rang. It was Yvette Howard.

"Hi, sorry for the delay in getting back to you. I have been absolutely swamped prepping for an upcoming wedding and am behind in returning my missed calls."

"Not a problem," I said, trying to sound gracious instead of impatient. "I know you must be a busy woman running your own business and all."

"It keeps money in the bank, so it's worth it. Anyhow, how can I help you? In your message you said something about being referred to me by Susan? I'm kinda booked up into early fall, but since you're a referral, I can try and work something out for you. I hate to turn away business."

I had to make a snap judgment on whether I wanted to lie about needing her services or just come out with the truth and pray for the best. If I told her what I was really calling about, there was a chance she might not be willing to meet me in person, and I really didn't want to do this over the phone.

Then again, what if Susan had already given her a heads-up that I would be calling? I decided to take my chances and lie after all. Remembering my backstory problems with Bryce, I thought fast.

"Well, my best friend's thirtieth birthday is coming up and I'd really like to do something big for her. I was wondering if you could help me with that."

"Oh! Thirtieth birthdays! I love doing those kinds of parties. What were you thinking? A house party? Or do you want to do something in a party room? I can get you prices for local restaurants and bars."

"Maybe a restaurant?" I sighed. "I don't really know."

"That's okay. Why don't we meet for coffee or something and I can show you some options."

We made plans to meet later that evening, and as soon as we hung up, I contemplated exactly how I would segue into the situation with Donna.

* * *

It was my lucky day because when I returned from dropping off the bank deposit, I found Lydia waiting for me at one of the booths. She was dressed in all black, holding a document-sized manila envelope and appearing slightly impatient.

"I was in the neighborhood so I thought I'd stop by with this paperwork," Lydia said instead of saying hello. "Turns out Eddie likes you, and said as long as all of these liability forms are filled out, he has no problem with Donna's terms." She handed me the envelope. "Nice place you got here."

"Thanks." I sat down across from her and turned the envelope over, bending the metal clasp through the eyelet on the back to get it open. I flipped through the paperwork, only understanding half of it. I noted the monetary values and was relieved that I didn't have to try to bribe Lydia or her boss with more money as Donna suggested.

Lydia leaned over the table and pointed to a page that I'd stopped on. "This is the consent form that Eddie had Meredith type up for these particular circumstances. We accept zero liability for anything that may happen to you during the duration of our involvement. You and Ms. Feng sign this one, and then I just need her signature on the rest. The front page has my retainer to get started. Then I charge per hour. Everything is documented, and I provide receipts for any expenses I may incur during the investigation."

I nodded along as she spoke, but truth be told, I wasn't entirely keeping up with anything besides the basics. The paperwork read like a lot of legal mumbo jumbo, and for one second, I considered having Anna May take a look at it, but then I realized I'd have to tell her what I was up to. If she knew things had reached the point of hiring a professional, there is no way she wouldn't rat me out to my parents.

"Okay, I'll get Donna to fill these out and get them back to you by tomorrow."

"Sounds great," Lydia said, slapping the table with both hands. "I've got a meeting in about forty-five minutes, so you'll have to excuse my abruptness. I'll be in the office tomorrow morning and gone by lunchtime."

"How much do you actually work in the office?" I asked.

"Not that much. I try to do mornings when my mind is the freshest, and then I'm out tracking people down, or meeting with clients."

"Do you like what you do?"

She smirked. "Why? You thinking about joining the life?"

I'm not sure why, but the thought of it made me blush. "Not really, just curious, I suppose."

Lydia stood up from the table. "Circumstances led me here; it's not what I originally thought I'd be doing. But yeah, I enjoy it. Someone has got to get answers for these people . . . and if I can help somehow, why not? There's much worse I could be doing with my time." She said goodbye and hurried out the door.

I sat at the booth for a couple of minutes thinking about her answer. Both of us had been led to a different life than we'd imagined. I guess we did have something in common after all.

CHAPTER
26

At six o'clock, I met Evie/Yvette Howard at the Starbucks on Clifton Avenue. The place was packed with people, and I shimmied my way through to the back of the line. I got my coffee and snagged the last empty table near the back and faced the door. I wanted to be prepared for her arrival.

A few minutes later, Evie walked in, and it took her only about a minute or so to recognize me. I could tell she was having a little difficulty placing me, but the familiarity was there. It was showtime.

She went through the line and got her coffee. On occasion she would turn to nonchalantly observe me. I pretended not to notice.

She was dressed in a casual suit jacket with skinny jeans and a V-necked silk blouse that was tucked stylishly into the front of her pants. She wore her hair down in loose waves and resembled someone you'd see advertising the casual-businesswoman look in a copy of *Glamour* magazine. She was carrying a fancy, brown leather purse that doubled as a workbag, and I imagined she'd brought an entire portfolio with her. I began to feel a little bit of guilt as I thought about the real reason for calling her here.

Once she'd gotten her drink, she slowly walked to my table and smiled. "You wouldn't happen to be Lana, would you?"

"Yes, that's me." I extended a hand and gave her a firm handshake.

She cocked her head. "I'm sorry, but we've met before, haven't we?"

"Yeah, you were the party planner for my friend Donna Feng."

Evie smacked her forehead and then sat down in the chair across from me. "Now I remember. You were the caterer."

"Yup, that's me."

"What a small world," she said. "How do you know Susan?"

"Actually, I didn't until recently," I admitted.

The pleasant smile that had been on her face since we'd made our introductions now dropped away. "Oh?"

"It's actually a funny story," I said, sipping my coffee.

She did not look the least bit amused. "How so?"

"I was looking into finding someone named Evie that I'd heard was friends with Alice, and what do you know? You and her are one and the same." I forced a laugh.

Her responding laughter sounded equally hollow, and she quickly occupied herself with taking a sip from her coffee.

"I really am trying to have a party for my best

friend," I lied. "But since we're already here, I wanted to ask you about something else as well. I thought maybe you could help me with a few questions I have."

"I can try," she said, sounding unsure.

"You were friends with Alice Kam, right?"

She nodded. "Yes, we knew each other."

"When I spoke with Susan, she told me that you guys were pretty close and that you would know more about her personal life than anyone else would."

"Ha! Oh, that Susan. They were really the ones who were close. That's how I met Alice . . . through Susan."

"Well, she did tell me that, but she said that you and Alice grew closer in recent months and that if anyone would know about Alice's relationship with Bryce Blackwell, it would be you. Was she wrong about that?"

For a moment, I thought I noticed relief pass over her features. "Bryce? What do you want to know about Bryce Blackwell?"

"Quite a bit, actually. But I guess the biggest question on my mind is, were they engaged at any point in their relationship?"

Evie stifled a laugh as if it was the most ludicrous thing she'd ever heard. "Not that I know of. I mean, Alice was a nice girl and all, but kind of timid for someone like Bryce." Her eyes lit up for a moment. "He's kind of on the adventurous side."

I raised an eyebrow. That was an interesting response for her to make. I made a mental note of her reaction. "Okay, so if they weren't engaged, do you know why they broke up?"

"I think it was sort of a natural progression. Bryce is a busy guy, and realistically, their schedules didn't match up. They started seeing less and less of each other as the newness of the relationship wore off, and Alice wanted to move on with her life. Neither one of them seemed that broken up over the relationship ending. Then she started seeing an older man a few weeks before she died. I assumed she had moved on."

"She did?"

Evie nodded. "She casually brought him up one day, but she didn't give me a name or many details. All I knew was that he had a lot of money and was more than willing to spend it on her. Alice was into that sort of thing. I think her dream was to go from nanny to rich housewife. She loved that circle of friends that Donna runs in and would talk about it all the time."

Her comment reminded me of the conversation I'd had with Brenda Choi, which seemed to have taken place forever ago. Brenda had said Alice knew what kind of crowd she ran in and that it equaled money. Maybe her plan the whole time was to find a sugar daddy. And with Donna at the top of the food chain, it would make sense for Alice to want to be by her side. Perhaps Brenda's financial status wasn't high enough for her liking.

Despite what Evie thought about the whole thing, maybe Bryce had a harder time getting over it than he let on. With the realization that she had started dating someone else, maybe he lashed out at her. Seeing her in person for the first time at the party might have made everything more real for him, and he just couldn't take it anymore.

"Can I ask you something?" Evie asked, breaking me from my train of thought.

"Sure."

"Why are you asking these questions about Alice and Bryce anyway? Did something happen?"

Even though Donna was a fan of Yvette Howard, the party planner, I wasn't sure how she'd feel about me telling her business to Evie, the gossiping friend. "Donna is just concerned that the police are looking in the wrong direction with this whole case and Alice's killer. She wanted me to see what I could find out about her background to get a better grasp on who she really was. When you come down to it, Donna didn't know much about Alice's personal life." There, that was sort of the roundabout truth, right?

"They're looking in *her* direction, aren't they?"

I stiffened. "She is a suspect, yes. But I can tell you she didn't do it."

She leaned forward. "How can you be so sure?"

"Do you really believe that?" I asked. "I know you don't have the same history that I have with her, but you worked for her. Is Donna Feng the type of woman you could imagine drowning someone in a pool?"

Her eyes slid toward the entrance and I turned to see who was there, but there was no one near the door.

She crossed her arms and leaned back in her seat. "I worked for her for a short time only, yes. And I can't claim to know all that much about her, but I do know that she is a powerful woman who shouldn't be taken lightly. Alice was having problems with her left and right. You tell me, if you were her friend, what would you think?"

"What about the recent house fire?" I threw back at her. "I'm sure you heard about that. Do you really think that she set her own house on fire?"

"It's insured, isn't it?"

My cheeks were warming. I decided I didn't like Yvette the party planner or Evie the gossiping friend. "Regardless," I said. "She didn't do it."

"No need to get offended. I was only asking." She held up her hands in defense. "Look, I'm not saying that she did, but maybe you shouldn't be meddling with police business, you know? They have their suspects for a reason. Aside from the older man she was dating, I don't know who else would hurt someone like Alice. She was well liked by everyone she crossed paths with."

"And you don't know anything about this older man?"

"No, she never mentioned his name to me. She kept it a secret for whatever reason."

I groaned. "That doesn't help me with much of anything."

"I wish I could be of more help." She took a sip of her coffee and then tapped the bottom of the cup on the table. "But I will say this . . . Brenda Choi's husband liked to cheat on her a lot. The Chois were at the party, and oh look, Alice used to work for Brenda."

My eye narrowed. "Are you insinuating that Alice was having an affair with Brenda Choi's husband?"

She shrugged. "I can't say for sure. But you tell me the real reason behind Brenda getting rid of her all of a sudden."

"I thought it was because her kids were getting too old for a nanny?"

"Does Brenda Choi seem like a mother type to you? Because she certainly doesn't to me. She seems more like someone to have a nanny until the day she ships her kids off to some fancy college in Europe."

I thought over that possibility. It was true. Brenda did seem to be a little too lavish to handle momlike tasks. Perhaps the maid she had on staff took over the other duties. Maybe Alice was sleeping with Brenda's husband and Brenda got wind of it.

"Just consider it," Evie said, shaking her now empty coffee cup. "I should get going. I have someplace I need to be." She stood up without giving me a chance to comment.

"If I think of something, is it okay if I call you?" I asked. "You've been a big help." Okay, I was lying, really she was leaving me with more questions than I'd arrived with, but I wanted to make her feel special so she'd be willing to talk with me again.

"Yeah sure," she said as she started to walk away. "You have my number."

I sat there for a while after she left, finishing my coffee and thinking. Something was bothering me. None of these stories matched up when it came to Alice and what her life was actually like.

I remembered that the papers from Lydia were in the trunk of my car. I decided to take a trip downtown to the Hilton and have Donna sign them.

"Mom's not back yet," one of the twins said to me, peeking from a crack in the door to their hotel room.

"Which one are you?" I asked. I wasn't even going to pretend I could tell the difference between the two girls.

"Hold on," she said, closing the door in my face.

I heard a metal hook slide and then the door opened. She stepped back to let me into the room.

It was a spacious room with modern art and sleek furniture that had a nice view looking out onto Lake Erie. The sun was beginning to set, and it sparkled against the waves of the lake.

"I'm Jessica," she said. "That's Jill." She pointed to her twin who was sprawled out on the couch. They were both petite girls with big doe eyes, button noses, and straight black hair that went well past their shoulders. They were both rail-thin as only teenagers can be, though they appeared more mature than other girls their age.

"Where did your mom go?" I asked.

"She was meeting with the electrician today. She should be back by now, but she probably made a few stops. You know how Mom is . . . always on the go," Jessica said with an eye roll.

"I see." I set the manila envelope on the narrow desk near the floor-to-ceiling windows. "I need her to sign these papers. Make sure she gets this envelope as soon as she gets back. I'll swing by first thing in the morning and pick them up."

Jessica eyed the envelope. "What are those?"

I knew that the girls were nosy, so I didn't want to make their curiosity worse. I decided it would be best to level with them. "They're documents to hire a PI who can help clear up what happened with Alice."

Jessica's head dropped. "Oh."

An obvious opportunity crossed my mind. Why hadn't I thought about questioning the girls before?

"What did you girls think of Alice anyway?"

Jessica lifted her head, her eyes wet with the beginnings of tears. "We liked her a lot. She was so much fun."

"Yeah," Jill said, hoisting herself into a sitting position on the couch. "She was way more fun than Mom. We went everywhere with Alice. We even went grocery shopping and stuff. She always made things super fun . . . even boring things. It's like we were always on an adventure or something."

My heart went out to the two girls. They had truly liked their nanny, and it seemed she must have made quite an impression on them, and perhaps even found a place in their hearts.

"Do you know how Rosemary felt about her?" I asked them.

Jill answered before her sister could get a word out. "That old hag? She's such a killjoy. She never talked to Alice. It was like Alice barely existed."

"Did you ever see them fighting or anything like that?"

The twins shook their heads. "No," Jessica answered. "Rosemary would like hardly even look at her."

I tucked that thought away and continued on with my questioning. "Do you remember the DJ that was working at your mom's party?"

"Do you mean Bryce Blackwell?" Jessica said, her voice raising an octave.

"He is a *total* hottie!" Jill added. "That's originally why we wanted to come downstairs. We were watching him from Jessica's room."

"Have you ever seen him at your house before? Before the party, I mean."

"No? Why would we?" Jessica asked, turning to her sister. "Did you?"

Jill shook her head. "No way, man. I would totally have noticed if Bryce Blackwell was at our house."

"Why would we?" Jessica asked, repeating her question.

"I heard that he was Alice's boyfriend a little while back. Didn't know if he ever stopped by to visit with her and maybe you guys saw the two of them together."

The twins looked at each other and their eyes widened.

"What?" I asked them.

Jill shook her head in disbelief. "Oh man, it makes total sense now."

My patience was dissipating. "What makes sense now?"

Jessica turned to me. "Alice overheard us talking about how cool Bryce was . . . she seemed to get kind of mad about it, but we couldn't figure out why. Then she told us to not drool over scumbags before storming out of my room. We figured she was totally PMS'ing."

"Oh really?"

"Yup," Jill confirmed. "Like I'm a total B when I'm getting my period, you know?"

I pursed my lips. "No, not that. That she told you that Bryce was a scumbag."

"Oh . . ." Jessica appeared dumbfounded. "Why does that matter?"

"No reason," I said, feeling the urge to think over this information in privacy. "I've gotta get going. Don't forget to have your mom sign those papers.

It's really important," I told them before shutting the door.

Bryce Blackwell, come on down, you just made the top spot on my list of suspects.

CHAPTER
27

That evening when I left the hotel, I went straight home, grabbed my notebook from under my mattress, and wrote in a flurry. I had so many thoughts and was having a hard time keeping up with them. Bryce had been bugging me this whole time. I knew that something about him and his relationship with Alice didn't add up. The only thing I couldn't figure out now was why Alice would hire him to work at Donna's party if she thought he was a scumbag.

Something must have happened in between the time she suggested it and the day the party actually took place. But what?

I also wrote down what Evie/Yvette, whoever she was, had said about Alice potentially sleeping with Brenda Choi's husband. Was that even a real possibility? Yvette had been the only one to mention it, and I wasn't convinced I could trust her.

My mind quickly rearranged the pieces into a few new theories: Bryce could have found out about

the affair and threatened to tell Brenda Choi. The
ex-couple then had a huge fight about it the night of
the party and Bryce lost his temper. Or he did tell
Brenda Choi, and Brenda herself was the reason Alice had ended up in the pool. And that would explain
why Brenda helped Alice get a job with Donna *and*
why Brenda wanted me to be suspicious of Rosemary. To ultimately take the attention off herself.

I felt hyper. I started to pace the length of the
apartment. Kikko followed me at first but quickly
grew tired of the fact that I wasn't going anywhere
useful.

I couldn't wait until the following day to take action. I tried Megan's cell phone. Not a good chance
she would pick up, but I didn't know what else to do
with myself.

She picked up on the second ring. "Hey," she
whispered.

"You answered. What the heck are you doing?" I
asked. "Why are you whispering?"

"I'm hiding in the bathroom," she hissed. "I had
to get away. This guy sitting at the bar is driving me
nuts. He keeps calling me toots, who even says that
anymore? But you didn't call to hear me complain
about work. So what's up?"

I told her about my visit with the twins and Evie/
Yvette.

"Weird for sure," Megan replied. "Also weird
how she came to Bryce's defense like that. Shouldn't
that be the opposite? You know, kinda like how I
hate jerk-face Warren?"

I cringed at the sound of his name.

"Speaking of," Megan continued. "What is the
deal? Have you dealt with him yet?"

"No, I haven't even had time to think about it. I really don't want to . . ."

"You need to do something," she said. "Either tell him to go away or have the talk and get it over with. Dragging it out like this isn't good for you. Land the plane already."

"I will, I just need to get through this Donna ordeal first," I said. It dawned on me at that very moment that I might be using Donna's situation to hide from my own problems. I kept saying I would deal with it once everything was done, but would I? Or would I find something else to hide behind? How long could I keep lying to myself? Megan was right: I needed it to be done and over with. Though I had moved on, there was still a part of me that was holding on to something. Once I talked things over with him, it would all be behind me. Isn't that what I wanted?

I groaned in frustration at myself and tried to shake the thoughts away.

Megan sighed, following along with my mental downward spiral. "I shouldn't have brought it up. You're right, deal with it later. This is more important."

"I need to talk to Bryce again."

"When I Googled him, I think I saw that he plays weekly at one of the small bars downtown. Do you want to go check it out?" she asked. "Maybe you can corner him there. I doubt he's going to willingly meet with you again now that he knows what you're questioning him about. Especially if he's guilty."

"I don't want to go alone . . ." I admitted.

"Damnit," she huffed. "I hate that I'm stuck here every day."

"I know, it's less fun this way. Are they ever going to hire someone?"

"There's a final interviewee coming in this week. I told them they'd better hire this person or I'm out of here. You realize I can bartend downtown and make way more money than I do here?"

"Yeah, but isn't the point to get out of bartending and become the manager? You've put in so much time there," I reminded her.

"Eh, I'd rather have the tip money than deal with these shenanigans for much longer. Anyway, I'll text you the place he plays at . . . I think he should be there tonight. Also, I never thought I'd say this, but take Kimmy with you."

"That's actually a great idea, she's always up for last-minute adventures."

"I'd better get back out there. I'll talk to you later."

I said goodbye and hung up. Ugh, Peter was going to kill me for this.

"This is gonna be awesome," Kimmy said from the passenger's seat of my car. "We are gonna work this guy over so good, he'll be beggin' for his mama."

I glared at her from the corner of my eye, trying to keep my focus on the road. "Kimmy, it's not that serious. We're only going to ask a couple of questions. We can't actually accuse him of anything. We don't technically have proof. Besides, it's not like he'll admit to us what he did. We just have to find enough evidence to take to the police."

When I had called Kimmy to tell her about confronting Bryce, she forced me to give her the entire scoop on what had been going on with the investigation. After I made her swear up and down that she wouldn't tell a soul, especially Peter, I agreed to give her as many details as possible without giving up Donna's real secret. She seemed content with the working theory that Alice had been possibly having an affair with Brenda Choi's husband and didn't question me too much after that.

"Details, details," she said, waving me off.

I stopped for a red light. "Kimmy, seriously, do not go accusing him of killing Alice while we're standing right in front of him. If he is guilty, that could cause us a lot of problems."

"Okay, okay, I won't," she said with disappointment in her voice. "You are forever ruining my fun."

Fifteen minutes later we were at a small bar on Euclid Avenue called the Cedar Room. It was exactly what you would expect from the name . . . a cedar room. There were advertisements on a board outside saying that it was industry night. A decent crowd had shown up for discounted drinks.

We sidled up to the bar after I had instructed Kimmy, yet again, to act casual. I discreetly scanned the room and found Bryce exactly where he should be, at the DJ booth. He was surrounded by a few men and women who were all holding shot glasses in the air and laughing about something that Bryce was saying.

I watched as they did their shots. Then the little grouping of people ambled away to find seats at one of the small tables off to the side.

While I kept an eye on Bryce, Kimmy ordered our drinks. I wasn't paying attention to what she ordered, and when I took a sip of my drink, I almost spit it back out.

"Kimmy! What the hell is this?" I yelled at her over the music.

"It's a Jack and Coke. You like that, right?"

"Did they put *any* Coke in it?" I noted the pale color of my drink.

She shrugged with a sly smile on her face. "What can I say? The bartender is friendly."

Inner groan. Yup, Peter was definitely going to kill me.

"So what now?" Kimmy asked. "That's our boy up there?" She nodded toward Bryce.

"Yup, that's him," I confirmed. "He hasn't noticed us yet, which is good."

"Oh, who the hell cares?" She gulped from her own drink and I saw her jaw slightly clench. "It's not like the minute he sees you he's going to run out of here screaming like a crazy man."

"You're right. He can't exactly up and leave."

"So just go up there and say what you gotta say. I'll be right behind you." She nudged my shoulder with her fist.

Taking a deep breath, I set my path through the small crowd and made my way to the side of the DJ booth. It took Bryce a moment to realize I was standing there, and when he saw me, he did a double take. He held up a finger signaling he needed a minute. I turned to Kimmy, and she gave me a wink.

I watched him push some buttons and turn some knobs before he slid his headphones off his head. "What's up?" He gave me and Kimmy a nod. "I don't take requests if that's what you came up here for."

Really? Did he not recognize me? Or was he just

pretending? I half expected him to ask me what I was doing in his place of employment. "No, we didn't want to request anything. I came to talk to you about something. I know you're working, but it'll only take a minute."

Agitation washed over his face, but it was so subtle that if I had looked away for even a moment, I would have missed it. "Can you give me like five minutes? I'll meet you guys out on the back patio."

"Sure," I replied amiably. No point in acting like I had an issue with waiting, even though I could feel my impatience creeping back up.

Kimmy and I found the back door to the bar and stepped out onto the patio. The evening air was warm but pleasant, and we found an empty picnic table to sit at while we waited.

Kimmy lit a cigarette and bopped her head along with the music that was coming out of the outdoor speaker. "When he comes out here, don't let him off too easy. I saw guilt written all over that pretty boy's face."

"You think?"

"Oh, for sure," she said, blowing out a puff of smoke. "He did something wrong. I know that look. I've *dated* that look."

We waited past the five-minute mark, and Bryce never came outside. Ten more minutes went by, and I started tapping my foot anxiously. I checked the time on my phone again.

"Drink your drink and chill, woman," Kimmy said, clinking her glass against mine.

"I have to drive," I reminded her. Flustered, I stood up. "Stay here, I'm going to see what he's doing."

Right before I left our table, the back door of the bar opened and Bryce stepped out, scanning the patio. When his eyes fell on us, he nodded and walked over. He was cool, calm, and casual. It reminded me a little of Warren, and my stomach did flops that told me to be careful. We were dealing with a charmer, no doubt.

I sat next to Kimmy so he would have to sit opposite both of us.

He took the seating cue and threw a leg over the picnic bench. "So, what's up?"

"I know you're short on time so I won't beat around the bush," I said.

"Good," he replied, checking his watch. "I have one of my friends covering for me at the DJ booth, and I told him I wouldn't be long."

"When we talked last time, you told me that your relationship wasn't that serious with Alice."

"Yeah, that's right. So what?"

"Well, why'd you tell Donna Feng that you two had been engaged?" I didn't bother telling him just yet that the only two people I knew to be friends with Alice had also said he was of no consequence.

"Yeah, why'd you do that?" Kimmy asked, pointing her cigarette at him.

He raised an eyebrow and then looked at me. "Who's this? Your wingman?"

"Never mind her," I said, not wanting to steer off topic. "Answer the question. Were you engaged to Alice or not?"

He let out a heavy sigh and ran a hand through his shaggy hair. "Yeah, okay, we weren't *actually* engaged. But I had proposed. It's no big deal really."

"How come nobody knew about the proposal

itself?" I asked. "I feel like that's something you'd share with your friends."

"Because she said no," he replied. "I didn't want anybody to know about it, so I made her promise not to tell anyone; it was super embarrassing for me. But when Alice . . . passed . . . I wanted Ms. Feng to know that someone had cared about her. I didn't want her stuff to sit in that house for weeks on end before it all got taken to a Goodwill, or worse . . . a dumpster."

"So you basically lied to get Donna to pity you?"

He leaned back, shock on his face. "What? No, I don't want anyone's pity. But I needed her to know that I was a legit part of Alice's life. Even if Alice said no to my proposal, we had still been in a serious relationship. It wasn't a total lie. I wasn't just some random guy trying to take Alice's stuff."

"And why did you want Alice's stuff anyway?" Kimmy asked. "I mean, if my boyfriend turned down my proposal, and then died, I wouldn't exactly want his things as keepsakes."

He turned to face her. "What business is it of yours?"

"Just answer the question," I said. "The sooner you answer us, the quicker we'll leave."

He huffed, shaking his head. "Fine . . . she kept the ring."

"What?" Kimmy and I asked in unison.

"Yeah, she kept the damn ring, okay?" He ran his hand through his hair again. "I'm not made of money, you know? I work hard for what I have. And I wasn't going to let that ring just go wherever."

"Why didn't you demand it back when she said no?" I asked.

"I told her to think about it," he said. "I thought that maybe if she held on to it and looked at it, she'd change her mind, okay? I know it's dumb, but whatever." For a moment he appeared sad over the memory. But with everything I'd learned recently, I had a hard time buying the act.

"So then why would she call you a scumbag?" I hadn't forgotten what the twins had said about their conversation with Alice. Right before she died, there was something about him that she didn't like, and I needed to know what it was.

"I asked her for the ring back when I saw her at the party. I told her I had someone else to give it to."

"You are a scumbag!" Kimmy yelled. "Who says that to a girl they supposedly love? You're lucky you're not my boyfriend, I'd smack ya one good and hard right across that smug face of yours."

"You're right, I am lucky," he replied sarcastically.

Kimmy gasped and started to rise. "You little—"

I grabbed her arm, pulling her back down.

Through clenched teeth, she said, "You're also lucky that my friend here is of the levelheaded variety, because I'd give you two black eyes to take back with you to the DJ booth."

He snorted. "Whatever."

"Okay, enough, guys," I said, scolding both of them. "Let's stay on topic here."

"That's all I have to say," he said, putting both hands on the table and hoisting himself up. "I asked her for the ring back, she wouldn't give it to me, end of story."

"Nothing else happened?" I asked as he walked away.

"Nope, and I still don't have the ring, either. It wasn't in her stuff, in case you were wondering."

We left shortly after that. On the way home, I couldn't tell how I felt about the exchange and whether or not I thought Bryce was actually telling the truth. Maybe he was.

There was still something that didn't make sense to me. It all came back to that thumb drive. It showed up on the same night that Alice was murdered. Bryce killing Alice because of jealousy or out of desperation didn't tie in with that. None of it did.

And I was frustrated with Kimmy losing her temper, because Bryce clearly cut the conversation short after that. I never got to ask him if he knew whether or not Alice was seeing someone else.

In the morning, once I got the signed papers from Donna and took them to Lydia, maybe she'd be able to make sense of this whole mess. Because I was just going in circles.

CHAPTER
28

- - - - - - - - - - - - - - -

The next morning, I was amazed by how soundly I had slept. So soundly that I had missed four phone calls from a number I didn't recognize. There were voice mails attached to them, and with my eyes still half closed, I listened to the first message.

"Hello, Miss Lee, this is Rosemary Chan. I am currently at the Hilton hotel downtown with Jill and Jessica Feng. Their mother has not returned from her meeting with the electrician. Please call me at your earliest convenience. Thank you."

Despite the calm and levelheadedness in her voice, my body went into an immediate state of panic. Donna had not returned from her meeting with the electrician?

I quickly called the number back, my heart pounding like a drum in my throat. "Rosemary!" I exclaimed when she answered the phone.

"Miss Lee, good morning," she said in a calm tone. "Thank you for returning my call."

"I'm sorry I didn't call you back sooner, I slept

through everything." Her first call had been around two a.m. I felt ashamed by the fact that I'd missed four calls.

"It is quite all right," she replied, maintaining her calmness. "I wanted to alert you that Ms. Feng is currently missing and I am watching over her children. Jill and Jessica are safe."

"When's the last time anyone spoke with her?" I asked.

"The last people to see her were the children, Miss Lee. She has been missing since that time. Mrs. Feng left to meet the electrician shortly after lunch yesterday. When she didn't return by late evening, Jessica called me to inquire if I'd heard from their mother. I came over here straightaway and attempted to call the police to ask for help, but they have time frames for this sort of thing. However, because she is a suspect in an ongoing murder investigation, it has been noted that she might be a flight risk."

I was still trying to wake up my brain to its full potential. Had Donna fled? Where would she have gone? Would she ever leave her girls?

"Miss, forgive me for saying so, but you must keep your wits about you and figure this out. She didn't say much to me, but I know that you are helping her with this situation and she has the utmost trust in you."

"I will," I said, sounding unsure. Was the electrician a hit man? Was the whole thing a setup to get her alone with him? How much would it take to orchestrate that sort of thing?

"Miss Lee? Are you still there?"

"Yes, Rosemary, I'm here. Can you give me the information on the electrician that Donna was using?"

"She has it written down on this notepad. Please hold for one moment." I heard her put the phone down and papers rustling. She picked the phone back up. "Here is the information."

She recited the company name, the electrician's name, and the phone number. I promised her that I would get to the bottom of this, and we hung up.

I ran into Megan's room, Kikko waddling closely behind. I shook Megan awake, and by the expression on her face, I could tell she was not happy with me. "What . . . Lana . . . what are you doing?"

"Wake up, it's important," I said, shaking her. "I think that Donna's been kidnapped!"

"What?" Megan slid herself into a sitting position and leaned herself against the wall. "Go slow. What happened?"

I told her about my conversation with Rosemary, how Donna had been missing since before I'd talked with the twins the day before, and about her supposed meeting with an electrician.

"Okay, first, you need to calm down," Megan said, wiping the sleep from her eyes. "You call the electrician and see what happened with them. Did this person even meet with her? I'll make coffee and then you need to call Lydia after that."

"But Donna didn't sign the papers."

"At this point, Lana, just forge them. If Donna was really kidnapped, it's not going to matter anyway."

Megan and I sat together at the kitchen table with our coffee mugs, Kikko at my feet. Megan had brewed coffee, made bagels, and let my dog out for her morning tinkle. I'd called the electrician, who sounded like a nice elderly man; he told me that Donna had never showed to their appointment. He thought it was strange since she'd been so adamant about them meeting as quickly as possible and him not being late. But he figured that she was probably a flighty person and didn't give it much thought after waiting for a while. He'd tried calling her cell phone, but she never answered or returned his call.

"I waited half an hour after I tried her cell. She'd call me back if she still wanted my services," he'd said casually.

One hand was on my mug, and the other was holding my head up. The room was spinning slightly and my heart was racing. I didn't know what to do. Either Donna had jumped ship and run away, or someone had kidnapped her before she even got to meet with the electrician. After talking with the elderly man on the phone, I highly doubted that he was a hit man sent by the Chinese mob.

"You have to call Lydia Shepard," Megan said softly. "She's going to be able to get a lot farther with this than we are."

I checked the time on my cell phone. "I have to call Nancy first. I can't go into work today. Not with this going on."

"What are you going to say?" Megan asked. "You can't tell Nancy that Donna is missing. She'll tell your mom and your mom will tell Esther and the whole thing will turn into an Asian epidemic."

"I'll just tell her I'm sick." I started to scroll through my phone for Nancy's number.

"You can't do that, either. Your mom is gonna come around asking questions." Megan shook her head and looked down at Kikko. "Kikko is throwing up everywhere and you don't want to leave. Your mom won't be as worried, but it's a good reason to stay home. You can't just have the dog puking everywhere all day."

I glanced down at Kikko. She grunted at me as if she knew what we were up to. "Okay, you're right, I'll go with that."

I hit the CALL button, and Nancy answered after a few rings. I quickly relayed my story to her, and she seemed to take it well without asking too many questions. Though I did get the distinct feeling that she didn't entirely believe me.

With that out of the way, I needed to decide what story I was going to tell Lydia. Did I tell her the truth—that Donna had been kidnapped and I had no signed contract papers, but I needed her help anyway? Or did I forge the contracts with Donna's name and give them to Lydia as if nothing had happened?

Of course, the second option had some problems, aside from the obvious legal and ethical issues. Finding Donna had just become priority number one, and I wasn't sure how Lydia could help me with that if I lied about Donna signing the papers.

"I need to get dressed," I said, abruptly standing from the table. "It's best if I discuss this with Lydia in person."

"Do you want me to go with you?" Megan asked. "I'll just throw on some clothes."

"No, it's okay, you have to work in a few hours. Go back to sleep," I said, feeling bad that I had woken up my friend. "We can touch base later."

* * *

An hour later I was out the door and making my way downtown to Price Investigations. I had called Lydia's cell phone to make sure she would be in when I got there, and she assured me that she would.

I found some off-street parking and hustled my way to the detective agency. Meredith greeted me in the reception area. "Well, hello there, dearie," she said when recognition set in. "It's nice to see you again. Lydia told me you were comin'. Want any coffee? I just brewed it fresh."

I remembered Lydia's warning about the bad coffee and politely declined.

"She's in her office," Meredith said. "You can go right on in."

I thanked her and moved to the closed door that was Lydia's office. I found her sitting at her desk, typing away on her laptop. She appeared to be pretty alert considering that when I'd called her she sounded half asleep.

"What's up, sunshine?" she said good-naturedly. "You look like you've been hit by a Mack truck."

"Donna's missing," I blurted. Okay, that hadn't gone how I'd planned. I originally intended to be a lot more smooth than that and tell her about the calls from Rosemary and my talk with the electrician, but between the three cups of coffee I sucked down and my already anxious mentality, that just wasn't going to happen.

"Whoa, what do you mean missing?" Lydia asked. "Like, for real gone and can't be found?"

I took a deep breath and started from the beginning, relaying the story to Lydia about how Rosemary had called me several times overnight and how previous to that I had thought she might be responsible for what was happening. I described how Donna had failed to meet with the electrician and also filled her in on my meeting with Bryce and the things that Evie had said about a potential affair between Alice and Brenda Choi's husband.

"Okay, slow down there, chickadee," Lydia said. "Donna didn't sign the papers, right?"

"No, she hasn't been seen since before I brought them over."

Lydia leaned back in her seat, folding her hands across her stomach. "Technically, I can't take on this case without some kind of contract." She chose her words carefully.

I felt my insides tighten. I tried to calculate how much I had in my savings account, which in truth wasn't enough to cover even a day's work of a private investigator. With business being as slow as it was, I hadn't been able to depend on tip money as much as I normally did.

"But I'll tell ya this, kid," she added after a few minutes of thought. "I like you. You've got sass, and I know you're in a real weird position. Hell, I've never seen anything like it, to tell you the truth."

"So you'll do it?" I asked, a little too eager.

"Yes, I'll do it," she said. She held up her index finger. "Under one condition."

"Anything," I said.

"Free Chinese food for a month," she said. "After all, a gal's gotta eat."

"Deal," I said, extending my hand.

"That's only half the condition."

"What? What's the other half of the condition?" I crossed my fingers that it wouldn't be anything too outlandish.

"I may need assistance on something in the future. Say I need an in with the Asian community. You got my back on that?"

I thought on it and decided it was an acceptable request. "Yes."

She stuck out her hand and gave mine a firm shake. "Then, Lana Lee, you have yourself a deal."

CHAPTER
29

-   -   -   -   -   -   -   -

I had to admit that I felt a huge sense of relief knowing that I had a private detective backing my play. I didn't feel quite so alone in this anymore. Not that having Megan on my side didn't make me feel better, but the stakes felt higher this time around and it was good to have a professional involved.

Before leaving Lydia's office, I'd told her about the notebook I kept of all the information that I collected. She told me she'd like to see it and that we should reconvene later in the day. She had a couple of things she wanted to do, and she also said I needed to calm myself. I wasn't going to be any good to her in my hyper state.

She wanted to set up another meeting with Brenda Choi and asked me for her information. While I went to retrieve my notebook and attempt to relax, Lydia was going to do some background checks on the Choi family along with some of the other major players. She agreed that something seemed amiss about Bryce but that more likely than not it was something mundane rather than relevant to the case.

She also stuck to the theory of a hit man being involved, but assured me that it was the least plausible of all the explanations. "A hit man wouldn't drag things out this much," she'd said. "But we'll keep it as an option until it's not an option."

I drove home and tried to keep myself in the present moment. It wasn't an easy task. I reminded myself that getting into an accident wasn't going to help matters. I needed to stay focused and alert. That was the best course of action.

When I got in the door, I made a point of spending time with Kikko, telling myself that I didn't have to rush. But the thought of Donna held against her will somewhere, away from her children and her friends, made me feel otherwise. I quickly let Kikko out for a tinkle and made myself a cup of hot tea when I got back inside.

Megan was still asleep and I tried my best not to wake her even though I wanted to. If she was going to work another long shift today, the last thing she needed was me bothering her every five minutes.

I retrieved the notebook from under my mattress and decided to sit down with it and review all my notes. I still had another hour and a half before Lydia wanted to meet up again.

With all the patience I could muster, I started with the first page and read everything I'd written line by line. That's when I saw something that caught my attention. I'd completely forgotten what the Mahjong Matrons had told me. Brenda Choi had also hired a private detective at one point.

I sent a quick text to Lydia to inform her of that fact in case there was any relevance to it.

A few minutes went by before she texted me back the following: *Hot damn! She used our agency. She was one of Eddie's clients. Getting the file now.*

It couldn't be a mere coincidence that both Brenda Choi and Thomas Feng had used Price Investigations, could it? But what did it mean?

My mind went into super speculation mode and I pictured Brenda and Alice trying to take Donna down together. Maybe Brenda knew that Thomas was using the agency and sent her a nanny-by-day, hit-man-by-night—Alice—to break into the server at Price Investigations to steal the information for her own malicious purposes. That seemed kind of far-flung and a little on the thriller-movie side of things, though. Could Alice really have been some kind of hacker for hire? I tried to picture her in that persona and couldn't make it work. I scolded myself for even having such ludicrous thoughts.

Then again, if Alice was a plant and she was blackmailing the rich widow, that would make Donna a suspect once again. I kept putting her on the table and taking her back off. I didn't want to believe that Donna could be capable of doing all of this. It would mean killing someone, setting her own house on fire, and then running away from her children, leaving them with no one but the maid. I couldn't believe that. If nothing else, she would never leave her children.

I pushed the whole idea aside. Maybe the excess caffeine had corrupted my brain.

While I sat there reading through my notes and

waiting for it to be time to leave again, Adam called. I filled him in on everything that had happened since last we spoke.

"Okay, that's it. You're definitely staying at my place tonight. Tell Megan she's welcome, too. I know leather couches aren't the most comfortable to sleep on, but it's all I've got, and I don't want you girls staying in your apartment in case this turns out to be something bigger than we think."

"Do you really think this is necessary?" I asked, feeling his anxiety drip onto me.

"Well, dollface, if this person was watching Donna closely enough to grab her before she planned to meet someone alone, then it's very possible that they may have noticed how chummy the two of you have been. They may have even noticed you talking to people from the party . . ."

"So you think that Donna is innocent then?" I only asked to confirm my own thoughts. I didn't know if I was trying to turn a blind eye because I knew Donna personally or not. I needed objectivity.

"Honestly, at first I thought it might be a possibility that she was guilty. But if anything gives away that something is wrong with this picture, it's the fact that her kids were left behind at the hotel. I don't know much about Donna personally, but you've made it clear that she's very prideful when it comes to her family. She'd never leave them to their own devices. No, if she was going to bail and run, she'd take her kids with her."

"That's what I've been thinking, too," I said, feeling a sense of relief wash over me. Though it was immediately followed by a sick feeling, because if Donna hadn't run off on her own, she was almost definitely being held somewhere against her will. We needed to find her, and fast.

"Pack a bag, and I'll pick you up tonight," he said. "We'll leave your car there so it looks like you're home. And then tell Megan to leave her car at the bar. We'll pick her up from work tonight."

"Are you sure about this?" I asked. "Two women in your house? Can you even handle that? Well, three, don't forget Kikko."

"On second thought . . . maybe you should fend for yourselves."

With the time I had left before meeting back up with Lydia, I packed a bag and put together travel arrangements for Kikko as well. I left a note on Megan's door telling her what the plan was and that there was no time to argue about it. I felt weird leaving her alone now that Adam had put the idea in my head; I could only hope that nothing would happen this early in the day. Besides, it was still just a theory.

Still, I left the apartment building with an overabundance of caution. I looked through the peephole before opening the door to make sure no one was standing outside waiting to kidnap me, too. Then when I got to my car, I made sure that no one was lying in the backseat. As I drove downtown, I kept checking my rearview mirror to make sure I didn't have a tail. I felt absurd, but if Donna's abduction had taught me anything it was that whoever was responsible for Alice's death wasn't done.

My mind eased when I was safely back inside Price Investigations. Meredith greeted me once again and told me to go right into Lydia's office.

I found Lydia at her desk, almost as if she hadn't moved since I saw her a few hours before.

"So I was skimming over the Choi file," Lydia said as I walked in. "And it looks like pretty standard stuff. She thought her husband was cheating on her and he was. Eddie got some great shots of Randall Choi goin' at it with this blond-haired woman who is much too young for him." She flipped the picture over so I could see.

I squeezed my eyes shut. "Oh yuck, I didn't need to see that." Though my glimpse had been brief, I was thankful it wasn't anybody I recognized. I'd had enough awkward encounters to last me a lifetime.

When I opened my eyes again, Lydia shrugged. She put the photo back in the manila folder. "Sometimes in this job you see things. The lesson here? People need to stop investing in sheer curtains."

"Was there any evidence of him having an affair with Alice?"

"Nope. If they were having an affair, then it wasn't exposed. At least not by us."

"So what are we going to do now?" I asked, eager to start the investigation.

"Well, I put some feelers out. I have a few connections throughout the city. I checked with the two major bus stations in the area, Greyhound and Lakefront Lines. I told my contacts to get back to me if they catch wind of a fancy Asian lady taking the bus outta town. So far, nothing from last night, so that's a good sign."

"Donna wouldn't take a bus if her life depended on it."

"Where's her car?" Lydia looked up at me. "And would you sit down? You're making me anxious."

"Sorry." I blushed, sitting down in the same chair I'd chosen last time. "I don't know. No one's mentioned anything about her car."

"Okay, call up Rosemary and ask her to check that out at the hotel if she can. See if she has a parking slip or something. We'll swing by the Feng residence on our way to Brenda Choi's house since they live near each other."

"But the electrician said that Donna never showed," I reminded her.

"We still have to mind our P's and Q's," she replied. "Best to check it out. We don't know if she got there a lot earlier than her appointment to give the house a once-over herself. It's possible she parked her car on the street and got nabbed after the fact. Plus, we have to be sure that this electrician is telling the truth. He could be a cover for someone else."

"You're so much more thorough than I am," I said with a bit of envy.

She winked. "It comes with the territory. With each case you make a mistake or two. And each case you learn something new because of it."

I nodded in agreement. Megan and I had found the same to be true ourselves.

"So here's our plan," she said, closing the file folder. "We head out to the Feng house, check on the car, and see if anything seems out of the ordinary. Check for potential signs of a struggle. Then we meet with Brenda Choi. I set up an appointment. I told her that we may have some more info on her husband's file."

"Really? What did she say?"

"She's really anxious to meet with me, I can tell you that. I didn't say too much else about it. She's going to be surprised that you're with me. I contemplated leaving you out of it totally, but A, you've earned this with the crap you've been through so far. And B, once I turn the tables on Mrs. Choi about why I'm really there, I'm going to need your help."

"Okay, and then what?"

"Nothing. We see what we can see, first. Then we decide." She stood up from her chair and stuffed her cell phone in her back pocket. "Let's go, I'll drive."

I followed her as she left the office. "Do you think that Brenda Choi could actually be involved in all of this? I can see her maybe killing Alice, but it doesn't seem to fit with the thumb drive and everything else that happened afterward."

She was walking a few steps ahead of me, and without turning around she shrugged and said, "It all depends. On the slim chance that a hit man is involved—which I am severely doubting at this point—then the Brenda Choi thing is a strange coincidence. But given that Alice worked for both women and both of them happen to be clients of Price Investigations, I have to wonder what the heck the connection is."

"Do you think a third party is involved that connects everything together?" I asked.

We entered a parking garage, and she led me through a maze of cars to a decent-condition Ford Mustang. It had a dent in the fender, but overall, it sparkled as if it had just been washed.

"Nice car," I said as we got in.

She shut the driver's-side door. "Thanks, it was my brother's . . . Mr. Hotshot Lawyer guy was too good to drive a Mustang. Now he has a Bentley or some such nonsense." She started the car and fastened her seat belt.

"Hey, what a coincidence, my sister's a hotshot lawyer, too . . . well, okay, not yet, but trying to be."

She smirked. "Get ready to have that shoved in your face every five minutes. Oh, and to answer your question from before: No idea is too far out of range to be considered. We have to look at every possibility. As the greatest private detective of all time said, *When you have eliminated all which is impossible, then whatever remains, however improbable, must be the truth.*"

CHAPTER
30

On the way to Donna's house, I called Rosemary and told her to search for a parking garage slip and whether or not Donna's car was missing. She agreed and said she would call me back when she found out either way.

By the time we reached Donna's house and failed to find her car parked in the street or in her own driveway, Rosemary called back to say that the car was not at the hotel, either. Lydia grunted at the information and we continued on to Brenda Choi's house after doing a quick walk around the Feng estate. We found nothing of importance to help us along.

The Chois' maid let us in and led us back to the pool where Brenda was lounging once again. She was dressed in a floral cover-up over a two-piece bathing suit and appeared to have been flipping through a fashion magazine, which she had abandoned on the empty chaise next to her.

When Brenda turned to face us, I noted the shock on her face at seeing me with Lydia.

"Lana," she said, removing her sunglasses and placing them on her head. "What are you doing here?"

Lydia answered for me. "Mrs. Choi, I'm Lydia Shepard, we spoke on the phone. I asked Lana to accompany me."

"Please, call me Brenda, Mrs. Choi is so formal . . . and old sounding." She gestured to the table. "Have a seat."

The three of us moved to the table. Lydia and I chose seats next to each other while Brenda sat across from us.

"What is this about?" Brenda asked. "If Lana is here . . ." She looked at me again. "Well . . . is this really about my husband?"

"You tell us," Lydia replied. "Was your husband having an affair with Alice Kam?"

Brenda blurted out a laugh. "Hardly!"

Lydia's eyebrows crunched together. "I'm not sure why that would seem laughable. Your husband doesn't have the best track record according to our files."

"That may be, Detective, but she isn't his type . . ." Brenda shifted her eyes toward the pool. "No, when he cheats, it's always with blond women. Leggy blondes with . . . well." She held her hands up to her chest. "Something to write home about, if you catch my drift. I assumed that you would have gathered that from your files. Mr. Price included several photos for my review."

"I see," Lydia said. "So nothing was going on with your husband and Alice. Then what was going on? I understand that Lana here had asked you some questions a few days ago, but from what she told me, you're keeping something out."

Brenda put a hand to her chest. "Now, why would you assume that? I have no reason to lie about anything."

It was then that it dawned on me that I had a sliver of information tucked in my mind that I'd completely forgotten about. On my last visit to the Bamboo Lounge, Penny Cho had told me she saw a woman in a blue dress slip upstairs at Donna's party. Either she went to talk with Alice or she was putting the thumb drive in Donna's bedroom. However, I didn't believe it was likely that she could have been leaving the thumb drive, since Lydia and I had recently established that the possibility for a civilian to get the information was next to impossible. So my money was on the fact that she went to talk with Alice.

"Why did you go upstairs after Donna yelled at Alice?" I blurted out.

Lydia glanced at me. "You didn't mention that . . ."

I shrugged. "I just remembered now." I turned back to Brenda. "Someone saw you go upstairs during the party."

"If you must know," Brenda said, lifting her chin. "I had to use the restroom and I didn't want to use the one downstairs."

"Why not?" I asked.

"Because." Brenda widened her eyes. "Why do you think?

"Oh!" I said, and then blushed a little. "So you needed more privacy."

She huffed and turned her head away. Her face was beginning to redden. "Nothing is more embarrassing than having stomach issues at a friend's party. I was trying to be discreet. The mixture of alcohol and seafood didn't sit well with me. I knew that Donna had a bathroom upstairs so I sneaked up there. I didn't think it would cause such alarm."

Lydia interjected. "Did you see anything strange while you were upstairs? Anybody up there that wasn't supposed to be?"

"No, I was in and out. I passed the party planner girl on the way down the stairs, but no one else."

"The party planner?" I asked. "Yvette Howard?"

"Yvette?" Lydia turned to me. "Who's Yvette?"

"Yvette is Evie," I explained.

Lydia looked down at the table in confusion.

Brenda started to fidget in her seat. Something was gnawing at her, I could tell.

"Brenda," I said, using my calm customer service voice. "If you know anything, or there's something you want to tell us, you can."

"It's just . . ." Brenda covered her face with her hands. "I didn't want to say anything because it will seem like I killed Alice, and I didn't." She uncovered her face and looked at us with pleading in her eyes. "I would never kill anyone, you have to believe me about that."

"Brenda, what happened?" Lydia asked, leaning forward in her seat. "You can tell us."

Brenda wrapped her arms around herself and rocked back and forth, her eyes focusing on something beyond us. "Alice was blackmailing me for money. She knew about Randall's affairs, she knew that my kids are heathens who steal whatever they can get their grubby little hands on." She sneered at the thought. "She knew it all. I have no idea how she knew it all, but she did. And she told me she'd tell everyone if I didn't pay her what she was asking for."

My heart skipped a beat.

Lydia sighed. "You're right, that doesn't look good for you. Blackmailing is a strong motive."

Brenda whipped her head around to face Lydia. "You think I don't know that? I'm the one who said it. But I wouldn't kill her. I paid what she asked for and I'd finally gotten her out of my house, it was over."

"So wait a minute," I said, holding up a hand. "That's why she wanted to get into Donna's house, isn't it? She was planning to blackmail her, too."

Brenda dropped her head in shame. "Yes. Alice told me that it was my final payment to her. All I had to do was get her into the Feng house and I would be free of her for the rest of my life. Donna was going to be her cash cow."

"You let a blackmailer into your good friend's house?" Lydia asked. "Some friend."

"I didn't know what else to do," Brenda whined. "I couldn't be humiliated by Randall's affairs. Or my children's actions. I've worked hard to get to where I am, and I won't be the pariah of the group. Donna already had rumors circulating about her, and she was still able to maintain her social status. I figured she's stronger and more prominent than me. She could handle it."

I shook my head in disgust. "Unbelievable."

Lydia tapped the arms of the chair. "Okay, so Alice was blackmailing you, her next target was

Donna, and then what? If you say you didn't kill her, then what happened?"

Brenda inhaled deeply. "Donna must have done it. That's all I've been thinking this whole time. And it's all my fault." She buried her face in her hands again. "I never should have allowed this to continue. I should have gone to the police as soon as I got Alice out of my house. But I wasn't thinking straight. I didn't know what she would do if I turned her in. So I was just biding my time to see how things played out. I never imagined that Alice would end up this way."

I glanced at Lydia, who jerked her head in the direction of the door. Nodding in agreement, I turned back to Brenda. "I'm glad you told us the truth," I said. "We may be able to figure out what really happened now."

Lydia rose from her seat and pulled a business card out of her back pocket. "If you think of anything else that might be important, any stray fact about Alice, please call me." She tossed the card on the table and turned to leave.

I said goodbye to Brenda, and we made our way through the house and back to Lydia's car.

Once we were inside the car, Lydia leaned her head back and stared at the ceiling, both her hands resting on the wheel. "So Alice isn't an innocent bystander after all."

"But you know what doesn't make sense to me?"

Lydia shifted her head in my direction. "What?"

"She never actually blackmailed Donna."

"How do you figure?" she asked.

"Donna told me that she found the thumb drive on her nightstand, and there were no instructions with it. No note, no anything. So Donna had no idea who it even came from."

Lydia turned the car on. "That's what she told you, but it doesn't make it true. And now that she and her car are missing, it doesn't look that great for her."

"When I found the thumb drive, it was in the bathroom," I told her as we pulled away from the Choi house. "She was planning to flush it. If she thought she was being blackmailed, would she really take that chance? The person—maybe Alice—might have had another copy, or could've told Donna that if she tried to destroy anything, they would expose her."

"Even if that theory is true, it's irrelevant. Alice isn't exposing anyone. She died before that could happen. There's still a chance that Donna could have killed her and then disposed of the thumb drive thinking all her problems were over . . . done and done. Unfortunately for her, she never got the chance to get rid of the evidence," Lydia said. "And there's no 'the person'; Alice is the one who had the information on Brenda Choi. She's the one who wanted access to Donna's house. It's her. She's the blackmailer for sure."

I turned to look out the window. Lydia was right about that. The thumb drive and Alice definitely had to be connected. The only question we had to answer now was who had actually killed Alice. Did Alice confront Donna after her outburst, threatening to expose her, and Donna killed her to protect herself? Or was Donna truly the victim in all this? Then there was also the small matter of finding Donna.

I thought back to my conversation with Donna

on the patio. She'd truly seemed confused on where someone would get this information and was convinced that a hit man was sent for her. Was Alice that hit man after all? She was the one with the insider information. And we had found nothing of importance about her. Nothing. Everything that Megan and I had seen on her social media showed that she was a normal girl.

But clearly she was not. Social media rarely tells the whole story about someone's life.

"What's spinnin' your wheels right now?" Lydia asked.

"I don't know," I admitted. "Something is just bothering me about this whole thing."

"Yeah, me too. I can't quite put my finger on it, though." Lydia took a deep breath. "Okay, let's regroup. Let's go back to my office and look through that notebook of yours from beginning to end. Now that we know Alice was the one doing the blackmailing, something might click that didn't before."

CHAPTER
31

On the way to Price Investigations, we stopped to grab coffees from Starbucks so I wouldn't be subject to the coffee that Meredith made at the office. When we returned, we sat in Lydia's office, and she reviewed my notes.

I felt a little self-conscious as she read because while writing it, I'd never had any intention of anyone other than Megan ever seeing it. It was embarrassing to now have a professional PI reading over the sloppy notes that I had taken, considering my rookie status. I thought back to when Adam had flipped through it and felt my cheeks warm.

"These are pretty good observations," Lydia said.

I sighed relief. "I'm glad you don't think I'm an idiot," I confessed. "Half the time I have no clue what I'm doing."

"This Bryce Blackwell guy," she said, pointing to his name on the page. "You've mentioned him before and you're right, his story is definitely all over the place. I'm inclined to believe he's hiding something, but I'm still having a hard time deciding if it's beneficial to our case or not."

"That's how I feel, too," I replied. "After he told Kimmy and me that he was embarrassed about the failed engagement, it started to make sense . . . mostly. If he's being honest about wanting the ring back, that explains him going to Donna for her things."

"But the ring wasn't in her things?"

"Nope. At least not according to him."

"And here's this Evie person again . . . Yvette." Lydia tapped the page. "Why is this name bothering me?"

"I don't know, but they're both connected with Alice, and they were both at the party. And Bryce was at Donna's house the day the fire happened, although my boyfriend pointed out that might be too obvious."

Lydia put her head on her desk. "Ugh, it's right here. I know it."

"Maybe, maybe not," I said. "Something is missing. Alice is the one with the information, that's all we know for sure. We don't know what happened after that, though. Bryce is suspicious, but if he killed Alice then the thumb drive placement is just a coincidence. Unless they were working together and something went wrong between the two of them. If not, and Donna did it, then . . ."

Lydia lifted her head. "Then what?"

"Then the whole thing fits together and Donna has truly lost her mind." It just didn't sound right to me. I couldn't wrap my head around the fact that Donna had killed someone and then gone on the run.

"I think we should take another stab at this Bryce Blackwell guy," Lydia said. "His background check came up clean, but who knows . . . criminals have to start somewhere."

It was getting late in the afternoon, and I wanted to go home and sit in an actual comfortable chair, take my shoes off, and just zone out. "Would you mind if I went home for a little while . . . I need to think."

"Sure, sure," Lydia said. "I get it. I do some of my best thinking when I'm alone. Go for it. I'll text you if I find anything."

I got home right before Megan had to leave for work. We convened on the couch, and I went through the day relaying all that I had learned from going back to Brenda Choi's house.

"Okay, so it's official. Alice is no saint," Megan said when I was done telling the story.

"Yeah, but now what?" I asked. "That just makes Donna look super guilty."

"Not necessarily."

"How so? You've had suspicions about Donna telling the truth the entire time."

"I know, but like I'm always saying, we have to consider every option." Megan tapped her chin. "So let's look at it like this. Donna was maybe kidnapped."

"Okay . . ."

"If Donna *was* kidnapped, then who would have the power to overtake her?"

"It would have to be a man, I would think," I replied. "If it were a woman, she may have been able to put up more of a fight and it would have caused a scene."

"Okay, let's go with that. And what man would do that?" Megan asked, attempting to lead me without giving her opinion.

"I suppose the only man we've come across so far . . . Bryce."

"Exactly what I was thinking. There's been something weird about that guy the whole time. He's at the party, he's Alice's ex-boyfriend, he was at the house the day the fire happened, and now Donna goes missing."

"But I saw Bryce at the Cedar Room after the fact," I reminded her. "If he kidnapped Donna, would he just go to work and leave her unattended? She could escape or something."

"Unless . . ."

"Don't say it," I said, cringing at the insinuation. I didn't want to think of the possibility that Donna might be dead already.

"Okay, let's flip the coin instead. Say Donna is guilty . . ." Megan proposed, changing the subject. "Then she wasn't kidnapped and Bryce is innocent and the whole thing is just one big coincidence. And that also explains why her car is missing."

"While it keeps her alive and well, that scenario doesn't make me feel better, either." I sank farther into the couch cushion hoping that it would swallow me.

"Well, on the bright side, at least we know Rosemary is innocent. That's one person we can cross off our suspect list."

"Unless this is part of her evil scheme," I said, attempting to make light of the situation.

"Wait, do you think that's possible?"

"No, that would make the least amount of sense.

If Rosemary killed Alice, it would be to get her out of the picture. If she kidnapped Donna and killed her, then she wouldn't have a job and killing Alice would have been pointless."

"Okay, no Rosemary," Megan said with resolve. She checked the time on her cell phone. "Well, I have to get going. You going to be okay here by yourself?"

"Yeah, I'll be fine."

"I'm kind of excited to see Adam's place. A home tells you a lot about a person."

"Text me when you're ready to be picked up," I said.

She gave me a thumbs-up and headed out the door.

An hour before Adam was planning to pick me up, I received a call from Lydia. She sounded as hyper as I had been earlier in the day.

"Lana! I figured it out!"

"Figured what out?" I asked.

"Why Yvette's name was familiar to me."

My stomach dropped. "Why?"

"Meredith took a leave of absence about six months ago. We had a temp working for us. And guess who that was?"

I gasped. "Yvette Howard?"

"Bingo. She always went by Yvette, so when you said Evie, it wasn't registering for me. Plus . . . well, it was six months ago and she wasn't that crucial to my life. I'd forgotten all about her."

"So she must have been the one working with Alice to blackmail Brenda and Donna, then!" I felt a sense of elation at the fact that we now knew where the information came from.

"She has to have been. It would explain how Alice got the files. Yvette must have stolen the information for her while she worked here."

"So what do we do now?" I asked.

"Well, unfortunately, this doesn't take Donna out of the hot seat. All it means is that we know where the information came from. This officially gets us out of the hit-man zone."

"Oh, thank God," I said. Because there's no chance on earth that Yvette would be a hit man . . . er, hit woman . . . right?"

"Not likely. I've dug into her past since I figured out the connection and it looks like she's lived a pretty basic life. She jumps from job to job. Previous to the whole party planning thing, she did a bunch of temp jobs. Seems like she had no particular direction career-wise, and she doesn't have any priors listed. No weird gaps of time missing. It's likely she just took advantage of a good situation that fell into her lap."

"Ugh, I can't believe this. Alice was her way into these houses." I started to wrap my brain around the two women working together. Susan Han had told me that Alice and Yvette had gotten closer in recent months. They must have been plotting their blackmailing business together that whole time.

"So now that we have this intel, we can guess that either something went terribly wrong between the two of them, or Donna got to her first."

"I hope it wasn't Donna."

"I'm going to do some tracking on Yvette. In the

meantime, you sit tight until I find something more concrete."

"But shouldn't I do this with you?" I asked.

"Not this time, chickadee," she replied. "This time you let the lady with the gun handle it. Just in case. I'll be in touch."

She hung up before I could protest any more.

I didn't like the idea of sitting on the sidelines. I didn't like the idea that Donna was potentially guilty after all. She had been set up by Alice and Yvette. Yet something still didn't feel right. It always came back to the kids. Donna would not leave her kids.

I began to pace.

Yvette was smaller than me. How would she overpower these people? How could she kill Alice? How could she kidnap Donna? It didn't make sense.

Also, how would she even set Donna's house on fire? Did she tamper with the wiring during the party, and it took that long for the fire to actually start? How would she even know that it would happen at all?

I thought about my conversation with Megan right before she'd left for work. Bryce. It had to be Bryce. Bryce could do the killing, the fire, the kidnapping, all of it. Then an alarm bell went off in my head. When I met with Evie, she'd spoken about Bryce as if she thought he was a swell guy. And Bryce had said he'd lied to everyone about his engagement because he was embarrassed. He'd told Alice that he had someone else to give the ring to. Was that someone else Yvette?

But Alice wouldn't give the ring back, for whatever reason—that part was unclear. And it wasn't in her things. So what happened to it? Again, I had to assume that Bryce was telling the truth and he didn't really have the ring in his possession. Why lie about not getting the ring back?

I checked the time. I only had half an hour before Adam came to pick me up. There was no way I'd be able to sit this out tonight. I needed to do something. Especially if Bryce was the culprit. It would mean he was holding Donna somewhere.

I did a quick search on my phone to see if I could find an address for Bryce Blackwell, which I did; I just didn't know if it was current or not. The information was from about three years back.

Hurriedly I texted Adam and told him I needed a bit more time to get ready because I was stopping at the store. If I told him what I was really doing, he probably wouldn't let me go. I felt guilty about lying because we'd promised that we'd tell the truth no matter how much the other one didn't like it, so I resolved to tell him about it as soon as he picked me up.

Before leaving the house, I went digging through my jewelry box and found a cubic zirconia ring that I'd purchased a while back from Kohl's. It would pass for an engagement ring and would be convincing enough for someone to mistake it as one. My plan was to tell Bryce I'd found it in Alice's room at Donna's house under the bed when I was helping Donna clean and turn it back into a guest bedroom.

I didn't know if anything would come of this or if I was wasting my time. But as Lydia said, I had to see what I could see.

* * *

Bryce Blackwell lived in a modest split-level house with an attached garage and decent-sized yard. I pulled my car a few houses past his driveway and turned in my driver's seat so I could stake the place out. It appeared unsuspicious. His car wasn't in the driveway, but it could easily be in the garage. I checked the street for Donna's car and found nothing. Although her car could also be in the garage . . . if he'd been the one to kidnap her.

There were no windows in the garage door, so I wouldn't be able to see what was inside. Plus there was still daylight left, and I couldn't exactly be sneaky with the sun still out.

I huffed. Now what?

If I went to the door and tried to strike up a conversation, it would be a little suspicious. How would I explain showing up at his house, tracking him down online? What could I possibly say as a reason for doing something so bizarre?

That's when the worst and brightest lightbulb turned on in my head.

I shut the engine off, grabbed my purse, and flung myself out of the car. I hurried to the door so I couldn't talk myself out of the plan. It was thin, but it was all I had. Maybe I'd be able to learn something while I was there, and I could take it back to Lydia.

I rang the doorbell and waited, my pulse thudding in my throat. My breath felt restricted, and I tried counting to five.

When the door opened, I almost jumped out of my skin. You see, Bryce Blackwell didn't answer the door. Yvette Howard did.

CHAPTER
32

"Lana?" Yvette asked, gawking at me as if I had sprouted two heads. "What are you doing here?"

Everything in my body told me to run far, far away, but my feet refused to move. I tried my best to pretend that it hadn't thrown me off at all that Yvette was standing in front of me. It was all coming together now. All in one fell swoop. And my brain was overloaded with the entirety of it all. Alice, Bryce, and Yvette had been working this entire blackmailing thing together. Something must have happened with Alice, and they decided to take her out. This had to be it. It just had to be. There was no other reason that Yvette would just so happen to be at Bryce's house. I knew right then that Donna Feng was, without a doubt, innocent.

"Oh hi, Evie, I came by to see Bryce. I had something of Alice's that belonged to him." I was planning to bargain my way into Bryce's house with the engagement ring that couldn't be found.

"Come in," she said, stepping to the side. "Bryce is in the basement, he should be right up."

I set one foot in the house, those alarm bells in my head going off again and telling me not to. I had this horrible image in my head that I would not be leaving anytime soon. *Turn back now*, my brain said. *This is the point of no return.*

Once I had taken that second step into the house, Yvette shut the door behind me and I heard her slip the lock into place. I assessed the living room, which was a sea of big beige furniture and similar-colored carpet. A giant flat-screen TV sat atop an entertainment center that was made of that cheap-looking wood grain so popular in the 1990s. Everything appeared normal and mundane. No blackmailers living here.

"It's nice to see you again," Yvette sang.

"Yeah, you too," I mumbled. I stepped off to the side with my back to the couch so I could face her better.

"So what brings you by?" she asked, folding her arms over her chest. Her lips twisted into a sadistic smile as if she knew her question would torture me. I had to assume she guessed at my involvement. Considering our previous conversation, I didn't think it would be that hard.

I maintained my poker face, if only to not give her the satisfaction she desired. "Like I said, I found something Alice had that I believe belonged to Bryce. He mentioned he was looking for it the other day and I happened to find it while I was at Donna's house."

"Oh, that's so nice of you." Yvette broadened

her smile, a little too wide for my taste. "I mean, to come all this way and not even be sure . . ."

"It's really no trouble. Why are you here?" I asked, trying to keep my voice from shaking.

"Oh you know, tying up some loose ends."

It sounded ominous, and I didn't like it. I took a moment to mentally beat myself up for thinking this was a good idea.

I heard footsteps coming up from the basement. Clomping, angry footsteps.

"If this is a bad time, I can always come back later." My eyes slid in the direction of the footsteps.

"No," a man's voice said from the stairwell I couldn't see. "I'd love to see what you think you're going to give me."

Bryce Blackwell appeared from the center of the house, holding a rather shiny-looking gun. The pulse in my throat quickened.

"Hey, Bryce . . ." I said. My left foot glided toward the front door. Without turning my head, I slid my eyes in the direction of the lock mechanism. I might be able to open it before he had a chance to aim. Keyword: *might*. "I found that ring you were looking for at Donna's the other day. I have it here in my purse." I started to reach into my bag.

Yvette cackled like a hyena. "She found the ring, Bry. Isn't that cute?"

"Real cute," he said with a snort.

Yvette extended a hand, rubbed my arm, and smiled sweetly.

I flinched. Gestures like that reminded me of psychopaths.

She closed her fist around my biceps and squeezed,

digging her nails into the backside of my arm. "Oh sweetheart, there was never any ring. You bought that story about them being engaged? I love it."

Try as I might, I couldn't keep the surprise from my face.

They both laughed.

"What I was really looking for was that damn thumb drive," Bryce said, stepping farther into the living room. "But don't worry, we found it. Donna had it this whole time. Kept it all nice and safe for us."

Yvette was still holding on to my arm. I tried to shake her off, but she wouldn't let go.

"Where is Donna?" I asked, channeling the bravest voice I could muster. "I assume you have her if you have the thumb drive."

"Do you wanna see your old friend?" Yvette asked in a baby voice. "Give her a little hug." She shoved me in the direction of Bryce, and he caught me by the shoulders and spun me around.

"Move!" he barked. I felt the barrel of the gun graze my back. "Don't get cute. I don't have the patience for it."

I held up my hands to show him I would comply and walked slowly toward the basement door. I took each step down with caution and wondered how the heck I was going to get myself out of this one. I listened to the footsteps of Bryce and Yvette as they followed behind me.

When we reached the basement, we turned a corner and there was Donna, sitting in a battered wooden chair with her hands tied behind her back and a bandanna tied around her mouth. Her hair was a disheveled mess, her mascara had bled down to her chin, and her cheek was bright red as if she'd been smacked in the face. Her eyes widened and muffled words came from her covered mouth as I came into view.

"Donna!" I rushed over to her, forgetting about the gun aimed at my back.

"See?" Yvette said. "Reunited. And it feels so good . . ." She snickered to herself.

"Are you okay?" I asked Donna, ignoring our two captors.

She nodded, her eyes closed and tears forming in the corners of her eyes.

"Oh, she's just fine for now," Bryce said. "Both of you are . . . for now."

I whipped around to face him. "What do you even want from this? Money? She'll give it to you."

"It's too late for that. She caught me rifling through her crap and saw my face. I can't let her go now."

"Stupid hag," Yvette spat. "Just had to be efficient and set up your little electrician appointment, didn't you? Other people might take their time with something like that. Maybe let the shock wear off. Maybe recuperate from almost being burned alive. But no, not you."

Donna glared at her.

I tried to plead with Bryce. "She's not going to tell anyone who you are. Not if you have the thumb drive. So just let us go. We'll keep your secret and you keep hers. It's a fair deal."

"Oh, you want to bargain, little girl?" Bryce laughed. "Is that what you think is going to happen here? I'm not stupid, you know. I know a thing or two about a thing or two."

"So what are you going to do then? Hide us out

in your house forever?" I asked. "You think that's going to work out for you? My boyfriend's a police detective, he'll figure it out."

"*My boyfriend's a police detective, he'll figure it out,*" Yvette said, mimicking me. "Shut up, you little brat. Your boyfriend isn't going to find you until it's too late, so stop hoping."

Bryce waved the gun at me. "No, I'm going to kill you both. It'll look like a mob hit."

"A mob hit in your house?" I asked, a little too boldly.

"No, dimwit. Later, once it's nice and dark out, we're all piling into Ms. Moneybags's car and we're gonna take a little drive . . . head out to the pier. It's a popular place for mob hits. I'm thinking execution-style, what do you think, babe?" he asked, turning to Yvette.

She clasped her hands together in mock excitement. "It sounds perfect to me."

"We'll leave the thumb drive with your bodies. The cops will figure out who Donna Feng really is, and they'll put together this whole big ordeal that didn't happen. Really, we have to thank Donna for making it so easy. If she hadn't lied about who she was, none of this would even be possible."

Chills ran up and down my arms. No one knew where I was. Not Lydia, not Adam, and not Megan. Adam would be showing up at my apartment right around now, and my only hope was that he would find it suspicious that I wasn't back yet. But how the heck would they figure out that I was trapped in Bryce Blackwell's house?

Lydia was onto the fact that Yvette was involved with the blackmailing, but part of Lydia still thought that Donna was guilty, and she didn't think that Bryce's bizarre behavior had any connection to the current situation. So would she even entertain the idea that Bryce might somehow be involved and come here searching for more answers? Probably not.

While I'd been contemplating my chances of survival, I hadn't noticed that Yvette had been digging around for some twine, which she promptly dangled in front of my face with pride. She pulled another ratty chair from the corner of the room and slammed it down next to Donna's. "Now be a good little girl and sit in the chair. I won't gag you if you promise not to scream like this old hag did."

With Bryce aiming the gun at me I didn't have much of a choice other than to obey. So I sat down in the chair and put my arms behind my back. Again the thought crossed my mind: *How am I going to get out of this one?*

CHAPTER
33

- - - - - - - - - - - - - - -

Even though it had only been hours since I first arrived at Bryce's house, it felt like days. Through the narrow basement windows, I had watched the day turn into night. I kept quiet as much as possible because I didn't want them to gag me, too. But there was so much I wanted to say. I couldn't lose hope now. No matter what the odds were against me, it wasn't over until it was over.

Donna's eyes flitted open and shut from time to time, and I imagined it was taking everything in her not to pass out.

Yvette had gone upstairs for a short time while Bryce kept an eye on us, never letting go of his gun. Not that I could have done anything had he put it down. My hands were tied behind my back.

"Why'd you do it?" I said, breaking the silence.

"I already told you, now shut up," Bryce replied.

"No, I mean, why did you kill Alice? I assume it was you who drowned her that night." I flashed back to the night of the party when he approached me in the kitchen. His clothes had been all wet, and he'd blamed it on the kids splashing in the pool. "Were you guys ever really together or was it all for show?"

He chuckled. "Yeah, we were together. For a time."

"So what happened? Is it true what Evie said, that Alice had gotten involved with an older man? Did she leave you for him and you got jealous?"

"Ha!" Bryce raised his eyebrows in amusement. "Me? Jealous? Hardly. That's a story Evie cooked up to buy us some time. She knew you were up to something and wanted to steer you away from us. She was hoping you'd waste time searching through Donna's group of rich biddies for an older man who would have an affair. There are a few of them."

I really despised the fact that Evie attempted to send me on a wild goose chase. I pushed my personal feelings aside and continued with my questioning. "Well, what actually happened then?"

"She couldn't handle it."

"Couldn't handle what exactly?"

"Why do you care?" he asked. "You're not making it out of this alive anyway. Buying yourself some time isn't going to stop anything."

"Because I don't get it. At least entertain me that much. If I'm not going to make it, then what's the harm in telling me?"

He shrugged and leaned against the washer. "She couldn't handle the job and it got in the way of our relationship. She didn't have the same vision that Evie and I had. Can you believe, Alice actually liked those damn kids? She thought this was going to be her life now and wanted out. But it was way too late for her to change her mind. She thought she was being smart by giving Donna the thumb drive, but it was the dumbest thing she could have done.

"She texted me during the party from her room and told me that she had left the thumb drive for Donna to find. Someplace she'd spot it before anybody else, and then Donna could dispose of it. Well, you can't get rid of me and Evie that easy. I asked Alice to meet me down by the pool so we could talk about it . . . I was going to reason with her. But she wouldn't listen. I guess I should have figured, she was kind of on the stubborn side.

"After the party was over, I was going to sneak upstairs to try and get it back, but I didn't count on Donna being so attentive with her kids.

"But whatever, I knew it was only a matter of time before we'd find the drive. Unfortunately, Donna here had to go and mess up the rest of the plan. Once I had it back, then I'd get my hands on the money we needed to get out of this rotten city."

"So you were going to try and blackmail her again?"

"*Try, try again*—that's what they say, right? If the old lady was smart, she wouldn't have held on to the damn thing to begin with. She had every opportunity to flush it, mangle it in the garbage disposal, throw it in Lake Erie . . . and what did she do? She held on to it. If you ask me, she deserves to die based on stupidity. Now shut up. We have big plans ahead and I need to center myself."

My stomach hurt and I thought I might throw up. I wondered to myself what Adam and Lydia were up to. Were they searching for me? Had Adam told Megan that I was missing? Was she worried about me? What would happen to Kikko?

I thought about the things I had left undone. I'd never gotten to tell that jerk Warren what I really thought about him and how he'd made me feel. I'd never gotten to hear his side of the story . . . what excuses he planned to come up with.

I thought about my family and how they would react. I thought about Donna's children losing both of their parents in the span of a year. What would happen to them? Would they go into foster care? Would a stray aunt or uncle adopt them and save them from a life in the system?

My mind was out of control. My thoughts were telling me that I had already given up even though I knew I couldn't. There had to be a way out of this, there just had to be.

They had taken my purse away from me, but thankfully my phone was in my back pocket. Not that I could get to it with my hands tied behind my back.

I heard Yvette clacking down the stairs in her heels. Despite the situation, she was still wearing stilettos. "Time to go, ladies," she said while clapping her hands.

Donna turned her head toward me, her eyes wild with fear. I tried to tell her telepathically that it was all going to be okay.

Bryce neared Donna's chair, began untying her hands, and hoisted her up. "You first, old lady."

She mumbled something at him through the bandanna, and he smirked.

Next he untied my hands while Yvette held on to Donna's arm. "Just a friendly reminder: Don't try anything cute. You can't outrun a bullet." He waved the gun in my face, and I felt sweat drip down my back.

"All right, we're walking very slowly to the garage, no tricks," Yvette warned. "Old lady goes first. Little brat, you go next." She shoved me forward.

I got behind Donna as she moved toward the steps. She took one careful step up, teetering back and forth. Donna also had stilettos on.

As the four of us slowly went up the steps, my instincts told me what I needed to do. If they got us in that car and to the pier, it was over for sure. I needed to time this just right. As Donna's foot touched the landing of the first floor, I braced myself and kicked back as hard as I could, hitting Yvette in the kneecap. She bellowed loudly and I kicked again; she swayed for a moment and then fell backward onto Bryce.

Bryce let out a string of swear words as he tried to steady Yvette. But thankfully he failed, and I heard them tumble backward on the stairs.

I yelled to Donna, "Run!"

Her scream came muffled, but she bolted for the door, and I sped up my pace behind her. Having my hands behind my back was screwing me up, but I tried my best to pick up speed.

I heard angry clomping up the stairs. As Donna neared the front door, I watched her turn and bend down, attempting to twist the lock open with her hands. We were running out of time.

Finally she got the door unlocked, but we had yet to open it. "Move over," I told her.

She moved and mumbled my name. That much I could make out. When I turned to get my hand around the doorknob, I saw that Bryce had made it up the stairs. "Sh—" I got the door open and Donna pushed through the sliver of door that was open. She was out.

However, I was not. Bryce was now inches away from me. I didn't see the gun in his hand, so I took the chance and slammed the door closed behind me. With all the power I had left in me, I leaned my weight against the door and flung my leg out, kicking him right in the unmentionables.

The pain on his face as he crumbled to his knees gave me satisfaction. On his way down, I kneed him in the head, pushing him back so I could open the door. I finally twisted the knob back open.

Right as I was about to exit the house, I heard Yvette come up the stairs. I heard the clicking of the gun. I made the split-second decision not to turn around and look back at her. I had to keep moving, and take the chance she would miss.

The bullet grazed right past my left ear as I stumbled onto the walkway leading to the house. My eyes took a minute to adjust to the dark; then I saw Donna standing at the edge of the driveway, hunched over and crying.

I ran toward her. "We have to move now, they're coming."

She stared at me, frantically, waiting for direction.

"This way," I hissed. I ran in the direction of my car. *Crap!* My keys were in my purse, and they had my purse in the house. I kept running. I turned around to see where Donna was—she was falling behind. I paused so she could catch up. While I did that, I saw Bryce come storming out of the house. "Donna! Come on!"

I ran through someone's yard and found a grouping of boxwood bushes. I shimmied myself between the house and bushes, I banged the house with my elbows a couple of times, hoping it would alert the homeowners, but I didn't have much strength left.

Once we were hidden, I told Donna to be quiet. We crouched and waited.

After a few minutes of nothing happening, I turned to the left, toward the street. I thought I saw someone walking down the sidewalk, but I couldn't tell if it was a passerby or Bryce. It definitely looked like a man's stature. That much I could tell.

I was pouring sweat, and didn't know how we were going to get help. I could tell by the way that Donna was hunched over, trying to breathe, that she couldn't run much farther. Would they find us in these bushes? How long would they look for us?

"Bend your head down more," I instructed Donna.

She did. I turned my back to her, lifting my arms at an awkward angle to pull down her gag as best I could. It was caught on her chin, but she could at least use her mouth again.

"Lana," she said, gasping for air. "What are we going to do?"

"I don't know," I whispered. "We can't stay here all night, it's too close. They have to know we didn't get very far."

"Does anybody know where you are?" she asked.

"No," I replied with defeat. "But I do have an idea. Turn your back to me, and I'll turn mine to you. My phone is in my right back pocket. Pull it out."

She nodded and we turned away from each other. I felt her hand blindly reaching for my phone.

"Okay, I have it," she said. "Now what?"

"Now hold it out," I told her. "I'm going to use my thumbprint to unlock it. And then I'm going to turn around and use the voice commands."

I pressed my thumb over the HOME button and saw the light brighten against the siding of the house as my phone unlocked. I shimmied myself back around and put my face close to the screen. "Siri, call Adam . . ."

"CALLING ADAM TRUDEAU . . ."

Siri said it so loudly that it was deafening in the otherwise quiet night and I immediately regretted doing it.

Donna and I heard rustling nearby. We glanced at each other.

"Drop the phone!" I hissed.

The phone plopped onto the ground and I covered it with my thigh.

Footfalls approached our hiding spot. I watched as Yvette's stilettos walked along the far side of the bushes. Bryce stayed on the side nearest to us.

"Hello? Lana!" Adam's voice yelled from my speaker.

I cringed.

"They're back here, Bry," Yvette said smugly.

"Come out here now or we'll just start shooting," Bryce threatened.

I prayed again that the homeowners were alerted by the sounds outside their house. "Okay, we're coming out. Don't shoot."

My phone had gone silent and I wanted to cry knowing that I had been so close. Now, leaving my phone behind, Donna and I shimmied out from behind the bushes and were greeted by Bryce and a cocky smile. Yvette came up from behind me and kicked the back of my knee, causing me to fall to the ground. "That's for kicking me earlier, you little b—"

"That's enough, Evie," Bryce barked. "Let's get them back to the house before someone calls the cops on us."

They ordered Donna and me to walk in front of them, and as we rounded the drive, red and blue lights illuminated the houses surrounding us. Three patrol cars, two unmarked cars, and one black Ford Mustang came barreling down the street and slammed their brakes a few feet from where we stood.

A police office got out of the car, his gun drawn, the driver's-side door his shield, and he yelled the infamous words no criminal wants to hear. "Hands up! We will shoot!"

Because Bryce and Yvette had been walking behind us, they used us as human shields. Yvette grabbed my hands and pulled me toward her while Bryce did the same to Donna.

"Don't shoot us!" I yelled at the cop. "We're the hostages!"

The cops glanced at each other. The one who'd gotten out of the car first spoke: "Let them go. This could go a lot worse for you if you don't."

"Yeah right," Bryce yelled to the cop. "We'll take our chances."

Out of corner of my eye, I saw Lydia's Mustang. She wasn't alone. I fully turned my head to see who was with her. It was Adam. The expression on his face was something I had never witnessed before. He was no longer my boyfriend; he wasn't even the original serious and professional Adam Trudeau I had met back on a day that now seemed so far away. No, he was someone else entirely. His eyes appeared hollow and cold, his jaw tense and lips clamped shut. His movements were robotic as he approached.

Lydia and Adam continued to inch closer. No one was paying attention to them. All eyes were on the cops with their guns drawn right in front of us.

I watched as Lydia raised her gun and aimed at Bryce. I stilled myself, hoping that she had good aim.

The gun went off, and I heard Yvette gasp. Blood splattered onto my arm as Donna fell forward. I yelled as I lifted my foot and stepped down hard on Yvette's foot with my heel. She yowled and released my hands. I fell forward, trying to figure out where the blood was coming from. Had Donna been shot? Had I?

The cops in front of us yelled for nobody to move.

I'd scraped my knee on the driveway cement when I fell forward, and I felt the stinging of the open wound as my eyes began to flutter. The world started to spin, and the last thing I saw was the stars in the night sky. Then everything went black.

CHAPTER
34

I woke up about an hour later in Southwest General Hospital. When I turned my head, the only person I saw in the room was Lydia. She was reading something on her phone; when she noticed I was awake, she put the phone away and approached the bed. "Hey, chickadee, how you feelin'?"

"Like I've been to war," I croaked. "What happened?"

"You passed out," she replied. "Not that I can blame you. You went through quite an ordeal."

"Was I shot?" I asked, inspecting my body while trying not to move my head. Everything ached. My head was pounding, my wrists stank, and my legs were sore.

"No, you weren't shot." She snorted. "As if I ever miss my mark."

I sighed relief. That meant Donna hadn't been shot, either. "Did you kill him?"

"Nah, just got him in the thigh."

"Where's Adam?" I asked.

"He's calling your family. Your roommate is already on her way."

Groaning, I asked, "Do I have to stay here?"

"No, you and Donna can leave soon. They just wanted to check you out one more time before they let you go. Donna is waiting on Rosemary to come pick her up. Everything is taken care of. You just relax until it's time to go home."

"What about my things?" I said, remembering that my purse had been in the house and my cell phone in the bushes.

"I took care of all that, too." She pointed to the chair opposite my bed. Then she stuck her hand in her pocket. "And I have this." She produced the terra-cotta soldier.

"Where did you find that?"

"It was in that dingy basement right by your purse. What an idiot." She laughed. "Don't worry, though. This never happened." She stuck the thumb drive back into her pocket. "Donna's secret will be safe with me."

"Do you think that Bryce and Yvette will tell?"

"From what I've heard, Yvette isn't talking at all. She's denying any involvement. I can come up with a list of what information she stole from the agency, though. I don't know about this Bryce guy, but I have a feeling he won't say anything. At this point, I don't think they'll want to admit to blackmailing Donna on top of everything else. We'll deal with it if the time comes. There are ways to doctor information, don't you worry."

"Thank you so much," I said. "Once we're out of the hospital, Donna will square everything away."

"I know she's good for it. Like I said, stop worrying."

There was a knock at the door. Adam stood in the threshold looking like his old self again. I smiled at the sight of him.

Lydia turned. "Well, knight in shining armor is here," she said playfully. "That's my cue to get on out. I'm sure we'll talk soon." She winked.

Adam gave Lydia a respectful nod as he stepped into the room. "Thanks for your help tonight."

"No problem." She punched his arm. "Take care of our gal here."

Once we were alone, Adam sat on the edge of the hospital bed and took my hand into his.

"I know," I said, feeling ashamed of myself.

"You know what?" he asked.

"I know that I was supposed to tell you the truth, and I didn't. I went behind your back and got myself into trouble, yet again . . . for the hundredth time."

"You think you know me so well," he joked. "Do you think I'm going to lecture you?"

I nodded. "Yes, yes I do."

"Well, you're wrong again, Lana Lee.

"What I was going to say is—" He squeezed my hand, bent forward, and kissed my head. "—What I was going to say is . . ."

"Yeah?" My heart started to pound.

"I love you," he whispered. "And don't do that to me again or I'll kill you myself."

I felt tears forming in my eyes and tried to sniff them away. "I love you, too, Adam."

He smiled and leaned in to kiss me.

We heard a loud cough in the background and I jumped.

We turned to see who it was and found my dad standing on the threshold with a goofy grin on his face. "There will be none of that mushy nonsense on my watch, folks." My dad laughed as he stepped into the room.

"I told him not to ruin your moment," Megan said from behind him.

My mom, sister, and grandmother followed behind, and everyone entered the room. The commotion quickly took over as my mom and grandmother doted on me and I began to feel claustrophobic. After about five minutes, my dad ushered everyone out of the room except for Adam. He patted his shoulder with approval before he left.

Alone again, I asked Adam, "How did you guys find us?"

"When I realized you weren't back yet, I contacted Lydia, and she did some digging around. The first place we checked was Yvette's house . . . when we saw that it was empty, Lydia remembered that you were still stuck on Bryce as a suspect. I knew right away that you'd go check him out. We got his address, found your car, and told the cops our story. Then we all came back around. I was already on my way to you when you called. How did you manage that anyway?"

"Long story," I said.

"Well, either way, I'm just glad to have you back. But I think from now on, I'm going to have a tracker attached to you permanently."

"For once, Adam, I agree with you. One hundred and ten percent."

EPILOGUE

A few days later, the recent happenings began to feel as if they'd been part of an action film rather than real life. Because of all that had gone on, my mother had insisted I take a few days off to recuperate. I didn't argue with her and spent a lot of time on my couch with Kikko in the crook of my knee. My mother and father took shifts handling the coverage at the restaurant . . . even Vanessa offered to help out.

Yvette Howard and Bryce Blackwell were safely behind bars, and so far neither one of them had spilled Donna's secret. They hadn't even mentioned that the whole thing had begun with blackmailing Brenda Choi. If Brenda Choi came forward for some reason, it could open a whole new can of worms. But I was guessing she didn't want her name to be associated with any of this. So for the time being, all was safe, but I had a feeling that Donna's secret would always be hanging over her head.

The past can be a tricky beast, and oftentimes we

allow it to rear its ugly head too frequently in our present lives. For Donna, she was kinda stuck with it. The burden was passed down to her through her mother's actions, and truly she would always need to keep one eye positioned over her shoulder.

I, thankfully, didn't have to let that happen to me. Though the door had been closed on Warren and me a long time ago, there was a drafty window still open, letting in whispers of things that we'd left unsaid.

In my head, I knew that none of it mattered. It was over and I was happy now. I had moved on and was in a great relationship with a wonderful boyfriend who loved me. There was nothing left for me from my past.

But my heart still felt slighted. I needed to move past that feeling and obtain the closure I felt was missing. And that's why I was currently sitting at a patio table at Fathead's Brewery across from my ex-boyfriend. I'd been listening to him ramble on for ten minutes straight and could feel my blood begin to boil.

". . . and she and I had just been together for so long, I didn't know how to tell her that I'd found you, so I planned to break things off with her, but then the holidays came and, well, you know, that's not the best time to end things with someone. She was fragile at the time and—"

"*She* was fragile at the time?" I said, my voice raising with each word. "*She was fragile?*"

"Well, yeah," he replied sheepishly.

"What about *my* feelings?" I asked.

The couple seated to our right popped their heads up from their menus at the sound of my raised voice.

Normally I'd care about that sort of thing. But today, I didn't.

"Your feelings counted, too, but I knew you could handle it better. You're much stronger than she is, Lana. It just wasn't our time . . . I had to be with her longer to realize that I wanted you. Now . . . *now* we can be together."

"Ha!" I yelled.

More people from around the patio turned to stare.

"*Now we can be together*?" I screeched.

A server came over. "Ma'am, is there a problem?"

"No, no problem," I said sarcastically. "Just the fact that he's a pompous ass!"

"Lana," Warren said, smiling apologetically at the server. "Let's go to the parking lot, okay?"

I stomped into the brewery and then all the way through it until I reached the back steps leading out into the parking lot. Warren had kept up with me and was standing directly behind me.

I whipped around and jabbed a finger into his chest. "Originally I planned to do this the mature way, but I've since changed my mind. You're a jerk. A good-for-nothing, lying, cheating jerk."

"Lana . . ."

"Shut up, I'm not done yelling at you yet," I snapped. "You are the most thoughtless, moronic piece of garbage I have ever laid eyes on in my life and you wanna know what? *I* don't want to be with you. I had no intention of ever getting back together with you. I didn't consider it for even one minute. You'd have to be an even bigger idiot than I thought if you considered for a millisecond that I would take you back."

"Then I don't understand. Why did you come here today?" he asked, confusion spreading over his face.

"To tell you this," I said, inhaling a deep breath. "You hurt me. Bad. Probably worse than anyone else in my life. But you know what? I found the upside of it all.

"I survived. I lived through it and found that I was stronger than I have ever thought I was. I've been through hell and back more times in recent months than I care to remember. But all it taught me is that you, Warren Matthews, were a blip on my radar. And now, now I say goodbye for the final time. Don't ever try and find me again. Lose my phone number, forget I exist, and for the love of God, learn how to treat a damn woman right."

He gawked at me, his mouth half open, unsure of what to say.

I smiled wide, flipped him off for good measure, and flounced off the steps in the direction of my car.

I drove with that same stupid grin on my face all the way to Price Investigations.

Meredith greeted me per usual and told me that Lydia was in her office. I gave a light knock before walking in.

"Well, if it isn't Lana Lee." Lydia beamed. "Come to bring me payment, I assume?"

"Yup," I said, pulling Donna's check out of my purse. "Sorry, I meant to be here earlier but I had some business to attend to." I handed her the check.

"Not a problem. The bank's still open." She took the check from my hand and smiled even wider. "It's been a pleasure, Lana," she said, extending a hand.

I shook it. "Don't be a stranger. Remember, I owe you a month's worth of Chinese food."

We said our goodbyes, and I walked out the door.

Eddie Price was coming in as I was walking out, and he stopped me before I could leave. "Lydia filled me in on your detective work, and I have to say, not too shabby for a rookie."

"Thank you," I replied.

"You know, if you ever consider taking this on professionally and getting licensed, I'd be willing to help you with all of that. I could add you to my staff. We could always use an extra set of hands around here."

In the background, Meredith groaned.

For a split second, I entertained the idea and tried to imagine what my life would be like as a real PI. I could actually get paid for sticking my nose into other people's business. I could right wrongs, solve mysteries, get closure for all those that needed it.

On the other hand, I thought about the paperwork, the long hours, stakeouts where peeing at your leisure may not be an option. The danger of snooping on the wrong person . . .

With a heavy sigh, I replied, "I think I'll stick to managing my parents' restaurant for the time being."

"Fair enough." He extended his hand.

I took it into my own, giving him a firm shake. A sly smile spread over my lips and I added, "But you never know what the future might bring."

Read on for an excerpt from

Killer Kung Pao

**The next Number One Noodle Shop Mystery
by Vivien Chien**

Available soon from St. Martin's Paperbacks!

"Lana Lee, you're the only person in this world that I know who actually *wants* to dye their hair gray on purpose," my sister, Anna May said, scrutinizing the hair photo I had been carrying around in my purse. "Are you sure this is a good idea?"

"First of all, it's not just *any* gray," I replied, grabbing the photo out of her hand. "It's gunmetal gray. And second, of course, it's a good idea. It's gonna be my best hair yet." I ran a hand through my pink peek-a-boo highlighted hair. The color was beginning to fade, and I was tired of keeping up with one of the weakest colors in the rainbow.

"I don't know why you can't just leave your hair alone. You've been on this bizarre hair-dying kick for a while now. Don't you want to give it a rest before you damage your follicles any further?" Anna May, who was slightly older and much more reserved than me, tucked a lock of smooth, glossy black hair behind her ear, exposing a dainty pearl-drop earring. Her typical hair length was always just a little past her shoulders, except on the rare occasions when she broke out a curling iron.

Everything about her was classic. Her makeup was forever neutral and almost appeared nonexistent. Her nails were either cherry red or French manicured— never anything besides the traditional white tip. And her style of dress often reminded me of things you might find in Jackie O's closet. But it worked for her, and begrudgingly I would agree that my sister was a beautiful woman.

However, I was the total opposite and refused to look anything like her. As previously mentioned, my hair is dyed random colors, lately more on the un-natural side. My nails are whatever color I feel fits my mood or the season, and my makeup . . . well, I own every color of eyeshadow that exists in the rainbow. As they say, variety is the spice of life.

I waved her concern away with the folded-up photo before stuffing it back into my purse. I wasn't going to let her sensibilities rain on my parade. After all, it was my favorite time of day. Five P.M. on a Friday, and I was getting ready to leave work. My job? I'm the manager of my family's Chinese restaurant, Ho-Lee Noodle House.

Was it my lifelong dream to end up working for my parents and to leave work smelling like sweet-and-sour sauce on a daily basis? No. But it was actually working out pretty well despite my original protests. Turns out that I like to be in charge of things. Even better, I'm good at it.

Anyways, like I said, it was the end of the work week, and after a long five days of managing the daily functions of the noodle shop and dealing with the public, I was thrilled for the weekend to begin.

The next morning, I would be pampering myself at Asia Village's salon, Asian Accents, and my stylist, Jasmine Ming, was equally excited to be dying my hair this stunning shade of gray.

You might be asking yourself, what's Asia Village? Well, it's an Asian shopping center located in the quaint suburb of Fairview Park, which—to give you some reference if you're not familiar—is about twenty-five minutes away from downtown Cleveland. If it's me driving though, I can make it in about seventeen. But don't tell my boyfriend, he's a cop.

The enclosed plaza has everything you could think of under one sky-lit roof. In one fell swoop, you can get your hair done, buy some books by your favorite authors, grocery shop, have dinner, update your cosmetic collection, enjoy a doughnut or three, and even sing some karaoke, if it tickled your fancy. I haven't even mentioned the fact that you can also stock up on tea cakes, or find the perfect supplements and herbs to complement your new healthy lifestyle. After all, you might need something to counter all the doughy goodness you purchased from Shanghai Donuts.

Our family's noodle shop has been at the plaza since before I was born, and I'd spent more time within these four walls than I'd care to admit.

Anna May had, in recent months, taken an internship at a prominent law firm in Cleveland, Andrews, Filbert, Childs and Associates, so her ability to help out at the restaurant had become extremely limited. But since our evening helper and resident teenage thorn in my side, Vanessa Wen, was currently out with the stomach flu, Anna May agreed to give up her Friday evening to help out. There's nothing worse than a twelve-hour workday in my book.

"Seriously, Lana, how long are you going to maintain this lifestyle? You're twenty-eight years old now, and before you know it, you're going to be thirty and you don't take care of yourself at all. Things don't get easier as you age, trust me. You eat horribly, you don't work out, and you're not even trying to look like an adult."

I swear that I tried to withhold my eye roll, but sometimes it just happens without me realizing it. This is what my sister is best at. Lecturing me. Even though she is a measly three years older than me, she acts like she's about ten. *And* she has all this "worldly" wisdom to pass down to her incapable younger sister. Lucky me. "I don't see what my hair has to do with any of this."

"It's a gateway, Lana. You're not taking life seriously, and it's showing in your hair."

I gaped. "That is the most ridiculous statement I have ever heard in my life."

"You refuse to grow up." She folded her arms over her chest and lifted her chin. "I think this new rebellion says it all."

"New rebellion?" I snorted. "Me dying my hair is not a rebellion. And I think I'm doing pretty well, considering. I mean, after all, I am running this restaurant. And doing a bang-up job, I might add."

"Henry says—"

I held up a hand. "Henry says . . . ? So, is your new love interest the reason why you're giving me this lecture? Unbelievable!"

Anna May had recently started "casually dating" one of the partners at her fancy law firm, which I was pretty sure wasn't the best idea, but did that stop her? Of course not. My sister often found justification in her own actions because she considered herself to be the most level-headed person on the planet.

She held her head even higher. "Henry says that personal presentation is everything. You are your own representative, Lana. Do you want people to view you as this immature young woman who constantly chooses to go against the grain of society?"

I started to dig into my purse for my car keys. She was just getting on top of her soap box, and I had plans to meet Adam for happy hour at the Zodiac, a local bar that my best friend and roommate, Megan Riley, bartended at. I didn't want to give up any more of my personal time listening to this drivel.

Anna May had continued spouting at the mouth while I tuned her out. I heard something about how I would have never fit into the lifestyle I had previously hoped for myself. And maybe she was right. A year ago, I'd daydreamed of being a glamorous businesswoman with a corner office and enough high-powered suits to overflow a walk-in closet. But that fantasy had died the minute I walked out of my previous job. After all, you can only take your boss flinging papers in your face so many times before you have to say enough is enough.

"I'm going now," I said, talking over her rant. "Adam is waiting for me at the Zodiac."

"Oh, don't even get me started on how you're always wasting your time at that stupid bar." Anna May uncrossed her arms and put her hands on her hips, mimicking our mother's lecturing stance. "I hope you don't have a drinking problem on top of everything else."

I let out a deep groan and flung my purse over my shoulder. "Thanks for helping out tonight," I said, unwilling to dignify her statement with a justification. "I'll talk to you later. Call me if there's an emergency."

I started to walk out of the restaurant, dropping my usual shuffling steps and taking long strides that I normally reserved for high heels. I'd manage to keep my cool and not engage in a screaming match with my sister, as I'd been well known to do. And she said I wasn't mature. Ha!

But my swagger was quickly ruined because just as I was about to exit the restaurant, Ian Sung, property manager of Asia Village, was walking in, and blocked my exit. Damn. So close to freedom.

"Lana." Ian, who was impeccably dressed in a navy blue Italian suit and polished light brown dress shoes, gave me a once over. "Are you on your way out for the day? There's something I wanted to discuss with you."

"Can we walk and talk?" I asked him. "I'm running late for an appointment."

Anna May snorted behind me.

Ian's eyes shifted to my sister and he regarded her with a stiff smile.

He didn't seem to like Anna May very much, but I had no idea why. I wish I could say the same for myself, but unfortunately Ian held a torch for a relationship between us that was never going to happen. It wasn't that Ian's a bad guy or anything, but there was something about him that I couldn't quite put my finger on that rubbed me the wrong way. Despite my mother's extreme interest in making him my boyfriend, I couldn't view him in that light.

Ian nodded in agreement and held out his hand, signaling for me to lead the way.

I turned to glare at my sister one final time before leaving.

Once we were outside the restaurant, Ian cleared his throat, loosening the tie at his neck. "So, I was hoping to discuss the end-of-summer sidewalk sale with you. Of course, it will be a longer discussion than what we can have on the way to the plaza exit, so maybe we could get together on Monday morning to have a real conversation. Perhaps we could grab some coffee and breakfast at Shanghai Donuts?"

I watched him from the corner of my eye, as I kept making my way toward the exit. Clever move asking to meet up at one of my favorite Asia Village establishments. The only thing better he could have said was for me to meet him at the Modern Scroll, the plaza's bookshop.

"I suppose I could ask Nancy to come in an hour early on Monday morning. I couldn't meet you until ten A.M., though." Nancy Huang was our only full-time waitress, and Peter's mom. Peter was the head chef at our restaurant and fell into the guy best friend category.

"That will work out perfectly," Ian replied. "I'll see you then."

"But why me?" I asked.

"What do you mean?"

"I mean, why me? Aren't the particulars of the sidewalk sale something you should discuss with the entire board of directors for the plaza, and not just me?" Okay, I was part of that board, but still, I was only one member. Why did he always have to single me out?

"Lana, I think you know the answer to that."

I cringed. I could guess, that's for sure.

"You're the only person on the entire committee that I trust implicitly. I know that you want to get things done just as much as I do, and I don't have to worry when I know you're involved with something."

"Wait, involved?" I blanched. "What do you mean *involved*?"

"Well, we can discuss all of that at our meeting on Monday morning," he said, suddenly in a rush to get out of our conversation. We had reached the main entrance and he stepped in front of me. "Allow me to get the door."

As he opened the door with a big smile, we turned just in time to see a dark gray Nissan abruptly back out of one of the employee parking spots and slam into a brand-new, white Cadillac sedan. My body jerked as the two vehicles collided and the sounds of metal scraping against metal caused my teeth to clench.

Ian stepped out on to the sidewalk in front of me, and I followed quickly behind him.

"Hey, doesn't that Nissan belong to June Yi?" I asked, pointing to the car.

He held a hand up to his head and massaged his temple with his thumb. "Ugh, of course it does."